D0501920

Cat Got Your Secrets

Also by Julie Chase:

Cat Got Your Cash

Cat Got Your Diamonds

Cat Got
Your Secrets

A Kitty Couture Mystery

Julie Chase

CROOKED
LANE

NEW YORK

Published in the United States by Crooked Lane Books, an imprint of The Quick Brown Fox & Company LLC.

Crooked Lane Books and its logo are trademarks of The Quick Brown Fox & Company LLC.

Library of Congress Catalog-in-Publication data available upon request.

ISBN (hardcover): 978-1-68331-283-3
ISBN (ePub): 978-1-68331-284-0
ISBN (ePDF): 978-1-68331-286-4

Cover design by Louis Malcangi
Cover illustration by Anne Wertheim
Book design by Jennifer Canzone

Printed in the United States.

www.crookedlanebooks.com

Crooked Lane Books
34 West 27th St., 10th Floor
New York, NY 10001

First edition: September 2017

10 9 8 7 6 5 4 3 2 1

To you, sweet reader, for making this dream possible

Chapter One

Furry Godmother's advice for business:
Get a PFA. Personal Feline Assistant.

"Hold still, please," I whispered to Penelope, the adorable black-and-gray tabby on my lap. Her striped paws kneaded my thighs in anticipation of freedom.

A pair of pint-sized silver wings bobbed against her back as she tried to bite my fingers.

"There." I snipped the thread and poked my needle into a stuffed tomato on my parents' dining room table. "You're officially the cutest little Cupid I've ever seen." I fluffed the length of her dress and tugged the sleeves. "Do you feel pretty?"

She leapt from my lap and skulked into the kitchen.

"Good idea. Test it for comfort."

I scrutinized the fit as she went. "How does it feel around the collar?" I asked her retreating figure. "Are the cuffs too snug? Why can't you talk?"

Mom cleared the remaining breakfast plates, stirring rich scents of buttery pancakes and syrup into the air. Her cream-and-olive wrap dress was modest, but elegant,

1

emphasizing her youthful figure without drawing attention anywhere specific enough to rouse a blush. "Have you given any more thought to making Penelope the face of Furry Godmother?" She followed Penelope into the kitchen.

Furry Godmother was my dream come true, a pet boutique and organic treat bakery in the heart of New Orleans's Garden District. The slogan *Where every pet is royalty and every day is a celebration* was chosen for its all-inclusive nature. At my shop *every* pet got the royal treatment, from turtle to tabby to terrier. No discrimination allowed. I didn't want to give the wrong impression by choosing a mascot.

"No." I rolled my head against one shoulder and let my heavy eyelids drop. We'd had this discussion multiple times.

"Why not?" she pressed. "Every successful business has a spokesperson. You need a brand. Something people can connect visually to your business. Why not use Penny?"

I forced my eyes open and pulled my head upright. "Furry Godmother is more than kitty couture."

Mom returned with an enormous mug of coffee. Her third since I'd arrived. "Fine. We can talk about it more later."

"You're having another cup of coffee?" Not that I was judging, but Mom lived to preach the perils of overindulgence. I should know. I was the poster child for her campaign.

She lowered gracefully onto the chair across from me, her bright-blue eyes avoiding mine. "I've been spring cleaning, and I'm exhausted."

I sensed there was a deeper meaning behind the words. With my mom, there usually was. "When you say 'spring cleaning,' do you mean you called a service?"

"No." She made a crazy face. "I mean purging. Out with the old and all that. For the record, I know how to do the day-to-day cleaning as well, Lacy Marie Crocker. I just prefer not to."

"Uh-huh."

"Besides, outsourcing boosts the economy and frees up my time so I can give back to the community."

"Yep." My mother was also known as Violet Conti-Crocker, sole living heir to the Conti fortune. To hear her tell it, Conti money had helped build the city, and she took her civic responsibilities very seriously.

I thought she tended to exaggerate.

She pursed her lips and held my stare for a long beat.

I looked like my mother, from her blonde hair and blue eyes to her narrow frame and ski-slope nose. What we lacked in classic beauty we made up for in spunk and chutzpah. Her chutzpah got on my nerves and vice versa, but we were learning to live with one another in the same city again.

I'd left for college nearly twelve years ago and rarely visited—outside the occasional holiday—until Pete the Cheat, my jerk of an ex-fiancé, broke my heart last spring and sent me running back to New Orleans. Specifically, to the Garden District, known for its stately historic mansions and megawealthy residents. As it turned out, I liked my new life here much more than I'd expected, and Mom was growing on me.

I smiled. "So hiring a cleaning service helps the economy, but you're doing the purging yourself?"

Her shoulders drooped away from her ears. Whatever she'd considered saying, she let it go. "This is different because it's personal. I'm going room to room boxing up anything I can bear to part with. A cleaner can't do that. So far, the work is endless, not to mention thankless, which is why I need the coffee."

"Room-by-room purging?" I did a long whistle and made a show of looking around the cavernous spread. The historic Victorian home had been in my mother's family for generations. It was a magnificent place to live— architecturally sound, immaculately kept, and in the most coveted section of the district, but it was stuffed to the frame with things no one needed. Five thousand square feet and nearly two dozen rooms with closets, cubbies, and built-ins. "Good luck with that." I worked through the information she'd given me. "Why are you doing this?"

She huffed, as if I'd somehow missed the obvious. "If I ever finish the insurmountable task, I'm going to redecorate." She curled both hands around her steaming mug and sipped. "I'm donating some things, and I have a pickup scheduled for this morning. I honestly thought she'd be here by now."

"Are all those boxes by the back door going out?" A sudden yawn split my face. I covered my gaping mouth with both hands.

"That's right."

"Wow." She had her work cut out for her. Mom was a certifiable packrat, exactly like her mother before her.

The attic alone was crammed with two lifetimes' worth of things she didn't need and couldn't part with.

She swept a thick swath of blonde and platinum hairs off her forehead and hooked them behind one ear. Mom had informed me long ago that our family didn't go gray. Those pesky white hairs that came along after thirty were called *platinum*. "There's a thrift shop on Jackson Avenue that guarantees anonymity and does pickups."

"A thrift shop?" I gawked. Who was this woman?

I'd recently caught her wearing jeans, and she'd changed her hair last week, adding waves and bangs to a shorter cut. The effect was drastic and glaringly opposite the sleek shoulder-length bob she'd worn for at least twenty years. Honestly, she looked nearly that much younger.

"What are you looking at?" She rolled her shoulders back and lifted her chin.

"I don't know," I marveled. "I guess I'm still getting used to your new look."

She raised a hand toward her forehead, but stopped short, opting instead to touch the new waves dancing against her cheeks. "I needed the bangs. You'll understand in twenty years. Sooner if you don't get some sleep."

"I sleep."

She hiked one perfectly manicured brow in challenge.

"I do." Not nearly enough, and normally after face-planting at my desk midstitch, but I slept. "And I love your new look."

A rare blush crept over her cheeks. "I think, perhaps, spending so much time with my daughter is changing my idea of beauty."

"What?" I made a show of looking over both shoulders. "Me?" I pressed a hand to my chest. "Well, clutch my pearls. You're getting soft." I rose to my feet and clamped my arms around her. "Now it's only a matter of time until my evil plan is complete." I rested my head on her shoulder.

"Get off me." She wiggled out of my grip with a peculiar grin. "Good grief. This is why I don't compliment you more often. You completely overreact." She grabbed her coffee and pressed it to her lips.

"I see you smiling."

"Do not."

I carried my cup across the threshold to the kitchen for a peek inside the boxes. "You didn't put any of my stuff in here, did you?"

"Not yet."

I didn't like that word, *yet*. I fingered the contents to be sure she wasn't lying, then lingered in the doorway between the two rooms. "Don't get rid of any of my stuff."

She rolled her eyes. "Do you mean the stuff you left here more than ten years ago? Why would I do that when you obviously use it so often?"

"They're memories. My memories."

"They're worn out books, of which you own multiple copies, and puzzles." She groaned. "Puzzles and games and brain teasers. I suppose you'd like to take those dusty things home and play with them again at your age."

I pulled my chin back. "Excuse me. I like puzzles." I shook off the bubbling frustration. "And I'm not old. I'm thirty and you're . . ."

She stabbed a finger in my direction. "Do not."

Penelope appeared at my feet, and I pulled her into my arms, carefully removing the little dress. "Grandma has had too much coffee, and it's making her grouchy." I set Penelope on her feet and folded the dress.

Mom ignored my jibe. "Who's the packrat now?"

"You."

She held a palm out. "Pot." And then the other. "Kettle."

I narrowed my eyes.

"New topic. Valentine's Day is next week," Mom said. "Have you made any plans?"

"Nope."

"Pity."

Yes. I was thirty and single, while every last one of Mom's friends was a grandmother. Heard it.

The back door opened and shut. Dad wandered into the kitchen and rolled his sleeves up to his elbows, then proceeded to scrub up as if he was preparing for surgery.

Mom moved to the doorway between rooms and cocked a hip. "Well, aren't you even going to say hello?"

He startled. "Oh. Hello, darling." He dried his hands on a dishtowel, then kissed Mom's cheek. "Sorry I'm late." He turned for the dining room and met me with a big hug.

"Everything okay?" I asked.

"Yes. Fine. Fine." His polite smile fell short, not quite reaching his normally bright eyes.

"He was out with Wallace Becker last night," Mom tattled. "He's probably hung over, but since he's finally chosen to bless us with his presence, we should talk about Friday night's award dinner and leave last night where it is."

Dad was the latest in a long line of Crocker men to fill the role of beloved Garden District veterinarian. He ran a private practice out of the renovated barn in their backyard, and he'd been nominated for a community service award. Mom was throwing a party to celebrate the fact. She'd celebrate the daily sunrise if she thought people would attend.

Dad forced the smile higher. "Great."

"Who's Wallace Becker?" I asked Dad.

Mom answered for him. "He's that man who runs the babysitting company for pets."

"The Cuddle Brigade?" The Cuddle Brigade was a fairly brilliant business concept—not a new one, but lucrative nonetheless. The pet nannies were vetted by a panel of local who's whos and rented out as in-home care to cover business trips and vacations. Some especially adoring pet owners hired the Brigade on a nine-to-five basis so their fur babies wouldn't be alone all day every day while they worked. Not every pet was as lucky as Penelope, who went everywhere I went. More or less.

"That's the one," she said.

"What a small world. The Normans are throwing their Saint Berdoodle a Bark-Mitzvah tonight, and I have twelve dozen dreidel-shaped doggy biscuits waiting in the car for delivery. I'm making a stop at the event hall next door to the Cuddle Brigade on my way to work."

She nodded. "That's Wallace's hall. The Normans are nice people. Their Berdoodle isn't bad either."

"How's Mr. Becker doing?" I asked Dad, enticing him to join into our conversation the way he normally did.

He set a kettle on the stove and cranked the gas. "Not good."

"I'm sorry to hear that. Is there anything I can do to help with your dinner Friday night?"

Mom made a crazy face. "Of course there is. I've already e-mailed a copy of your duties. I thought you said you got it."

"Right." I tapped my temple, pretending to have forgotten. I didn't always open Mom's e-mails. "Sorry."

She rolled her eyes. "Since you obviously haven't read it, dinner is at the Elms Mansion at eight. Be there at seven. Bring a date. Your cat doesn't count. And wear something pink. I'm playing off the valentine theme. Love for animals. Love the community. All we need is love. That mess. I don't want you to clash."

"Got it." I packed my things and pulled Penelope's carrier onto the table. "I'd better get going so I can make that delivery." I caught Penelope as she tried to slink past and stuffed her into her travel pack. "Time to go." I kissed Mom's cheek and motioned Dad to walk me out.

He followed me silently into the warm Louisiana day, carrying Penelope in her pack.

I stopped to beep my car doors unlocked. "Are you sure you're okay?" I asked, squinting against the sun.

He kissed my head and loaded Penelope onto my passenger seat. "I'm fine." He buckled the seat belt around her carrier and forced a tight smile.

"Why don't I believe you?"

An older model SUV appeared at the end of the drive before he could answer. The vehicle crunched over loose gravel and stopped behind my Volkswagen. A woman in her forties fell out, stumbling for balance and mumbling under her breath. She straightened her blouse and elastic-waist pants over the lion's share of her curves. Her fuzzy brown hair fluttered in the wind. She gasped when she finally noticed me.

I did a finger wave and wondered if she was lost.

"Mrs. Crocker?" She fumbled in my direction, hand extended. A powerful cloud of essential oil scents wafted around her. "I'm Claudia Post. It's nice to meet you."

I held my breath against the olfactory assault of lavender and rose hips.

Mom bustled outside and down the driveway toward us. "There you are. I'm Mrs. Crocker. This is my daughter, Lacy Marie." She motioned for Claudia to follow her and turned back for the house. "I've got everything by the door for you."

Claudia returned a moment later with her hands full.

Dad jerked to life. "I'm so sorry. Let me help you." He hustled to her SUV and opened the hatch. "I'll carry the rest. Just a moment."

"No. It's no problem, Dr. Crocker." She slid the box inside and hurried after him.

Mom came to join me in the gravel and beamed. "Isn't this wonderful?"

Wonderful? Maybe Mom wasn't the hoarder I thought she was. "Yes?"

"I'm told Claudia's the best," she whispered. "She guarantees complete anonymity for donors. Finally, I can get rid of anything I want and trust it won't be gossiped about at the next big event."

"What do you have that people would gossip about?" *Dare I ask?*

"Please." She clasped her hands over her belt. "No one needs to know my dress size or what I keep in my closet. Can you imagine?"

"Not really, no." I wore a size eight, and I'd never considered it a secret. Also, I didn't want to know what was in Mom's closet.

Dad and Claudia loaded the final boxes into her SUV. She shut the hatch and approached me with an apologetic expression. "Sorry about the mix-up earlier."

"It's okay. People mix us up all the time," Mom lied.

"Well, if you ever have anything you'd like taken off your hands, just give me a call." She handed me a shiny white business card with curly pink letters in the center. "Resplendent," I read. "New Orleans's premiere thrift shop."

"Thank you, Mrs. Crocker. Dr. Crocker." Claudia wrenched open her squeaky driver's side door and climbed onto the seat with a little effort.

I kissed my parents' cheeks before following Claudia's SUV down the driveway and around the block where we parted ways. I zipped along the picturesque residential roads of our district, eager to make my delivery and get to work. More than that, I was dying to know what had my normally jubilant dad so melancholy. I would have blamed Mom, but she seemed sincerely clueless.

Penelope rode quietly beside me, ears rotating like tiny satellite dishes as the sounds of our district wafted in on the breeze.

A crowd came into view outside the reception hall.

"Uh-oh," I told Penelope. "Something's wrong."

Police cruisers blocked the parking lot entrance, forcing me to pass my destination in search of an empty space along the curb. A firetruck sat beside an ambulance outside the hall where my delivery was expected.

I parked two blocks away and powered the windows up halfway. "Wait here," I told Penelope. "I'll be back in a minute. I need to find out what happened so I know what to do with these dreidel biscuits." If there was a fire, I'd have to deliver them somewhere else, which meant throwing my day off schedule more than it already was.

I jogged back to the lot entrance. Lookie lous lined the sidewalks, snapping photos and buzzing with anticipation. I sidled up to a man standing outside the hoopla. "What's going on?"

"I'm guessing fire." He crossed his arms and rocked on his heels. "Could be a robbery or vandalism, I suppose. I'm not sure what they keep in there."

The hall was the big empty kind that folks rented out for special occasions. Unless the family holding the Bark-Mitzvah had stored something of value for the party tonight, I couldn't imagine any reason to break in. I snapped a few pictures with my phone. Photos had helped me sort things out in the past, and this felt like a moment to remember or at least document.

I lifted onto my tiptoes for a better view of the firetruck. Several men in New Orleans Fire Department T-shirts leaned against the giant vehicle, scanning the crowd and posturing. No gear or hose in sight. I ducked under the crime scene tape and went for a closer look.

"Hey," the man called from behind me. "You can't go in there."

I waved him off. "It's okay. I have a delivery."

I hustled through clusters of men and women in uniform, passing cops, firemen, and crime scene investigators with my chin up and shoulders back. A gust of wind whipped through the scene, sending goose bumps down both arms. New Orleans in February could be forty-five or seventy. Sometimes on the same day.

A knot of workers in matching uniforms huddled near the side entrance. "Hi," I said. "Sorry to interrupt, but I have a delivery for the party tonight. Is it okay if I leave the boxes with one of you?"

A puffy-eyed woman burst into tears.

The man beside her gave me a cold stare and pulled her into a hug. "Party's cancelled."

I cast a look at the not-burning building. "No party?" I had twelve dozen Jewish dog biscuits in my car. How the heck was I supposed to unload those if not for the Normans' Bark-Mitzvah? "I'm confused," I admitted. "What happened here?"

"I tried everything," the woman cried. "I was too late. He was so cold."

My gaze jumped back to the building. Fear prickled the skin along my collarbone. "Who was so cold?"

"Wallace Becker," the man said, pulling her closer. "She found him in there this morning."

I blinked long and slow at the woman sobbing against his chest. Behind her, a pair of EMTs drove a gurney into the back of a waiting ambulance. A closed body bag balanced on top.

"A real shame," one EMT told the other as they snapped the doors shut behind the body. "Wallace Becker was the nicest guy on earth."

It felt like ice slid down my spine and into my sandals. Dad was with Mr. Becker last night.

And now Mr. Becker is dead.

Chapter Two

Furry Godmother's advice on personal baggage:
Donate it to charity.

The world seemed to burst back to life. People bustled in every direction. Voices filled the humid air with white noise. I stumbled over my feet, processing an influx of self-ish thoughts. I knew what this meant for Dad. I'd been through it last summer when a body was found outside my shop, and I'd been the last person to see that man alive. For me, the days immediately following had been a night-mare. Dad was already in a strange funk, almost as if he'd known . . . but that was impossible. He'd never hurt any-one intentionally, and if he knew someone was hurt, he'd call for help. His mood and his friend's death weren't con-nected. They couldn't be.

A scrawny guy with a blond goatee and black horn-rimmed glasses moved in front of me and extended his hand. "I'm Robbie." He had a polo shirt and khakis on with black Nikes and a rubber-banded wristwatch.

"Lacy." I choked the word free from my suddenly dry mouth. "Do you know what happened in there?"

"No." He tipped his head away from the group and motioned me to follow.

We moved several paces to the left.

Robbie scanned the scene over my shoulder when we stopped. "We're the morning crew. We come in and scrub the place on days when an event's scheduled, which is most days. Lana got here first today."

I glanced at the little circle we'd left behind. "Lana's the one who found Mr. Becker."

"Yeah."

I, too, had found a body this year. I'd planned to create a pet companion line for my favorite fashion designer and personal hero, Annie Lane, but she was dead when I'd arrived for my appointment. I never got the chance to meet her, but I thought of that moment nightly. My heart went out to Lana. She'd never forget this day.

I rubbed the goose bumps off my arms. Someone had killed Annie Lane, but this wasn't like that. I had no reason to assume murder. I shook off the effects of my personal baggage and gave the situation a more sensible appraisal. Wallace Becker was at least sixty. He could've had a heart attack or an aneurism. Maybe a stroke. The coroner would know soon. None of this had anything to do with me or my dad.

Robbie dashed the toe of his shoe against the asphalt. "I heard the medical examiner say it was probably a heart attack."

My shoulders relaxed by a fraction. "Oh, good."

Robbie raised his brows.

"I mean, not good, but . . . it wasn't a robbery or anything violent."

"No. Nothing like that. He was locked in the freezer. I guess that triggered the attack. I don't know."

My eyes widened. "What?"

"Yeah. Weird, right? Lana saw the emergency light on when she got here. The doorstop was wedged underneath the door from the outside. Total fluke. She kicked it away and found him on the floor. I heard her screaming when I pulled into the lot. I thought she was hurt, but I found her in the freezer trying to wake him. I called nine-one-one and started CPR, but he was already gone. The police told us to stay here until they spoke with us. We've been standing around for almost an hour."

I stumbled away on wooden legs. Mr. Becker was locked in a freezer? So this could be murder after all? My chest burned. The urge to flee overcame me. I needed to escape before I became part of whatever had happened here. When I'd lingered too closely in the past, these things had a way of growing claws and dragging me in.

"Hey, lady," Robbie called. "Lacy? You okay?"

"No." I shook my head and applied the breathing techniques I'd learned in therapy. "I have to go."

Dad had been in a horrible mood this morning. Had he and Wallace had a disagreement? *Oh, Lord. Please don't let them have had a fight.* I turned my eyes skyward in a silent plea. A fight, even a verbal one, was considered a possible motive for murder, and Dad would be in the crosshairs of the New Orleans Police Department, not to mention local media and the gossip mill.

Robbie darted ahead of me and blocked my path. "Hey, are you driving? I don't think you should drive like this."

My tummy coiled. "Penelope!" I jogged back across the lot and under the police tape. Thankfully, I'd opted for polka-dotted ballet flats instead of heels this morning. My navy A-line dress fluttered against my thighs with every broad stride. The brisk winter winds threatened to re-create the famous Marilyn Monroe moment if I took my hands off the hem.

Robbie stayed at my side. "Hey, I'm not supposed to leave."

"So don't." I stopped at my car and heaved a sigh of relief.

Penelope was on her back in the travel pack, sunning herself in narrow beams of light flickering through the window. Irrationally, tears stung my eyes. She was okay, and I was okay. Everything was okay.

Except that Mr. Becker was dead. He wasn't okay.

Robbie watched me with blatant curiosity. "Let me at least call someone to drive you. You don't seem well."

"No. I'm fine." I pressed a clammy hand to my pounding chest. My fingertips landed in the deep V of my neckline, further chilling my skin. "You're very kind, and it's nice to see chivalry isn't dead, but I have to go."

"I'm a volunteer firefighter." He shrugged. "I worry about people. Probably more than I should. It's a curse."

"No," I said. "It's really not."

Cursed was coming back to my hometown after a decade away and finding myself at the scene of three murders in less than a year.

I climbed behind the wheel and gunned my little engine to life. I gave Robbie one last look. "You'd better get back before the police notice you're missing."

I pulled away with a jolt, leaving him alone on the sidewalk, and made a dent in my gas pedal motoring down Magazine Street toward Furry Godmother. I needed to call Dad before someone beat me to it. I also needed as much information as I could get about what had happened last night. With enough pieces, I could solve any puzzle, and the stakes were high on this one. Dad's friend was dead, and Dad would soon be a suspect. Maybe he'd feel like talking when he got this news.

I careened onto Magazine Street, the heart of the Garden District and location of my shop. Robust baskets of red, white, and pink flowers hung from lampposts along the six-mile stretch of charming shops and delicious food, anchored by matching "Fall in Love with the Garden District" flags and golden silhouettes of Cupid and his bow. Shop owners pulled sale racks and chalkboard signs onto the sidewalk, enticing shoppers inside for Valentine's Day sales. Magazine Street was my district's answer to the French Quarter's Bourbon Street. Maybe not the main attraction, but definitely not to be missed.

I slid into the first available curbside spot and grabbed Penelope and the dreidels. We made a run for the store, hopping over ministreams and rivers where water from window washing and plant watering swirled on the sidewalk. Two months from now, the little puddles wouldn't stand a chance against the searing Southern heat.

I bumped the front door open with my backside and spun into my adorable little shop. The bell dinged overhead, announcing my arrival. Wide wooden flooring stretched in every direction, from the turtle tank to the bakery counter. White built-in shelves lined the walls. Tiny chandeliers hung in tidy rows overhead. A soft pink-and-green color palette gave the room a perfectly whimsical feel.

"Mornin', Miss Lacy." Imogene, my former nanny and current shopkeeper, met me with a bright smile. "I didn't expect to see you so soon. Your mother said you were having breakfast with her today." Imogene and my mom were best friends, and if that wasn't enough, Imogene was a bit of a mystic, painfully aware of the general dispositions and intentions of everyone around her. I'd gotten away with nothing when Imogene was my nanny, and very little since she'd taken the position as my faithful employee.

"I left early to make a delivery at the reception hall next door to the Cuddle Brigade offices." I set the box of doggie dreidel treats on the counter as evidence. "I need to find out where these go now." Thankfully, the Normans had paid in advance.

"Oh." Her voice fell an octave. Color rose in her latte-colored cheeks. "I heard about what happened over there."

Imogene knew everything that went on in the district, despite the fact that she lived on the other side of the French Quarter in Faubourg Marigny. I supposed the grand number of shamans and whatnots in her lineage gave her an advantage. "Well, what did you hear?"

"Someone locked poor Mr. Becker in the freezer and left him for dead."

I pointed to my nose. "Now I have to tell Dad, but I don't want to. They were friends, and Dad was already upset this morning."

Imogene hummed a long note and sauntered back to the bakery display. "Well, in better news, you had a crowd outside when I opened. Folks around here can't get enough of these little valentine boxes." She lifted one of the small heart-shaped boxes that I'd filled with organic pet treats. "I must've sold ten in ten minutes."

"Excellent." I unloaded Penelope and set her on the counter. "Where's everyone now?"

"How should I know?"

I pulled in a deep breath and found my cell phone. "Right." I dialed my mom and waited.

She answered on the first ring. "Violet Conti-Crocker."

"Hi, Mom." I shifted foot to foot. "How are you?"

"Fine." Water ran in the background. "What do you need?"

"Is this a bad time?"

"No. I suppose you called to tell me about Wallace Becker."

Imogene chuckled from across the room.

I puckered my brow, unsure how she could hear both sides of my conversation, but certain she could. "How did you know about that?"

Mom huffed into the receiver. "It's my job to know what happens around here."

That was true enough. After all, a socialite without a grapevine was like a cat without an attitude. Nonexistent.

"How's Dad taking the news?"

"Fine, I guess."

I chewed my bottom lip, unsure how to proceed. "Have you called your lawyer about this?"

"No. Why would I? Are you in trouble again?" The sound of running water ceased.

I lifted and dropped a hand in defeat. "Not for me. For Dad. Dad was with Mr. Becker last night."

"So?"

I glanced around the room for support. Only stuffed animals and my turtles looked back. "So," I dragged the word out for several syllables, "he's probably a suspect, or he will be as soon as the police find out he was with the victim immediately before he became one."

"Be serious," she scoffed. Pots and pans clanged in the background. "Listen. I can't talk. I'm baking Mrs. Becker a casserole, and this phone is too tiny to sit on my shoulder. I'm making a mess."

I dropped my forehead onto the counter. Proper Southern etiquette dictated that friends, families, and neighbors provide food when someone was hurting, healing, grieving, or sick. Also if they were new to the neighborhood, got engaged or married, had a baby, or a hangnail. No occasion was too small for a casserole and/or a pie. I'd broken my leg at the hands of a madman last Thanksgiving, and the food didn't stop coming until New Years.

"Shoot," she snapped. "Now I need to change. I hate this tiny phone."

"Please call your attorney before you go to the Becker home."

"Nonsense."

I raised my head fast enough to make it spin. "I'm serious."

"So am I. I'll talk to you soon, sweetie. Right now, I have a widow to feed and comfort." She disconnected.

I stared at my phone.

I brought up a search engine and looked for articles about freezer deaths. Horrified, I sent a series of text messages to Detective Jack Oliver, my one and only contact on the police force. Lucky for me, he worked homicide. If he hadn't been assigned to this case, then it wasn't flagged as foul play yet, which meant I had time to prove it wasn't before Dad wound up at the police station.

Imogene sang under her breath as she hung a tiny satin shirt in my window display. I'd created a faux garden, planted red hearts on sticks, hung puffy cotton clouds from above, and featured my cutest valentine designs on the clothesline. "My granddaughter would love this little tunic. She's just like you were at that age, except she dresses her Yorkipoo like a yuppie." Imogene shook her head. "That dog loves satin."

"You should take one home to her. What's her dog's name?"

"Beyoncé."

I chuckled. "In that case, you'd better take two. How's Michael doing these days?" Michael was Imogene's oldest son. He and his wife had at least six kids. I'd lost track while I was away. Her youngest son was Sean. She didn't mention him often.

"He's good. Working hard and loving that family."

"I always liked him."

Her smile grew. "He's a good boy."

I hauled a box of little skirts and cardigans onto the counter and plugged in my iron. "Who's to say it wasn't an accident? Maybe he happened to be in there when he had the heart attack from completely natural causes. There's no reason to assume foul play."

I checked my phone. Jack hadn't responded to my texts.

Imogene stopped working and looked at me like a specimen for study. "Who said anything about murder?"

I dragged my mind back to the parking lot, Lana's account, and my exchange with Robbie. "No one, I guess."

I texted Jack again.

No answer.

"How long do you think it takes to determine the time or cause of death?" I asked Imogene. My fretting mind couldn't recall the time frame from past experiences or anything else useful at the moment.

She made a thinking face. "Hard to say. I guess it depends how busy the coroner is. I'm guessing Mr. Becker wasn't the only one to die in New Orleans this week."

I spread a small skirt on the counter and placed a heart-shaped appliqué on top. I skated the iron over the material, careful not to stop anywhere too long, then flipped the skirt inside out and repeated the process.

The front door swung open with a flourish, and I nearly burned my fingers.

My best friend, Scarlet, marched toward me on three-inch platforms. "Hey, ladies." Her skinny capris paired perfectly with her royal-blue baby-doll top. She had giant white-framed sunglasses on her head and the newest addition to her growing brood on one hip. Poppet was baby number four in the Hawthorne clan, a princess with three big brothers. Both ladies had hair the shade of red that women sold their souls for and smiles to charm the pearls off a church lady. The Hawthorne men were defenseless against them.

"Where have you been?" Scarlet asked. "I stopped by your house last night and you weren't home. I thought about letting myself in and waiting in the dark to scare you, but this one was riding shotgun, so no fun for me."

"Good job, Poppet." I kissed her cheek. "Mommy thinks it's funny when I wet my pants."

Scarlet laughed. "I told you not to give me a key and the alarm code. I won't rest until I've used it for evil."

Someone had to have a spare key to my place, in case I ever went missing or worse, and I wasn't giving a key to my mom. Scarlet had seemed the logical choice until I remembered how mischievous she was.

Scarlet and I had been best friends since we were in diapers. Then she married Carter Hawthorne at nineteen, and I went to college. She doubled her net worth through marriage, and I went broke, rejecting my family's money in search of independence and a path I could control. Fast forward several years, and I was back where I'd started. Funny how life works sometimes.

I stroked Poppet's chubby cheek and gave Scarlet a one-armed hug. "What are you doing out so early?"

"Ha," Scarlet deadpanned. "It's almost ten. We've been up for four hours. Carter took the boys to the French Market to get their faces painted, so I thought Poppet and I would come see you." She jostled Poppet until she laughed. "I think they're looking for valentine gifts for me, and the market was a ruse."

"Nice. What did you get Carter this year?"

She shot a pointed look at the tiny person in her arms. "You know these don't really come from the stork, right?"

"Yes." I blushed, stupidly, as if Poppet might have read my mind.

"So what's going on?" she asked. "Anything new?"

"Wallace Becker is dead," I blurted. "He died inside a walk-in freezer last night. Dad was with him before it happened, and he was acting weird this morning. Dad, not Wallace, because . . . you know." Wallace would never act weird, or any other way, ever again. I bit my bottom lip. "I'm nervous."

Scarlet turned one hip away, separating Poppet from the awful conversation, and dipped her head. "You don't think your dad . . ."

"No!" I covered my mouth. "No. Of course not. I'm just worried about the implication. He's being given a community service award. Something like this could ruin his practice. Is there any chance you can get some more information for me?" I whispered. If anyone had access to the local scuttlebutt, it was Scarlet.

"Absolutely. Have you tried Jack?"

My expression must've answered for me.

"Right." She bounced Poppet higher on her hip. "I'm on it. I'll call you later." She blew Imogene air kisses and turned for the door.

I followed her onto the sidewalk, waving to Poppet as they walked away.

Jack had been AWOL more than he'd been around lately. It might've had to do with a personal investigation he'd started last year, but I couldn't be certain. He'd brought me in for help last fall, but I hadn't learned anything useful, and he was tight-lipped on his findings.

I turned back for the door.

A sharp wolf whistle pierced the air and I smiled. Chase Hawthorne, Scarlet's brother-in-law, clapped his hands slowly as he approached. "Darlin', you need a sign on that dress to warn men that you're coming. Tell me the truth. How many wives have slapped their husbands since you've been standing here?"

I lowered myself onto the bench outside my store and crossed my ankles. Chase made me weak in the knees. I had no intention of letting him know. His ego was too big already. The man would probably float away or fall over if his head got any larger.

He took a seat beside me and stared.

"What are you doing?"

He pointed a finger at my face and grinned. "I'm trying to be a gentleman and keep my eyes up here."

"Fine. I'll try to be a lady and not arch my back."

His gaze dropped.

"Sucker."

"That wasn't fair," he drawled. His bright-blue eyes twinkled with mischief. "You planted an image."

"Don't you have to be somewhere?" I teased.

Chase was an attorney at the Hawthorne family law practice, possibly the most powerful firm in all Louisiana—definitely the most influential in our parish. He had free reign, and I knew it.

"Yes, but I'm chasing an important lead. I need to know if you'll be my date to your father's fancy dinner next weekend."

I leaned my head against his broad shoulder for a quick beat. "Mom says I have to work the dinner. She sent me a list of instructions. Actually," I remembered, "one of my jobs is to bring a date."

"Done. What else is on the list?"

"I didn't open it."

He laughed. "I accept. Half the work. Twice the fun."

"Deal." I lifted my head to smile at his handsome face. Chase had left professional volleyball last year to put down roots in the district. Despite his endless charm and playboy reputation, he'd never missed a night at my place while I recovered from a broken leg. He'd kept me company, carried everything I couldn't, and let me cry when the frustration of needing so much help had gotten the best of me. He even watched my favorite romantic comedies without complaint. I wasn't sure how, or if, he'd found time to date during those couple months, and I didn't ask. Truthfully, I didn't want to know.

I hated to admit it, but Chase had cracked my betrayal-hardened heart with his unyielding presence. So much so, I'd nearly made good on a certain promise many times since Christmas. Last summer, he'd helped rescue Penelope from Pete the Cheat. The agreed-upon payment was one kiss. The only condition on the kiss was that *I* kissed *him*, and that I had to want to do it. I'd agreed in haste, only thinking of holding Penelope again, but lately, I'd toiled over the possibility more than I cared to admit. I absolutely wanted to kiss Chase, but where did it go from there? Our families were Garden District royalty. Chase and I couldn't play around at being a couple. The inevitable breakup would

leave marks and wrinkles on everything and everyone we loved. Neither of us were ready for that kind of pressure.

"Your lips are drifting toward mine," he whispered slowly, as if not to frighten me away.

I froze, inches from his mouth. "I didn't realize," I whispered back. Scents of his shampoo and cologne muddled my thoughts.

"You aren't retreating." He smiled. "Is this the moment I've been waiting for? Should I meet you halfway or are you still deliberating?"

I let my lids fall shut. "Shut up, I'm thinking."

"All right then." His breath washed over my face and my body went slack.

If he'd touched me, I'd have slid onto the sidewalk.

"Lacy?" His bottom lip brushed mine as he spoke. "People are starting to stare. I think a guy just dropped a dollar by my feet."

I smiled, letting my nose touch his.

A car door slammed nearby and my phone began to ring on my lap. Jack's ringtone.

"You want to answer that?" he asked.

My eyes popped open. I pulled back to glare at the phone, suddenly furious. I'd texted Jack thirty minutes ago. He couldn't be bothered to respond for half an hour? Really? And how long did it take to answer my questions anyway? Why call? What if I was with a customer?

I rejected the call. Much as I needed to speak with Jack, I also needed a minute to collect my marbles.

"Lacy." Jack's voice echoed through the air.

I twisted at the waist, befuddled.

He closed the distance between his truck and our bench in long, pretentious strides.

I jumped away from Chase. "What are you doing?"

"What are *you* doing?" he parroted back. He stared down at Chase and me, hands on hips, judgmental frown on lips. Sunlight glinted off the silver detective badge hanging around his neck. "We need to talk."

Chase kissed my cheek. "Looks like you two have business. I'll leave you to it."

"Wait." I grabbed his hand. "I think I might need an attorney present."

Chase barked a laugh and crossed his arms. He kicked back on the bench, apparently ready for a show. "All right. Go on, Detective Oliver."

Jack shot him a droll look before turning his crystal-blue eyes on me. "I'm here as a courtesy."

"What's this about?" Chase asked, suddenly serious.

Jack crouched before me, elbows on knees, regret on his brow. "Wallace Becker was found dead this morning, and your father was the last known person to see him alive."

"And?" I challenged.

"I'm on my way to your parents' house to bring Dr. Crocker in for questioning."

He turned his expressionless stare on Chase. "She's right. It'd probably be wise if he had an attorney present."

Chapter Three

Furry Godmother's advice for changing the world:
Start with your outfit.

The police station smelled like bratwurst and sweat. Men and women wearing stoic faces and navy uniforms ghosted around me, desk to desk, room to room, oblivious to my distress. Near-constant white noise and chatter spewed from walkie-talkies on officers' hips and shoulders.

Chase rubbed Mom's back as she chewed her thumbnail and stared down the hall where Jack had escorted her husband.

I'd opted for a seat on the bench across from a green-faced partygoer. The man was handcuffed to his bench and alternating between creepy winking in my direction and dry heaving into a wastebasket at his feet.

"Are you sure you don't want to sit?" I asked Mom for the tenth time.

She pivoted on her toes for another lap through the waiting area, her designer heels snapping and clicking against historic marble. She'd changed into a flowy black tunic and pencil skirt before leaving home. A far cry from the incessant pantsuits I'd found her in when I returned home ten months ago. "I'm too nervous. I can't be still right now."

She couldn't sit down and I couldn't stand up. Panic didn't set me in motion; it stole my wind and rendered me useless. So I sat, deflated, on a questionable bench, imagining the absolute worst scenarios my mind could conjure.

Chase left Mom to pace and returned to my side on a long exhale. "How are you holding up?"

"I want to smack him."

"Jack?" he guessed correctly.

"Yes." Jack had been nice enough to allow my parents to ride with Chase and me to the station. Chase behaved as if the offer was glorious and remarkable instead of common courtesy. The last thing my parents needed was to be seen leaving home in a homicide detective's truck. I ground my teeth at the thought. As if my fifty-five-year-old, community-advocate father could somehow be a killer.

I rubbed a shaky hand over my forehead. "Everything about this day is ridiculous. Why are we here? Jack knows Dad wouldn't hurt anyone."

"True, but don't fault the guy for doing his job. This is procedure. Your dad isn't being treated any better or worse than anyone else, and that's good. If Dr. Crocker appeared to be given special treatment, this would all go south fast."

"I still don't know why you couldn't go back there with him. You're a lawyer."

"I'm not *his* lawyer."

No, a portly cream puff of a man who specialized in veterinary malpractice, but also handled my parents' general needs, was Dad's attorney. If Dad ended up on trial for murder, his attorney wouldn't know whether to scratch his head or wind his watch. My cheeks scorched as the reality of Dad's situation grew heavier on my heart. "He needs you. Our family attorney doesn't even practice this kind of law."

Chase wrapped his hand around mine. "Your folks only hire the best. You know that. Besides, it's not as if I've ever handled a case like this either. I help rich people hide things for a living."

I snapped my hand away and curled ten fingers against my scalp.

"Hey," Chase cooed, "there's no reason to take this out on your hair."

I dropped my hands into my lap.

Chase slung an arm across my shoulders and dipped his face to my ear. "Everything's going to be fine. I promise. Your dad's tough, and Jack respects him. It's not like he's being tortured."

"It's no fun in there," I said. Last summer, I'd sat across from Jack in the interrogation room. The experience was horrifying. "I cried."

"Well, that's because you're a girl."

I kicked his shiny black shoe with my ballet flat. "Don't try to distract me with misogyny."

"Aw, come on. A good feminist rant could take your mind off things."

"Maybe later." I tipped my head against his shoulder. "Thanks for being here for this."

He leaned his cheek into my hair. "Where else would I be?"

My phone buzzed with a text from Scarlet. "Finally." I swiped my thumb over the photo of Penelope in a black flapper costume and read the message. "Scarlet says there's a rumor going around about Mr. Becker. The gossips say he was seeing one of his Cuddle Brigade workers." I made a quiet raspberry. "Men."

Chase stiffened at my side. He lifted his head off mine and angled toward me until our knees bumped. "Who said that?"

"I don't know. One of Scarlet's contacts." I sent a return text, thanking her.

Chase stared at the side of my face.

"What?" I asked after dropping the phone into my purse.

"Don't."

"Don't, what?"

"Please don't look into this. You've got a vested interest in learning the truth, plenty of motivation to get the right guy in cuffs, and you've already sent Scarlet on reconnaissance. You're looking into the murder, and that never ends well for you."

I guffawed. "I hardly think one text from my best friend is anything to get worked up about."

"Did you ask Scarlet to look for gossip on the victim?"

I looked away. "So?"

Clearly, I had no future as a defense attorney. What I had was years of mandatory debutant training. I straightened my spine and tossed a mile of blonde curls off my shoulder. "Checking in with a few known gossips doesn't qualify as 'reconnaissance.'"

"Using finger quotes doesn't make that true."

I dropped my hands back to my lap. "Okay, but think about it. If Mr. Becker was seeing someone besides his wife, I can think of two women who had motive to lock him in a freezer."

"Remind me never to cheat on you," he murmured.

I gave him the stink eye.

Mom wandered closer and shook her phone at me. "Everyone knows we're here now. I'm putting out fires left and right at the gossip mill."

"I'm so sorry." I tested my noodle legs. Mom needed me. The least I could do was give her a reassuring hug.

"If anyone asks," she sniffled, "your father and I are here to pick you up again."

I pursed my lips and closed my eyes so I could roll them privately. No hug for her.

"What'd you do this time?" Chase asked me.

I lifted a fist in his direction. "I think I might've assaulted a lawyer."

He leaned away from me, bright smile gleaming.

I turned to Mom. "Scarlet heard Mr. Becker was seeing one of his employees."

She gasped. "That's fantastic."

Chase dropped his head back and sighed at the ceiling.

I swiveled to face him. "I think you need to help Dad with this. I don't care if you don't practice criminal law. I trust you, and I know you'd represent him with gusto. Please?"

He lifted his face, looking years older than he had a moment ago. "I"—he looked at Mom, then back to me—"can't."

"Can't or won't?" Mom asked. Her voice hitched. "He doesn't need you. I'm just curious." Her pale cheeks whitened further, already washed out against the black blouse.

Chase rubbed massive palms over bobbing knees. "My firm represents Mr. Becker."

I reared back. "What?"

He ducked his chin. "We represent his company."

"When were you going to tell me this?" I asked, slowly filling with misplaced rage.

"Never."

"Why not?"

"It's uninteresting and irrelevant."

I crossed my arms in protest. "That stopped being true the moment Jack hauled my dad to the police station." Something else came to mind. "Is that why you told me not to look into Mr. Becker's affair? You didn't want me to find out you're his attorney?"

"I told you it's because you have a track record of getting yourself hurt." He turned pleading eyes back to Mom. "You don't need my help. You have incredibly strong connections, if you need them, which you won't."

"I already told you he doesn't need you," Mom said.

I went to stand shoulder to shoulder with Mom and glare at Chase. "Why do you represent his company? Was there a pending lawsuit? Someone angry with him about something? Are there allegations of wrongdoing against the Cuddle Brigade? Can you think of anyone with motive for his murder?"

"Jeez." He kicked back against the icky police station wall. "No."

"Then why'd he hire a powerhouse firm like yours? Anyone could've handled the company's employee disputes and taxes."

"I believe our retainer was a precautionary measure. That's all. I'm not at liberty to discuss anything about the relationship, and honestly, I don't know anything worth telling." He gave me a mean face. "Ever consider that maybe this is why I didn't voluntarily tell you about the situation? You overreact."

Why did people keep saying that?

"I'm motivated." I broke the words into syllables, hoping to help Chase catch up. "This is a big deal. My dad's life is at stake."

"I feel like your statement is making my point."

"Oh. I see." I clamped trembling hands over my hips. "I'm overreacting because you've already told me everything will be fine, and I didn't accept that as gospel, is that it?"

"Yes."

Mom spun back toward the hallway. "Thank heavens. What took you so long?"

I tore my anger away from Chase to see where she was going.

Jack, Dad, and the family attorney sauntered toward us, speaking softly among themselves. Dad's shoulders were rolled forward, and Jack reeked of guilt. As he should.

"Detective Oliver," I snubbed. "What? No cuffs?"

Dad took my hand and pulled me into a hug. "No need to be harsh, pumpkin. He's doing his job." He kissed the top of my steaming head. "Now, what do you say we go home?"

"Hallelujah." Mom headed for the door, matching pace with our attorney.

I stepped out of Dad's embrace. "Okay. I'll be there in a minute."

Chase, Jack, and I waited in silence until Dad vanished into the sunlight.

I turned on Jack. "Well? Are you satisfied my dad isn't a murderer?"

He lifted his brows. "You're still mad about this?"

I chomped my lip. Tears swam in my eyes.

Chase moved behind me, close enough for me to share his strength. "Give her a break, man. She's scared for her dad. Surely you get that."

Jack shifted his weight and locked Chase in a venomous stare. "I'm well aware of why she's upset, Attorney Obvious. I didn't want to do this any more than she wanted me to, but it's my job to follow the facts. Don't you have some millionaire you need to pander to right now?"

"You mean someone exactly like you?" he snapped.

Jack's mouth fell open. It wasn't common knowledge that the broody detective had inherited the Grandpa Smacker estate not long ago, and he liked to keep it that way. Grandpa Smacker was a megacorporation established more than seventy years ago by Jack's grandfather. Grandpa Smacker sold jams, jellies, and sweets of every sort to people across the country. Jack was insanely rich and too innately stubborn to give up detective work and enjoy the money. Jack was too stubborn for most anything. Including giving up on a hunch that his grandfather's death wasn't an accident.

The medical examiner was a friend of his grandpa's, and he'd hidden a few things from the press after the autopsy. For one, his heart attack was likely caused by ongoing small doses of GHB, a date rape drug found in his stomach along with some wine. Jack believed his grandpa's live-in girl-friend, Tabitha, had been secretly administering the drug. The question was, why? I'd suggested the little doses might have been enough to loosen his lips and not actually meant to kill him. Maybe she wanted to extract trade secrets or his bank account numbers. I hadn't worked out the details, but Jack and I had been exploring the theory together, until he started pushing me away. And accusing my father of murder.

Chase looped an arm protectively around my back.

Jack stared at Chase's fingers in the curve of my waist and worked his jaw until I worried his teeth would crack. He moved his gaze to my face. "We don't think Mr. Becker's heart attack was an accident. We suspect it was a direct result of being locked in the freezer."

I gave him a pleading stare. "My dad didn't do this. Have you checked the security cameras yet?"

"Parking lot surveillance shows your dad's car. No one else's. We've got him at the crime scene until ten."

"When was the time of death?" I asked. "Are we sure Mr. Becker was in the freezer when Dad left?"

Jack pressed his thumb and forefinger against his eyes. "I don't know anything for sure yet. That's why I'm asking questions."

"Any interior cameras?" Chase asked.

I'd nearly forgotten he was there.

Jack shook his head and dropped his hand from his face. "The only internal feed covers the bar."

I contemplated the new information. There wasn't a camera pointing at the freezer, but there was still hope.

"You said he was locked in, but did you check the freezer's safety mechanism? Walk-ins have measures in place to prevent things like this from happening."

"There was a mechanical issue." He bit out the words.

Why was he being coy? "I've already spoken with Lana. The light was on when she got to work."

"Sure, the exterior light alerts workers that someone is stuck inside, but he was only stuck because the . . ." Jack stopped midrant. His eyes stretched wider. "Did you say you spoke with Lana? The woman who found Mr. Becker?"

I needed a change of subject before I got another lecture. "Was this really a routine questioning, or is my dad a suspect?"

Jack raised his chin, apparently caught off guard. "I asked him not to leave town."

My heart clenched. Nothing about this scenario made any sense.

Chase's fingers pressed against my waist, reminding me again that I wasn't alone.

"I can't believe a person could die from a few hours in a freezer," I complained. I wasn't premed long, but I'd stuck it out enough semesters to know Mr. Becker should've lived, maybe with a little frostbite or hypothermia, but he should've lived. "I don't understand why he had a heart attack."

"Well," Jack rocked back on his heels. "The ME will have an official report soon, but Wallace Becker was definitely locked in the freezer, and he's absolutely dead."

I bit back the urge to swear and sweetened my voice instead. "Even if my dad's car was in the lot last night, why does that matter? They were friends. They went out. Neither of those facts should make him a suspect."

Dad eased into view. "We had a fight in the parking lot."

I jumped. I hadn't heard him return. "You and Mom?" I asked. "Why?" I craned my neck to see where she was.

"No. Wallace and I."

The implication of his admission crashed over me like a bag of rocks. I jerked my eyes to Jack's, hoping he hadn't heard that.

Jack watched Dad.

Dad moved into my personal space. "Our disagreement was caught on the security feed."

Chase released me, and I grabbed Dad's hands. "What happened?"

He tipped his head and smiled sadly. "Wallace invited me inside for a drink, to talk things through in private."

"Dr. Crocker," Chase warned, "you shouldn't say anything else without your lawyer present."

"It's okay," Dad said. "I've told the police everything I know. This is on record with the authorities. I thought it was time I put it on record with my family."

"Daddy." I pressed my lips into a tight line. I hadn't called him that since high school. Even then, I'd only used the endearment when I was truly frightened.

Jack moved toward Dad, bringing himself back into view. "The camera pointed at the bar caught the whole thing. Parking lot cameras show your father leaving a few minutes later. Alone."

"That's why you were acting so strangely this morning," I whispered. "You had a fight with Wallace."

"I tried to call him when I got home, but he wouldn't take my calls. I woke this morning thinking he'd be ready to talk, but the calls still went to voice mail. I thought the things I said to him had ruined our friendship." Dad's voice wavered. "I thought I'd said too much. Been too far out of line to turn back, and he might never speak to me again. I had no idea how true that would be."

Chase set a hand on one of my shoulders and one on Dad's. "Let's talk about this somewhere else. Yes?"

We nodded in unison.

Jack shook Dad's hand. "I'll keep you appraised as details come available."

Lies. I glared at Jack. He planned to tell a murder suspect about new clues in the case? Yeah, right.

Chase steered me out the front door to where Mom waited at his car. He loaded us inside and rolled slowly away from the station.

Jack stood at the front door as we passed. He slowly mouthed the words, "I'm sorry."

Yeah, so am I.

Chapter Four

Furry Godmother protip:
If you want something done right, do it yourself.
Just don't get caught.

Chase dropped me off at work after taking my parents home. No one had spoken a word after leaving the police station, and I'd found myself thinking irrational things that were still with me an hour later. *What were Dad and Mr. Becker fighting about? What if Mr. Becker threatened Dad physically, and Dad pushed him into the freezer to get away from him? What if Dad's disposition at breakfast was the result of more than a verbal dispute between friends? Why wouldn't he talk to me about it?* I shook off the nonsense for the hundredth time. Even if Dad pushed Mr. Becker into the freezer, which he never would have, he certainly wouldn't have kicked a doorstop in front of the door. Good grief. No, Dad didn't hurt Mr. Becker, but he was definitely keeping a secret.

Imogene bagged another box of valentine treats and handed them across the counter to a smiling customer. "Y'all come back."

She gathered a fresh cloth and spritzed the glass display. "Don't you just love meeting people from all over the world, Lacy?" She wiped crumbs off the bakery counter in wide sweeping circles. "I traveled for a whole year in the seventies. Did I ever tell you that? Just me, my best friend, her boyfriend, and the occasional hitchhiker, all in a psychedelic love bus. We went to concerts and protests. Met all sorts of people. It was a time of free love and open rebellion. How's that for complicated?" Her smile faded when her gaze landed on me.

I tried imagining Imogene in bell bottoms and rose-colored glasses. It wasn't happening. My mind kept snapping back to Dad and all the trouble he was facing.

She discarded the bottle of cleanser and dropped the cloth. "Hey, now. You can't think that way. You'll pollute fate with that stinking thinking." She swung her hips in my direction and stopped a few feet away. "Hey. Stop that."

I tried smiling but felt the creases in my forehead tattling on me. "I didn't say anything."

"You didn't have to say anything. Those ugly thoughts are written all over your face."

I blew out a long breath and sucked in a new one. "You're right. I'm overthinking. Jack's a great detective. He'll find the killer, and Dad will be fine." I worked up a more natural smile. "I was pretty mean to Jack earlier. I probably should apologize."

Imogene patted a palm against my shoulder blade. "I'm sure he understands. You've been through a lot these last few months. This must bring back some tough memories. Not to mention you're a daddy's girl through and through."

She dug into her apron pocket. "I've got something in here to help clear your mind."

I stepped back. "Oh, no thank you." Normally, I accepted whatever Imogene pulled from her apron, purse, or pocket because it made her feel better to help, but the last couple of times I'd welcomed her mystical interventions, my messes had gotten a lot bigger. This one was big enough already.

She frowned.

I flipped my phone over on the counter in search of a distraction. "I met a guy this morning who works at the hall where Mr. Becker was found. If I can find him, I bet he'll shed some more light on the crime scene." I searched for a list of local fire departments.

Imogene went back to digging in her apron, unfazed by my initial refusal. "I could've sworn I put it in here this morning."

I did my best not to wonder what "it" was.

The door sprang open with a fresh round of shoppers, and I made my getaway. "I'm going to make a few phone calls. Would you mind keeping watch?"

"Of course." She went to greet the little crowd with open arms and a thick southern Louisiana accent. "Welcome to Furry Godmother, where every pet is royalty and every day's a celebration."

I ducked into the stock room.

Penelope was seated atop Spot, the Roomba robotic vacuum, when I arrived. It seemed Spot had returned to his base for a recharge, and Penelope didn't like it. She pawed his start button, uselessly.

"What are you doing, sweetie?" I asked. "Is Spot ignoring your commands?"

Her green eyes widened, begging me for help.

"Sorry, hon. Even robots need a break sometimes."

I dropped onto the chair at my desk and dialed fire station phone numbers until I connected with someone who knew a volunteer named Robbie, who also worked for Mr. Becker's event hall. I hadn't found his station, but the guy on the other end of the line was more than happy to hand out Robbie's cell phone number when I confessed how much I regretted not asking him for it when we met.

I danced my fingers across the keypad while kicking my feet in victory. Too easy.

Robbie answered on the first ring.

"Hey, Robbie," I started. "This is Lacy. We met this morning. I was being weird. Sorry about that."

"I remember," he said. "Not that you were weird. I remember that we met. The situation was definitely weird."

"Yeah." I chewed my lip, mulling my words. "That's why I'm calling. Now that I've had time to think about what happened to Mr. Becker, I have a couple questions. I think you can answer some of them for me."

"I didn't know Mr. Becker, personally. I just clean and set up for events at the hall."

"That's okay. My questions aren't about him. Can you tell me about the freezer?"

He laughed. "Um, okay. What do you want to know? Make and model? Capacity? Are you looking to buy?" he teased.

"No." I smiled against the receiver. "What can you tell me about how it worked?"

"It's a standard walk-in deep freeze. It stays colder than a walk-in fridge." He paused. "I'm not sure what you want to know."

"I'm more interested in how Mr. Becker got trapped in there. You mentioned there was a doorstop blocking the door."

"That's true, but the safety latch has been broken for a while too. The doorstop was overkill." He went silent. "Sorry. Bad choice of words."

"It's fine. You said the safety mechanism on the door was broken?"

"Yeah. The door is supposed to need an extra push to cause the lock to engage, but the weight of the door is enough to do that, so the crew and I use the doorstop to keep from getting stuck in there."

I tapped the end of my pen against my forehead. "Do you think Mr. Becker knew that?"

"I don't know why he would. I'd never seen him at the reception hall before Lana found him there this morning. He owned the building and rented it out, but it wasn't like he spent time there or anything."

Was it still possible that his death was an accident? Could he have gone into the freezer and let the door shut without knowing he'd be trapped? "Any ideas why he'd go inside the freezer?"

"None."

Spot revved to life, nearly giving me ten consecutive strokes. He backed off his charging station with Penelope sitting on top, tall and proud. They bumped into stock boxes and spun toward the open doorway.

"Lacy?" Robbie asked. "Are you okay?"

"Fine. Sorry."

"You gasped."

"Cat," I said by way of explanation. "Can you tell me what happens now? Is the hall closed for the night? A week?"

"I'm not sure," he said. "Are you worried about your delivery? I can call Lana and see if she knows what's happening with the party."

Yikes. I'd forgotten about all those dreidel biscuits. "No. That's okay. I'll take care of that. I meant, what happens to the freezer? Will it be replaced? Cleaned out? Scrubbed down?"

"So you *are* in the market?" He chuckled.

I released a guilty sigh. "I'm just wondering. Curiosity is an affliction of mine."

"I guess they could clean everything out and rebuy the stock." He didn't sound sure. "As far as I know, there weren't any contamination issues, and the Swensons' sixtieth wedding anniversary party is still on for Monday with a kitty entourage. A crew will go in and scrub the place before then."

"A crew? Not you?"

"No. I'm on call at the firehouse tonight and tomorrow."

My phone beeped with an incoming message from Scarlet.

"Okay, thank you." I rushed off the call with Robbie in case there was an emergency and flipped the phone around to check my texts.

Caution: Becker's death made local news.

I logged into the laptop on my desk and brought up the Chanel Six website. "Oh, no." Somehow, surveillance footage from the reception hall had found its way out of police

47

custody. A grainy image of Dad and Mr. Becker anchored the frame. Both men waved their hands and made angry faces. This wasn't good.

The comments were impossibly worse. Dozens of people with usernames that began with CB, presumably for Cuddle Brigade, had already left presumptuous and tersely worded remarks about my dad's guilt. They accused the police of negligence and favoritism because Dad cared for most of the officers' pets.

I logged out and called the Normans about their doggie treats. I sighed in relief to learn Mrs. Norman would send someone for the dreidel biscuits right away.

Back out front, curious faces turned toward me as I entered the room. Had they seen the news?

My heart sped. My throat went dry. My mouth was gummy. The beginnings of a panic attack had become all too familiar since being tied to a stage prop last summer and threatened at gunpoint. Thrice. I grabbed a bottle of water from the minifridge behind my counter and cracked it open.

My therapist's words rushed to mind. *Engage the intellect, control the emotion.* Expensive words that sounded a lot like *try not to think about it* to me, but Mom claimed Karen was the best therapist this side of the Mason–Dixon Line, and it was nice to vent to someone and know that what I said wouldn't get back to my mother. Anywhere else in the district, the chances were iffy at best. Eavesdropping was a sport here.

I dropped my phone on the counter and performed a search on my phone for freezer-related deaths. As suspected, Mr. Becker's death was unusual.

"Lacy?" Imogene called from behind the bakery counter. "Telephone."

I cheerfully took an order for the Creative Cavies Easter Celebration. Ten bunny costumes for guinea pigs. Exactly what I needed to keep my mind busy. Sometimes my life was kind of perfect.

I flipped through design books, marking pages. Then I grabbed a new spool of elastic for perfect one-size-fits-all creations. An hour later, my first mock-up bunny costume was finished, and the steady flow of customers through Furry Godmother had fizzled.

"What do you think?" I asked Imogene, raising the tiny white fabric into the air.

"What is it?"

Mom swept dramatically into the shop before I could answer. She was wearing big black sunglasses and a matching floppy hat. If she was trying not to be noticed, she'd failed. I wasn't sure if it was the black swing coat or leggings that put the whole high-end ninja look over the top, but it was something.

"Mom?"

She scanned the empty shop. "Good. We're alone." She stood guard by the front window, gaze traveling up and down the sidewalk outside. "Come here."

I dropped the fuzzy material and approached her with care. "Everything okay?"

"No!" She whipped the oversized glasses off her face.

"What's wrong? Why are you dressed that way?"

"I'm lying low. The local news and the CB have painted your father as a monster."

"What's a CB?" Imogene asked.

"Cuddle. Brigade." Mom spat the words. "They're making everything worse."

I peeked through the window at her side. "You think someone followed you here?"

"I don't know. I'm humiliated, and I'm worried about your father. He's not speaking. He hasn't left his office since we returned from the police station."

"I'm still unclear about the outfit," I said. "Are you a ninja or is this supposed to be slimming?" It certainly did nothing to help her blend in. Magazine Street was an artsy and colorful display of local shops and native blooms. She stood out like a weed in a rose bouquet.

"I'm on my way to deliver Mrs. Becker's casserole. Black is the traditional color of mourning. I'm dressed to show support."

"Really?" I checked the time on my phone.

Mom left the window, apparently satisfied she hadn't been followed. She rounded the counter where I was working and lifted my bunny costume mock-up. "Very nice."

"Thanks."

She turned the piece over in her hands, examining the stitches and seams. "If I were someone you listened to, I'd suggest creating a collection of your favorite designs. Everything that screams Furry Godmother, and I'd get it together as soon as possible."

"Why? What have you heard?"

She did her best to look aloof, but I knew her. She had information, and as long as someone asked her for it, she wasn't gossiping. She was simply being polite. "The National Pet Pageant finally decided on this year's location."

I held my breath. This was the moment I'd been waiting for. I'd checked their website for months, but with all that had happened today, I'd forgotten.

"They're coming to New Orleans this summer."

"Yes!" I dropped my head back and did a silent scream.

When I righted my face, Mom didn't look half as excited as I was. I tried and failed to tone down my enthusiasm, but her news was huge. "Do you think I should make some show pieces? Were you suggesting a portfolio?"

"That's what I said, isn't it? Every pet owner in the district is climbing over one another to get the perfect outfit and venue for a party. If you handle this properly, you're guaranteed to have more business than you can manage."

I pressed my hands into prayer pose. "Where did you hear this? Is it on the website? Are you sure this is solid information?"

Mom dropped her patent-leather Kate Spade bag on the counter and gave me her exasperation face. I'd seen that one a lot since coming home. "The National Pet Pageant Welcoming Committee." She spoke slowly, waiting for the words to mean something to me.

"Who?"

"I told you I formed the committee. I even asked you to join us so you'd know everything about the pageant before anyone else. You refused."

"You were serious?" When she'd told me the idea at Christmas, I'd assumed she'd had too much eggnog. The National Pet Pageant had made it clear they wouldn't reach a decision on the next location for months. Why start a committee for an event that might not even happen on the same side of the country?

"We have to be preemptive, Lacy. It's our Southern duty to exemplify hospitality. I daresay the pageant chose New Orleans, at least in part, thanks to the efforts of our committee. Now they're coming, and this district needs to wow those NPP people." She smiled. "The ladies and I are calling them the NPP to save time. It stands for National Pet Pageant."

I did a slow nod. "Got it."

"We need to show the NPP that they made a wise decision by choosing New Orleans. We can't just wing it and hope for the best."

"Remind me why locals are throwing parties?"

Her mouth fell open. "This is exactly why I keep telling you to get more involved in the community. You're so busy working you don't know what's happening under your nose, and this pageant has to do with you."

I waited. There was nothing I could say without egging her on. Clearly, I was failing as a proper Southern woman, daughter, business owner, and other unnamed things.

Mom shot Imogene a look before turning her attention back on me. "The NPP Welcoming Committee is choosing a local face for the event. An ambassador, if you will."

"Your committee is choosing an ambassador. For the NPP event?" I let that sink in.

"Of course. It's basic good manners. The ambassador will give us one more method of making the NPP feel welcomed. Our local pet ambassador will have his or her face on every NPP flyer, poster, brochure, and flag made by the committee. We're designing them now. We'll use them to drum up local enthusiasm."

The concept disturbed and invigorated me. Sure, the competitive culture in our district was borderline certifiable, but I was about to be buried in an avalanche of design requests. "Are you entering Voodoo?"

Voodoo was the Crocker family cat, a typical black with big green eyes. Like the others before her, she was adopted as an adult when her predecessor became ill or died. Dad's family had been replacing Voodoo for decades. To the outside world, she was ageless, mystical, the epitome of New Orleans's culture. To us, she was family.

Mom frowned. "No."

"Why not?"

"I don't do this for the glory, darling. I'm only here to help others. Besides, how would it look if the committee chose one of the members' pets as ambassador? People would think we were self-serving." Mom hooked her bag in the crook of one arm and squared her shoulders. "I've got to go. There's a widow in need of dinner out there." She adjusted her floppy hat and glasses before striding away.

I flipped the "Open" sign to "Closed." "She's so dramatic."

Imogene hiked both eyebrows into her hairline. "She is?"

"Yes." I flipped the dead bolt. "I know she's your best friend, but she's over the top."

Imogene chuckled. "Mm-hmm."

"What?" I tidied shelves of bedazzled Shih Tzu tutus and Swarovski-encrusted turtle tiaras.

"Pots and kettles," Imogene said.

"Now who sounds like my mom? I heard the same thing from her this morning."

She chuckled.

I straightened a shelf of Banana Bacon Pupcake mix and thought of my conversation with Robbie. What if he was right, and I wasn't the only one cleaning up right now? What if an entire crew descended upon the event hall to scrub it down before I had a look at the crime scene? What if the police missed something?

Imogene flipped the overhead lights off, leaving the setting sun to light our space, and moseyed in my direction. "I see those wheels turning, and I think you're plotting trouble."

I focused on my shelves. "No, I'm not."

"Mm-hmm." She cocked her head over one shoulder. "Probably you and that little red-headed sidekick of yours."

"Scarlet!" I had an idea so fantastic it couldn't wait for shop cleaning. "You're brilliant, Imogene." I kissed her cheek and hugged her tight. "I know what to do next."

"Calling Scarlet?"

"Yep." I grabbed Penelope on her next pass through the shop. She straightened her legs as I lifted, attempting to continue her ride on the Roomba. I tucked her against my chest and grabbed her travel pack.

"Come on, sassy. It's time to visit my favorite Hawthorne."

Chapter Five

Furry Godmother's advice on friends:
The best ones will drive your getaway car.

I dropped Penelope off at home, then made a beeline for Scarlet's place. Hers was the massive estate surrounded by painted garden stones and the vibrant blooms of cherry trees. Evidence of her young family spilled from the property's seams, brightening the sidewalks and faces of passersby. Tiny soccer nets and plastic golf clubs lined the walkway, and a row of tricycles shared a spot in the driveway.

I pulled against the curb and waved to her husband, Carter. He bounced haphazardly across the lawn dressed as Clark Kent, carrying three of their four offspring. The high-end suit was probably standard business attire, but his Man of Steel impersonation was spot-on. Dark hair, black-framed glasses, kind eyes. One pint-sized boy laughed wildly in each of Carter's arms while a red cape and a third tiny smiling doppelgänger hung around his neck and down his back.

Scarlet stopped to kiss their faces on her way to the sidewalk. She met me on the curb with a baby strapped to her chest.

I dragged my attention to Poppet's sleeping face and powered down the passenger window. I leaned across the console and stage whispered, "What are you doing?"

Scarlet bent forward for a better view through the open window. She cradled the baby's head in one palm. A white eyelet bonnet covered Poppet's wispy red hair. "Park here. Okay? I'll drive."

"Why?" I cast a wayward gaze to Carter and the other offspring as they collapsed into a roaring heap of laughter. Shouldn't he be collecting the baby?

Scarlet made a show of peering into my back seat. "I don't see a rear-facing infant seat with five-point safety harness."

She had me there. No five-point harness. Also, no baby to necessitate whatever that was. "I keep one of Penelope's spare cat carriers in the trunk," I offered.

She shot me a droll expression. "I'll drive."

Scarlet headed for the white Lexus SUV in her open garage while I parked my eight-year-old VW on the street.

"Ready?" she called as I approached. She unloaded Poppet from the sling and positioned her into the bizarre three-strap seat belt with mind-boggling ease. The complicated safety harness looked like something out of the space shuttle or a professional race car and incredibly out of place on the bulbous little infant seat.

I rounded the vehicle to the passenger door and climbed aboard. My grown-up, single-strap seat belt seemed suddenly like a ruse.

Scarlet slid behind the wheel. "Sorry for bringing the baby. She has separation anxiety, so I have to take her everywhere now."

I gave my friend a long look. That sounded exhausting. "How are you doing?"

"Okay." She slid designer sunglasses over her eyes and heaved a sigh. "You know. Living the dream."

I smiled. "You really are. And hey, they're only babies for a little while, right?"

She reversed out of the drive with a hearty laugh. "As long as they weren't born with a Y chromosome."

"Well, that seems unfair." I smiled at the spread of male Hawthornes on her lawn.

"Apparently you've never seen a grown man with a cold. Or a papercut. Or just out of reach of the remote control." She merged into traffic with a smile. "Where are we headed? Your call was a bit cryptic."

"How do you feel about crashing a crime scene?"

"Like I thought you'd never ask. The reception hall beside the Cuddle Brigade offices?"

I raised and lowered my chin in exaggerated movements.

"Excellent. This is exactly what I needed. A little excitement. An adventure."

I turned the stereo on low and brought up my favorite station. "I aim to serve."

"You aim to misbehave," she corrected.

Occasionally, that too. Sunlight warmed my face and arms as we traveled along the familiar streets wrapped in nostalgia, whisper-singing to songs from our high school days while Poppet slept in the back.

Scarlet pulled smoothly into a space behind the reception hall and settled the engine. "What's the plan?"

I wobbled my head. "No plan."

"Goal?"

I released my seat belt and angled to face her. "I want to know what the police saw in the freezer. I can't get a look at Mr. Becker, but I can explore the crime scene before it's scrubbed down and restocked. I want to know what kind of 'evidence' the police might try to use against my father." I popped my door open. "Do you want to wait here?"

"No. Why?"

I cast a pointed look into the back seat. "We can't risk getting Poppet arrested."

"She can't get arrested. She's a baby."

"Still, that would be the epitome of setting a terrible example."

Scarlet rolled her eyes and hopped out. A moment later, she swung Poppet's sling over her head and swaddled the baby inside. "Think of this as a lesson in true friendship. Poppet and I are out here supporting you and finding justice for your father. Two noble causes."

"Way to twist the facts. It's as if you married a lawyer."

"The very best."

"Good." I eyeballed the cleaning crew swarming in and out of the open back door like honeybees from a hive. "Get him on speed dial so we don't wind up in jail."

"Pft." She puffed air into her wavy sideswept bangs. "We're two nice ladies and a baby. No one's going to think we're up to anything."

I followed her through the open rear door, moving upstream against workers in white overalls hauling boxes of frozen items to the truck outside. Broken crime scene tape fluttered along the frame as I passed.

Ahead of me, Scarlet tipped her baby's head back and futzed with her hat.

"What are you doing?" I asked.

"Looking for Poppet's lost bonnet." She untied the string and slipped the cover from her baby's head. Red hair stretched skyward in a haze of static electricity. Scarlet tucked the bonnet under Poppet's body and looked around. "Which way to the freezer?"

"Follow them." I motioned to the men and women angling past us in the hall.

We moved through the passageways between the kitchen and manager's office until the freezer came into view. A large calendar was taped to the wall outside the office. Apparently Mr. Becker's event hall was as big of a hit as his nannies. I trailed my gaze over the weekend dates. Someone had drawn a red X through tonight's Bark-Mitzvah. Dark-blue ink scribbled over something written in the box beside it denoting Friday's events. I inched closer, squinting at the tangle of looping lines. I scratched the page with my fingernail, as if I could somehow pick the top layer of ink away. "Can you make out what's written here?" I asked Scarlet. "Someone scratched it out."

Scarlet nearly pressed her nose to the paper. "I can't read it. What do you think it says?"

"I'm not sure. Are those ones? It's hard to make out, but there might be a number eleven under all those curlicues." I snapped a picture with my phone.

A woman appeared at the end of the hall and headed right for us. Alarm stretched her eyes into saucers. She pressed her palms together and stopped to admire the baby. "What are you doing here, little one?" she cooed at Poppet. "Oh, she's sleeping." The woman spoke more softly. "A true Sleeping Beauty. Just look at you. You tiny angel baby girl." She lifted her animated expression to Scarlet. "She's beautiful. How old is she?"

"Four months."

"She's precious." Her hands hovered in the air, desperate to touch, knowing she shouldn't.

Scarlet smiled sweetly and stroked Poppet's pink cheeks. "That's so nice of you to say. Thank you." Her voice grew sugary and her accent more pronounced. "Are you the supervisor?"

"Oh, no." She shook her head and stepped away from Poppet, seeming to recall she had a job to do. "Not me. No. Frank's out front."

Scarlet tipped her head in a show of appreciation. "Thank you so much. You've been ever so helpful."

The woman's smile grew. "You're quite welcome."

I waited until she'd sashayed away before turning to Scarlet. "What was that about?"

Scarlet turned wild eyes on me. She shoved my shoulder, pushing me toward the freezer. "You go check out the crime scene. Poppet and I will distract the manager."

I marveled at the tiny Hawthorne. "Is there anything she can't sleep through?"

"Yeah," Scarlet answered coldly. "The night."

I stifled a laugh. "Okay. Go." I slipped into the freezer for a quick look around, careful to check that the doorstop was secured on the right side of the door. The temperature dropped immediately. A thin layer of frost covered most of the shelves and remaining stock. The interior structure was a monochromatic ode to silver. Silver floor. Silver walls. Silver shelves.

The throng of workers barely glanced in my direction as they continued the circuit of load-up-and-leave. Gray dust clung to the threshold and doorknob, likely evidence of the crime lab's attempt to pull fingerprints. I dragged my toe over something pink on the floor. It was too flat and brightly colored to be gum, but it didn't budge. I crouched for a closer look. I snapped a picture with my phone. Nothing else in the room was that shade of pink. I rubbed the pad of my finger over it. There were no visible markings on the little wedge of adhesive, but it must've been the remains of a sticker.

"Hey!" A burly man with angry eyes and a handlebar mustache filled the doorway. "What are you doing in there? You don't belong here." Colorful tattoos of fire and scantily dressed ladies climbed his forearms and disappeared beneath his rolled-up sleeves. According to his name tag, this was Frank.

"I'm looking for something," I explained. "My friend lost her baby's bonnet."

A few workers gave me strange looks, but stayed out of my mess.

"Found it!" Scarlet trilled from somewhere beyond the mountain-sized man before me. "Found it. Here it is."

Frank advanced on me and snapped a hand out in my direction. He was quick for his size, but I was faster.

"No!" I jumped back. "No touching."

His bushy eyebrows lowered to a tight V over his broad nose. "I'm calling the cops." He spun in place and nearly fell over. "Whoa!"

With Poppet strapped to her chest, Scarlet blocked the doorway, business face in place. "No cops."

Frank looked from her to me and back again. His expression simmered somewhere between mistrust and anger.

I dashed to his side. "Please don't call the police. I didn't touch anything, and I didn't take anything." I lifted my palms to prove my innocence. "Promise."

He curled back one side of his mouth, so I slid into the doorway, shoulder to shoulder with Scarlet.

"Move." Frank demanded.

"No problem," Scarlet said. "We're leaving now, but you don't need to make any phone calls about us. We haven't done anything wrong. How does fifty bucks sound as incentive?"

He sucked his teeth and thought it over. "Sounds like you have something to hide. One hundred and I don't call the police, but you have to leave now, and you can't come back. I'm not losing my job over whatever you two are up to."

She narrowed her eyes, looking oddly dangerous for a baby-toting woman with freckles. "Fine. One hundred and you don't mention you saw us. To *anyone*."

"Why?" He flicked his gaze to me. "What'd you do in there?"

"Nothing." I glanced at Scarlet for help.

She lifted her brows.

I flipped through a mental list of potential lies and went with the only one that didn't involve me slipping into a British accent. "I own a pet-friendly reception hall in Shreveport. This place is our biggest competition, and I wanted to see what the fuss was all about."

He groaned. "You business owners are the worst. Fine. Give me the money." He presented an open palm to Scarlet.

She made an apologetic face at me. "I don't have my purse."

"What?" I gasped.

"I forgot it. I keep my driver's license and a black AmEx in my back pocket, but you should try wearing a baby in a sling and toting a decent handbag. It's impossible."

Poppet fussed at the sound of her mother's strained voice.

"Fine." I shooed her with one hand. "I'll take care of it and meet you at the car."

Scarlet nodded, turned on her toes, and bounced Poppet gently away.

I dug into my wallet and tossed out old receipts and sticky notes in search of money. "Here we go. There's twenty." I slicked the wadded bill against his palm, flattening the wrinkles. It sprung immediately out of shape upon my release. "Forty. Forty-five." The bills were getting fewer and harder to find. I fanned the pages of my checkbook in search of more. "I don't usually carry cash," I apologized for my lack of available bribe money. "Here. This makes sixty-five. Sixty-six, seven, eight, nine . . ." I shot him a look. "I don't suppose you take credit cards."

He curled his meaty fingers around the cash and crossed his arms.

I kept digging. Quarters rolled onto the floor. "Oops." I handed Frank a few more ones and squatted over my still-falling coins. I gathered and stacked quarters into fours. "One. Two . . . fifty. How much do you have now?"

"Get up, lady." Frank shoved my cash into his pocket. "Keep your change. Go back to Shreveport, and maybe get a better paying job once you're there."

"Will do." I cleaned up my mess and hustled toward the door. A crowd of workers in white overalls gawked from the sidelines, having witnessed the entire debacle. "All righty. Thank you. Bye."

Scarlet was in the driver's seat, car running, windows up, and singing to whatever was on the stereo.

I climbed inside and pretended to pass out. "What is wrong with us? We're like Lucy and Ethel, except we're never lucky enough to wind up in a chocolate factory."

She turned the volume down on a Kidz Bop version of "Head, Shoulders, Knees, and Toes." "I love those ladies. I'm Lucy."

I laughed. "Yeah right."

"I have the red hair." She reversed her car away from the reception hall and pointed us toward home. "Besides, Ethel was the sidekick."

"I'm not a sidekick," I insisted. "Poppet can be Ethel."

"Then who are you?"

"I'm thinking."

She turned onto her street with a giggle. "Find anything useful in the freezer?"

"Not really." I flipped through the handful of pictures on my phone. Nothing had struck me as notable, except the scribbled-out calendar and remnants of a hot-pink dot of paper glued to the floor. Though, I had no idea if either was significant.

My stomach sank impossibly further. How could my Dad be a murder suspect? I needed a way to save him before his reputation and veterinary practice were ruined, or worse. I shook my phone in frustration and dropped it into my newly cashless purse.

The SUV stopped behind a pile of scooters in Scarlet's driveway. "Can you stay for dinner?"

"No, thanks. I'm going home to clear my head and bake until something makes sense in my life again."

Hopefully that would be soon rather than after my poor father was locked behind bars.

I climbed into my car and pulled away from the curb with care. Traffic had picked up on the main roads, slowing my progress and raking my nerves. Something bounced off my roof. I adjusted my mirrors and crept along with traffic.

Ping!

I put one hand over my head instinctively as the sound recurred.

Ping! Bing! Bump! Cubes of ice slid down my windshield. I hit the wipers and checked my mirrors again.

A yellow truck on my driver's side flank rolled dangerously close to the car in front of it, tires on the dotted line between lanes. The word *Tonka* was painted over the wheel well in black. The tinted passenger window powered down and an arm came out. Chunks of ice battered my window.

My heart kicked into high gear. I hit my signal and took the next right, away from traffic and the crazed ice wielders.

Horns honked behind me.

I watched the truck in my rearview, unable to follow, trapped in traffic as I barreled away, and I hoped the ice wasn't a warning after my trip to the freezer.

Chapter Six

Furry Godmother's advice on meal planning:
Start with wine.

Chase arrived at nine. I waited on the porch when I saw his headlights flash over my front window. An anvil of stress fell from my shoulders at the sight of him.

He climbed the steps at a turtle's pace and kissed my cheek without enthusiasm. "Hello, gorgeous."

"Hey. Bad day?"

He forced a smile that didn't reach his eyes. "It's getting better."

I hooked my arm in his and led him into my living room. I'd been counting on his charm and wit to cheer me up, but seeing him down only motivated me to provide that service for him. Maybe he'd let me help. Unlike my father.

I'd called for Dad twice since dinner, but he claimed to be with a patient both times.

"Coffee?" I locked the front door and reset my home alarm.

Chase dropped his briefcase on the floor and toed his shoes off beside it. "Wine."

"Done." I motioned for him to follow me into the kitchen, though he was as comfortable at my place as I was. Like the others on my street, my shotgun home was squat, narrow, and historic. The structures were originally built to house workers at the turn of the last century and meant to be utilitarian, but New Orleans had other plans. Now the uniquely Southern properties were colorful works of art, reflecting the individuality and taste of their owners.

Chase tucked a barstool beneath him and rested his elbows on the counter. "I love coming here at night. Your place always smells like heaven."

My new granite countertops overflowed with fresh-baked treats and evidence of my restless labor. Unhinged cabinet doors and removed drawer fronts leaned against the updated island, waiting for me to finish the fresh paint job I'd started. I opened the new wine fridge tucked neatly beside the stainless steel dishwasher. "Tell me your troubles."

I'd first met Chase during my senior year of high school when Scarlet started dating his brother, Carter. Chase was a sophomore then, already a volleyball player and exceptionally handsome. Pride alone kept me from showing interest in an underclassman. Heaven knows my parents and best friend would have supported the connection.

He broke into a flirtatious smile. "You first," he said. "How are you holding up?"

"You know me." I poured another glass of wine for myself. "I'm staying busy."

"Apparently." He swept a palm in front of him like a game show host, indicating the rows of fresh-baked treats. "You did all this after closing up shop?"

"I even made a pit stop at the reception hall." I sipped my wine and watched as the statement settled in.

His eyes widened. "Should we order dinner?"

"No." I set the available island space with plates of cheese, fruits, and crackers, then caught him up on my evening shenanigans. "Overall, I'd say it was a bust. I'm out $74.50, and on my way home, a lunatic in a big Tonka truck chucked ice out his window at me. I came home to bake and clear my head."

"Harassed by a Tonka truck?" He swirled his glass of pinot. Deep-violet liquid clung to the sides. "I can't decide if that's my new favorite story or if you need a personal security team to follow you around the city. Anything else?"

"Yes." I moved to the seat beside him and popped a red grape into my mouth. Every time I'd shoved a batch of goodies into the oven, I'd used my laptop to research freezer deaths while I waited. "Very few people die in big walk-in freezers. I can't figure out why Mr. Becker didn't survive. If it was you or me, we'd have come out the next morning with a little hypothermia and a bad attitude, but we would've lived. He had to have done everything wrong to die in there between ten, when Dad left him, and the next morning when the cleaning crew arrived. He probably shouted for help all night and exercised to keep warm. Those are both bad ideas because they drain the body of oxygen." I lifted my fingers to tick off the mistake moves I'd learned. "When he got tired, he probably sat on the floor, also a bad idea because the cold metal would've lowered his body temperature at a faster rate."

"He was hit on the head," Chase said. "The ME hasn't released an official cause of death, but head trauma was noted in the police report. That could've been a factor."

My chin dropped. A long line of questions queued in my mind. "I thought you couldn't help us with this case."

"Public records." He sampled another cheese chunk. "I picked up a copy of the report while I was at the station on business for the firm."

"What sort of head trauma? Can I see the report?"

He leaned as far back as possible on the stool without falling off and pretended to reach for his briefcase in my living room. Scarlet's line about men beyond the reach of their remote came to mind.

"Jeez." I fetched the case and set it on the stool beside him. "You're exhausted. What's going on?"

"My dad's slowly working me to death. He says things like, 'Justice doesn't sleep and neither should we when we're on a case this big.' Which would be fine and good except that we're *always* on a huge case. When I point out the fact that I'm sleep deprived and more likely to make errors in this condition, he says, 'No rest for the best,' or, 'There'll be plenty of time to sleep when you're dead,' then claps my shoulder and goes home for a nap. He's already put in his time. He's earned his sleep. I, on the other hand, am the wayward son returning to prove my worth."

I ran an arm over his shoulders and tugged him against me, taking a seat at his side. "I have a parent just like that. If I can do it, you can do it. And for what it's worth, I'm glad you came home. I'd have gone full bananas by now without you."

He feigned shock and pulled away. "Not full bananas."

"Yep."

"Well, we couldn't have that." He tugged his tie loose and unfastened the top two buttons on his shirt. "I miss professional volleyball. The clothes were more comfortable, and my coach was nicer." He snapped his briefcase open and handed me a thin stack of papers.

I skimmed the text. "Mr. Becker might've died before entering the freezer." I worked the new information around in my head. "I don't think that helps my case. Dad could've whacked him on the head and dragged him in there. Anyone could have. Or maybe he was already in there when he was conked."

Chase made a little cheese-and-cracker sandwich. "Maybe. The report's preliminary. No new news, other than the head injury. Cause and time of death have to come from the ME. That's a report I'd like to get my hands on. It'll include a description of what he might've been hit with."

I fumed inwardly. Why hadn't Jack returned my texts? It'd been hours since I'd first asked him for some simple details. We were friends. Weren't we? "I should've known about the head injury. Why didn't anyone tell me sooner?"

Chase sat back with a sigh. "Anyone like Jack?"

I climbed off my stool, clutching the papers, and paced the floor. "Would it have killed him to text me?" I blurted. "There's never been anything more important than this, and he can't poke his phone screen a few times for me?"

I skimmed the document slowly, hoping something new would stand out. "Whoever put the doorstop in front of the door must not have known the lock was busted."

"A reasonable assumption."

"I think I can rule out any workers with knowledge about the freezer. Unless the stopper was put there to throw us off their trail."

"You might be overthinking now."

"Okay, but what about the emergency light? Oh, no." I cringed. "If the knock on the head didn't kill him, then he regained consciousness at some point and knew he was trapped. He turned on the emergency light and waited for help that never came."

Penelope dashed under my feet, nearly scaring me senseless. She wound around Chase's ankles and darted away before I could catch her for a snuggle. The row of newly painted cabinet doors clattered into a pile.

"I don't know why you don't pay someone to rehang those," Chase said. "You're too busy to remodel your kitchen." He laughed. "Who does stuff like this?"

"My dad." I restacked the doors. "He made me try everything before I was allowed to ask for help. Now I can do all kinds of things, like remove, prime, and repaint these doors. I'll rehang them too, as soon as I have time. It's not like I tried to hang the cabinets. I'm just refinishing them." I knocked on the granite. "Don't tell Dad, but I didn't even try to install the new countertops. I made one phone call and presto. Free delivery and installation."

"Rebel." Chase turned curious blue eyes on me the way he did whenever the subject came up. "Speaking of massive renovation funds, how's it going with Grandpa Smacker?"

"Things are good."

"Uh-huh." He sipped his wine and watched me squirm. "You sold some of your recipes to Grandpa Smacker's Homemade Preserves for a pet-friendly companion line to their bestselling spreads."

"Correct."

"You were paid a sizeable advance and remain on staff as a consultant until the line rolls out this summer."

I pressed the wine glass to my lips and sucked. "That sums it up."

"I see." He wiped his mouth on a napkin. "Tell me the part you're keeping from me."

I tried to rearrange my expression and failed. "What do you mean?"

"You're keeping something from me," he mused, "which is fine. Even the closest friends keep a few things to themselves, but you, Lacy Marie Crocker, are a sharer. An oversharer, really, and I can't help wondering what this is about." He pointed at my face.

I bit my tongue. He was right, but this secret wasn't mine to tell. "I'm not an oversharer."

"Wrong. You tell me *everything*. I know more about you than I want to, yet anytime the topic of Grandpa Smacker comes up, you go mum. Why is that?"

I rested my arms at my sides. Crossed them. Dropped them again. What did I usually do with my hands? Why were they just hanging there?

He held my gaze another long beat before changing the subject. "I don't want you to worry about your dad. He isn't going to be convicted. He didn't do it, and our local detectives are sharp. Plus, if they somehow manage to charge him, he has the means to retain a top-tier defense attorney."

I stopped pacing. "He's my dad."

Chase joined me in the room's center and caught me by one wrist. "I know." He pulled me against his chest and set his chin on top of my head. "He's going to be okay, and so are you." He lifted my heavy arms and placed them around his waist.

I buried my cheek in the valley of his chest and inhaled the scents I'd come to associate with safety.

"Did you know your dad taught me to drive?" His deep voice vibrated my cheek.

"What?" I pulled back for a look at his face.

"I was fifteen and a half, praying for sixteen, and my parents were busy worshipping Carter. They were never home. Always looking at colleges with Carter, attending his baseball games and academic debates. Fretting over his future."

"Don't sound bitter or anything."

He released me on the heels of a hearty laugh. "I'm not *now*. Now he's my best friend, but back then, I hated the guy. I loathed him throughout my entire adolescent life. Everyone thought Carter hung the moon, and I was an emotional drain on the family. Everyone was right on both counts, of course. I couldn't even yell fraud. He was perfect, always striving to please our parents, while all I wanted to know was how soon I could leave their unyielding grasp." He rubbed a hand through his hair. "One night, your dad came by looking for my dad, but he'd gone somewhere with Carter. So your dad came back a few days later.

Same thing. The second time, he stayed and waited. Dad didn't come home for two hours, but your dad stayed. He asked me about my most recent suspension for fighting and how volleyball was going. Eventually, he ordered fish tacos and took me with him to pick them up. On the way home, we started talking about driving, and I confessed I hadn't had a lesson. He drove us straight to the lot behind Armstrong Park. We ate tacos and talked about the gauges on the dash, what they meant, why they're important. When we finished, he handed me the keys."

That sounded exactly like my dad. "Where was I?"

"Who knows?" Chase gave me a sad smile. "He worried a lot about you back then. I was troublesome, but you were practically a delinquent."

"Was not." I was more like a teenage Houdini who'd mastered the art of vanishing from her room after curfew to kiss boys who lived outside the district. "Okay. Maybe I was a tad rebellious, but I never meant to worry Dad." I stepped away from Chase. "I'd only intended to upset my mom."

He nodded. "Well, for what it's worth, I kept your dad's mind off of whatever you were up to at least once a week for a couple months. He picked me up every Saturday after that for tacos and a driving lesson."

My heart swelled with love for my father, appreciation for Chase, and a million other things I couldn't name. "I can't believe I never knew that."

"Your dad's like that with everyone. It's who he is and everyone knows it. No one's going to believe he killed Mr. Becker. They might be clamoring for gossip right now, but in their hearts, they know."

I moved back against his chest and laid my cheek over his heart. "Thank you."

"It's no problem. It's the truth."

I wrapped my arms around his middle and inhaled the comforting scents of fabric softener, mint gum, and cologne. "Thank you for being there for him when I wasn't. For taking his mind off his obstinate daughter. And for being his friend."

His strong arms curled more tightly over me. "You want to kiss me now?"

I laughed. "Yeah. A lot," I confessed. Maybe I *was* an oversharer.

He released me with a cocky grin. "Good." He pinned me with a ready stare. A cocky smile slid into place. "Go on." He lowered his voice to a smooth whisper. "You can do it."

Time slowed to a crawl, and for a moment, every thought in my head seemed vacuumed away. He didn't move as I pressed my mouth to his, allowing me complete control and, more important, the opportunity to abort. Tension leaked from my body, and my eyelids fell shut.

My phone erupted with Mom's special ringtone.

I pulled back on a sharp intake of air. "It's like she knows," I whispered, pressing shaky fingertips to my mouth. I grabbed the phone and hoped for good news. "Hi, Mom."

"Lacy? This is your mother."

Chase watched as heat spread over my cheeks and neck. There was a wicked gleam in his eye.

"Hi, Mom," I said more slowly. "How's Dad? Have you heard anything more from the police or your attorney?"

"Of course not. Your father's in his office pretending that none of this is happening, and I'm out here handling things."

"What do you mean by 'things'?"

"For starters, I've hired a personal security team to watch the perimeter."

"That sounds smart. Anything else going on?"

She huffed into the receiver. "I tried to deliver my sympathies to Mrs. Becker, but she wouldn't accept my casserole. Can you believe it? She flat-out refused it and sent me off her porch in front of God and everyone."

"Who else was there?"

"No one. What do you mean?"

I rubbed my forehead. "I'm sure she just needs a little time. She's probably in shock. You can't fault her on lack of congeniality today."

"I didn't expect her to offer me tea in her best china, but she could've at least taken the darn casserole. She could've thrown it in the trash when I left, but she should have accepted it."

"Mom," I started, unsure how to say the thing she already knew, "she's hurting. Grieving. Her husband died last night." Or this morning. I couldn't be sure, since Jack wasn't speaking to me for some reason.

"She can't possibly believe your father hurt Wallace." Her voice cracked, a rare loss of composure.

I softened my voice. "Give her time."

"It's asinine." Mom sniffled.

I agreed, but I'd also never lost a husband under any circumstance, especially not any as strange as these. "What exactly did she say?" Maybe Mrs. Becker knew more than I did, and she'd let a little something slip.

"Well, for one thing, she said to count her off the District Welcoming Committee for the NPP. Now you're going to have to fill in for her. I'll get a schedule of meetings to you tomorrow."

Not the information I was looking for.

I filled one of the empty glasses with wine and took a gulp. "You put me on the Pet Pageant Welcoming Committee."

"As a Crocker, you have certain community obligations."

I tossed back another mouthful of wine. I'd heard this particular speech all my life. The only difference being that since moving home, I'd been trying to live up to her expectations, which meant I was stuck. To make it worse, she was right. I owed my district for a growing list of things. The powers that be had supported my business, rescued my trashed shop after a break-in last summer, and welcomed me home with open arms after a ten-year sabbatical. "Okay."

"What do you mean?"

"I mean I will cheerfully join you on the committee. I'm glad to help."

"Good," she said after a long pause. "I also need you to do your thing with Jack. Bond. Flirt. Use your feminine wiles if necessary, but get this insane allegation against your father squashed before the rumors do permanent damage."

I turned my back on Chase at her mention of me using my "feminine wiles." "Don't worry. I'll figure out who did this."

"No!" she shouted. "Don't do that. For heaven's sake, you practically got yourself killed the last time you poked your nose into a murder investigation. I don't care if they find

Wallace's killer. I just need to clear your father's name before I can't undo the damage. I swear my mother's probably turning over in her grave to hear such things said about this family." Her voice dropped to a rattling whisper. "You know she never wore a skirt that didn't cover her ankles, and look at us today—showing off our rear ends!"

"Mom!"

"It's true, isn't it? Oh, here comes your father. Be here for dinner tomorrow. He needs some cheering up." She disconnected without a good-bye.

I dropped the phone onto the counter and refilled my glass. "Well, that was my mother."

Chase smiled. "I gathered. I also hear you joined a new committee."

I dropped my head onto the counter. "She's practically swearing now. Nothing good can come from that. Mom never gets that worked up. It's unladylike and not respectable at all."

"I believe I've heard one or two zingers out of your mouth."

"Sometimes the crown slips."

We stared at one another in a strange heated silence. We'd finally kissed. I'd officially repaid my debt for the safe return of Penelope. Now what?

"Are you thinking about kissing me again?" he asked.

"Yes." I loaded cooled pet treats into bakery boxes lined in pink-and-green paper to keep my hands busy.

"Good."

I released a long, slow breath and sealed the final box with a fleur-de-lis sticker.

"What're you going to do now?" he asked.

I turned in a slow circle, looking for something to keep my harried mind occupied. My pink canvas tote came into view. "Since there's no chance I'm sleeping tonight"— I pulled the tote into my arms—"I guess I'll start the mock-ups for Mrs. Neidermeyer. She asked me to make seven vintage military tutus and tops for her Shih Tzus. They're performing to *Boogie Woogie Bugle Boy*. I didn't ask at the time, but they're probably dancing for the NPP Welcoming Committee." I kneaded the aching muscles in my neck and shoulders. "I guess that's me now."

"What branch are the Shih Tzus serving in?"

I wrinkled my nose. "She didn't say."

He laughed. "Why are they performing for the committee?"

"The winners will be crowned as our local ambassadors for the National Pet Pageant."

"Ah." Chase stretched to his feet. "I'm going to leave you to it." He kissed my head on his way to the front door. "I'd try for a kiss goodnight, but I don't want to press my luck. Also, I call a do-over. I'm falling asleep sitting up, so that wasn't my best work."

Not his best work? I'd kissed him twenty minutes ago and my toes still hadn't uncurled. "A do-over?" I squeaked.

"Yep."

I followed him onto the porch. "When?"

He rubbed his eyes and made a frown face. "Wait a minute. Won't making costumes for contestants in an event you're judging create a conflict of interest?"

Not the response I'd wanted. I gave his question a quick deliberation. "Probably, but there's no way I'm not making those costumes. Besides, Attorney Hawthorne, this isn't a court of law. It's the Garden District, and serving it is my civic duty." With any luck, I'd be hired to make all the competitors' costumes as well. Maybe I could use the conflict of interest angle to get out of judging.

Chase moved onto the sidewalk with a broad smile. "It also helps that your mom is the ruling queen of this place, and you're the fair princess."

"You didn't answer my question," I called.

He winked and dropped into his shiny new sports car.

I ducked inside and set my alarm. I'd just gotten through one highly anticipated kiss and he wanted another? I wouldn't survive it without an endorphin-induced coma.

Chapter Seven

Furry Godmother's advice on burning the midnight oil:
Save some for morning.

I flipped the "Closed" sign to "Open" at Furry Godmother and arranged my vintage military uniform mock-ups on a rolling rack for Mrs. Neidermeyer. Despite the occasional local rubbernecker, come to see the killer veterinarian's daughter, there was a steady stream of genuine shoppers buying valentines for their pets. I could've used a little help from Imogene, but she claimed Sunday was the Lord's Day and meant for rest. I happened to know she was planting a garden and having lunch with her friend, Veda, in the French Quarter. According to Imogene, Veda ran an enchanted cookie shop off Royal Street, and I was dying to know if it was the shop or the cookies that were magical. Imogene was too tight-lipped to give me a decent clue.

Shoppers filled the space around my bakery display, oohing and ahhing at the little pastries inside and emptying the shelves at a record-breaking pace. The line at the register made quick work of my prepackaged mixes and elastic Cupid wings for pets under twenty pounds. I'd never been so thankful for my favorite cushioned wedges. I'd come scarily close to wearing open-toe red lace pumps. If I'd worn those, I'd have been barefoot before lunch.

Eventually, the bright Louisiana sun began its descent. Happy hour slowly lured my shoppers away, tempting them into local cafés with cheap drinks and underpriced appetizers.

Penelope climbed onto Spot the moment I released him. I didn't like her to ride in an overcrowded store. Someone was bound to trip, and my shop owner's insurance didn't cover *cat*astrophes. She batted wildly at the spiral of pink pipe cleaner antennas I'd added for her entertainment. Spot bounced off a tiara display and headed in another direction.

I went to the back room to gather inventory for restocking the shelves.

When I returned, Jack's big black truck was seated at the curb outside my window, throwing shade over my front door. He strode into the shop with heavily tinted aviators over a carefully controlled cop face. A day's worth of stubble covered his cheeks. He walked inside with a bag of ice in one hand. A tear in the top threatened to spill the fast-melting contents. Red syrup dripped through the bag. "Is this yours?"

I stumbled back a step and emptied my arms on the counter. "Where'd you get that?"

"It was leaning against your front door. There's melting ice all over the bench out there and puddles on the sidewalk. You want to tell me what's going on? Don't say 'nothing' because I can see on your face that this means something to you."

It meant the person chucking ice at me from the Tonka truck hadn't been a random hoodlum. That ice had been a threat, and now someone had left another much larger one on my doorstep.

A cold twist of nausea spiraled through me. Whoever was responsible for the ice knew what I drove and where I worked.

"Lacy?" Jack's deep tenor pulled me back to the moment.

I forced what I hoped was a congenial expression and met him in the middle of the room. "You're dripping." I pushed him to the door.

He set the bag outside. "Talk."

I grabbed a roll of paper towels and mopped up the floor. "Some crazy person in a big yellow Tonka truck was pelting my car with ice yesterday."

"Why?"

I finished the job and stood. "Because they're crazy?"

He didn't look convinced.

"I don't know, and I'm trying not to read too far into the ten-pound bag with blood-colored syrup."

Jack scowled over his shoulder at the front window, where the tip of the bag was still visible outside.

I needed a change of subject. "I've texted you a half dozen times. You didn't answer, and I was starting to worry."

"There was a shooting in the Lower Ninth Ward. I was tied up late into the night."

I simmered in silence, torn between my need for information and a broken heart for whoever had been involved in the shooting. "I'm sorry to hear that. I hope there weren't any casualties."

He dragged his slow gaze over me, and I tried not to overthink my outfit. The blue pleated skirt and white V-neck blouse were adorable, district appropriate, and slightly boho chic.

Jack, on the other hand, looked like trouble. His overall vibe was more renegade cowboy than urban crime fighter.

I crossed my arms to keep from fidgeting. "I heard Mr. Becker had a knock on the head. Was that the cause of death?"

He raised his eyebrows. "How do you know that?"

"Police report," I hedged. "Public record."

Jack leaned forward, bridging the significant gap in our heights. "I'm handling this." He furrowed his brow.

I stuffed my thumbnail between my teeth and gnawed. "What was the official cause of death?"

"If I tell you, will you stop digging?"

"I'm not."

He peeled the glasses off his face and tucked them into his shirt pocket. "You pulled the police report."

I bit into the tender skin along my cuticle to keep from tattling on Chase and opening another can of worms.

He rubbed his square jaw, pulling my attention to the peppering of tiny white scars hidden beneath the stubble. One more of his many secrets I'd never know. "It could be another day or so before I get anything official back from the ME."

I dropped my hand to my side and hid my throbbing thumb inside my fist. "Okay. At least tell me you're done looking at my dad as a suspect."

"I'm following up on all leads. That's my job, even when you don't approve of the direction it takes me." His voice was patient and tender, worrying me further.

"This is my dad," I pleaded. "What about your gut? What does that say?"

He cocked a hip and rested one hand on the butt of his sidearm. "My gut can't keep your dad out of jail. I'm hunting admissible, irrefutable evidence."

I blew out a shuddered breath to calm my jarring fear.

He scanned the empty store. "I'm looking into Becker's finances. Maybe that'll take me in a new direction."

"It was probably his wife. It's always the spouse."

"I'll keep that in mind." His cheek twitched.

I smiled. "Did you know Mrs. Becker refused my mother's casserole? Who does that?"

Jack's cheeks lost the battle to stay somber. His lips curled into a handsome beam. "It's no wonder. She thinks your dad killed her husband. Tell your mama bourbon works better on Mrs. Becker than food. No one enjoys a stiff drink more than a 1975 rodeo cowgirl."

"No!" I pressed cool fingers to my lips, trying to imagine a young Mrs. Becker riding bareback.

Jack's smile turned sly. "Everyone's got secrets. Some are just a whole lot easier to dig up than others."

"Speaking of secrets." I spun on my toes and headed for the slightly more private space behind my counter. I bent my finger for him to follow. "Any news on the other thing you're looking into?" In other words, had he gotten any further in his search for Grandpa Smacker's ex-girlfriend?

Jack had been looking into his grandpa's death for more than a year. He'd specifically taken an interest in Tabitha, his grandpa's former live-in girlfriend, but she was a ghost. So far, all we knew for sure was that she had no job, a mysterious bank account that never depleted, and a nearly untraceable past. I'd signed on last fall for a little friendly espionage assist. On the surface, I'd sold a few organic pet recipes to the Grandpa Smacker company and hung around infrequently to advise on branding and alternative ingredients that might save the company money during production. Secretly, I spent a couple hours a week on site hoping to overhear something Jack might find useful in his quest for truth. Sadly, so far I'd failed. I hadn't seen or heard anything the slightest bit shady in months of working there. Either the employees were all Walt Disney–grade happy, or I was a lousy sleuth. For Dad's sake, I hoped it wasn't the latter.

I'd get back to helping Jack once Mr. Becker's killer was found. For now, all I could think about was keeping my father out of jail.

Jack jerked his head around, double-checking for eavesdroppers. "No." His expression was grim when he turned back to me. "Nothing since she moved out at Christmas. What about you? Have you overheard anything suspicious at my company?"

"Nope. Everyone's sugary sweet." Almost to a fault, as if their hiring paperwork didn't allow for any other emotions while on the premises. "Plenty of female employees wish you'd come by more often, but whatever." I gave him a delicate smile to hide the irrational note of jealousy in my tone.

Jack's expression turned cocky. "Is that so?"

"Yep."

He pulled the phone from his back pocket and stared at its screen. "I've got to go."

I hopped to attention. "Was that the ME?"

He slid dark sunglasses back over his eyes and tucked the phone back into his pocket. "For the record, I know it was Chase who pulled that police report, and I'm proud of you for taking a step back on this case. It shows you trust me to handle it and that you've learned something from your last two run-ins with psychotic lunatics. There's hope for you yet, kitten."

"Well, Karen's definitely earned her pay," I muttered. "And I don't like when you call me that."

His eyebrows crowded together behind the dark lenses. "You're still seeing the psychiatrist?"

"She's a licensed family counselor specializing in trauma recovery." A hot poker of frustration burned through me. "You know if I had any idea how to help my dad, I would, and that has nothing to do with trusting you."

He lifted a palm and hovered it between us before shoving it into his front pocket, as if he'd considered touching me and changed his mind. "You're helping him by letting me handle this. Don't forget I said that." He crossed the shop in four long strides and launched onto the sidewalk at a jog. A moment later, he and his big truck were nothing but taillights. Whatever was in that last text message had put a fire in his boots.

I would've dwelled on the mystery longer, but something else he'd said sneaked back into mind.

Mrs. Becker likes bourbon.

* * *

I parked across the street from the Beckers' Greek Revival home and applied fresh lip gloss with the help of my rear-view mirror. I'd gone home after work to drop Penelope off; feed Buttercup, my betta fish; and swap my lively pleated-skirt-and-blouse combo for a vintage black dress with a high collar and low hem. I'd even found stumpy but sensible two-inch pumps at the back of my closet for a more modest and unoffending look. After twisting my hair into a tight bun and stopping at the liquor store, I was ready to play the role of supportive neighbor to Mrs. Becker.

I met a couple on the narrow sidewalk leading away from her home. They stepped into single file with matching sober expressions as I approached. The woman pressed a handkerchief to the corner of one eye. The man nodded.

I climbed the front steps with controlled effort, staunching my desire to rush in begging for answers about the tragic night's events. If anyone had all the facts, surely it was the widow.

The front door swung open before I knocked. A trio of women spilled onto the porch with tear-stained faces. "We love you," they sang in near unison. "If you need anything at all, don't hesitate to ask." They stumbled against one another, blowing air kisses and trailing the sweet scent of liquor in their wake.

I pressed a hand to my nose, practically drunk on the air.

A grim-faced woman stared at me from the interior side of a storm door. "Who are you?" she asked through the glass. Her gaze halted on my empty hands. "Are you an insurance agent or a lawyer of some kind?"

"No, ma'am."

"Reporter?"

"No. I'm a neighbor. I grew up in the area, and I wanted to pay my respects." All true, but I also had some questions.

She rocked back on her heels, crossing her arms over a threadbare Kentucky State T-shirt and jeans. "Name?"

"Lacy." I bit the insides of my cheeks to keep from adding the "Crocker" to my introduction as Mom had taught me. Normally, our last name was a point of pride that spoke volumes on our behalf. This time, those two little syllables were the surest way to get myself kicked to the curb.

Mrs. Becker wiggled her ultrathin eyebrows, apparently waiting for something.

"Oh!" I unzipped my handbag and reached for the bottle of authentic Kentucky bourbon inside. "I thought this might help with your day."

Her glassy eyes lit up. "Well, why didn't you say so?" She pushed the door open and let me pass.

"Thank you."

She accepted the bottle of amber liquid with eager hands and padded deep into the house. I followed, trying to imagine the narrow, middle-aged woman before me in cowgirl chaps.

Wide wooden trim outlined the cavernous rooms with twelve-foot ceilings. Gray walls and white woodwork showcased brightly colored, magazine-worthy displays of fine art and local culture. Her home was a masterpiece where each item accented another. Either Mrs. Becker had an extremely talented interior designer or she was an artist. "Your home is remarkable," I said, shuffling along behind her, taking in the beauty.

She ignored my compliment. It was probably one she heard often.

I paused to appreciate the high-polished beams underfoot. "These floorboards are magnificent."

"The floors are antique heart pine," she said. "They were reclaimed from the port of New Orleans." She stopped in a comfortable parlor and set two tumblers on an antique sideboard.

A chubby gray cat pranced into view and led me to an armchair in the corner. Mrs. Becker extended a glass of bourbon in my direction. "That's Dimitri Midnight Gregori. He's a Russian Blue." She sipped her drink. "Dimitri was sired by the award-winning Dominique Alek Gregori of Tampa."

"Ah." I accepted the drink with a small smile.

"Do you like cats?"

"I love all animals. I have a tabby."

She finished her drink before falling onto an antique loveseat surrounded by castoff tissues. "You said you're from the neighborhood?"

"Yes. All my life." I allowed my gaze to wander the room, taking in family photos on the broad fireplace mantle and hung in elaborate groupings on her walls. She and Mr. Becker seemed genuinely happy in every shot, often accompanied by a young man at various ages. I smiled at a photo of the man tucked between his parents and dressed in a cap and gown. "Your son?"

"Yes." She sighed. Her glossy eyes batted heavy tears as she poured and threw back another shot of bourbon.

Something caught her attention, and she set the glass aside. She stretched the hem of her shirt for a better look at

the seam. A fleck of hot pink protruded from the materia
attached, it seemed, by little more than static electricity an
misfortune.

My heart leapt. Whatever it was looked a lot like the
thing that had been on the floor of the reception hall freezer.

Mrs. Becker frowned and tried to flick the offender
away, failing several times before it fluttered to the floor on
its own.

I rolled my glass between my palms, watching the little
pink scrap and wondering if I really had seen it before.

"Hello," she drawled long and slow.

I yanked my attention to her face. "Sorry. What?"

"Did you know my son? You both grew up here. You
must've known one another."

"We didn't," I assured.

She shuffled her feet, successfully drawing my attention back to the floor. The little pink sticker had vanished
among the piles of crumbled tissues. She must've cried all
day to make such a mess.

My heart broke at the thought. "I'm truly sorry for your
loss, Mrs. Becker. I didn't know your husband, but from
what I understand, the world has lost a good man."

She finished shot number three and managed to look as
if I'd shoved a lemon in her mouth. "A good man? Is that
what you've heard?"

"Yes. I think so. Why?" He must've been. Dad chose his
friends with care. "Wasn't he?"

She poured another shot, though the others already
seemed to have a good grip on her. "Everyone loves to hype
up his accomplishments, but no one ever asks how he managed them. No one asks what the woman in his life has

done to make those things possible." Her speech slurred slightly. "I gave up everything to be his wife, and he had the nerve to cheat on me. And at his age? Shameless!"

"I'm so sorry. I had no idea."

Her head swayed and her eyelids drooped. "With some blonde woman half his age, no less."

I couldn't help thinking of Jack's grandpa and his too-young, blonde pinup girlfriend that had conveniently vanished when Jack began focusing on her as a suspect for murder. Was it pure coincidence that the district's tight circle of wealth had experienced another unusual death so soon, and that the current victim also had an excessively young mistress? "Sure sounds like Tabitha," I mumbled.

Her eyes popped open. "Who?" A sliver of clarity slipped into her eyes. "What did you say?"

"It's nothing." I patted my handbag. "I thought I heard my phone. Maybe I can make you some coffee?" I offered. "Are you staying here alone now?" Surely someone her size shouldn't drink anymore. I silently cursed my decision to bring the bourbon.

"I'm all alone tonight." She made a weird face. "Wallace always had a thing for blondes like you. I used to color my hair, but once I learned he was a no good snake in the grass, I decided to wear it how I liked." She combed the wavy, salt-and-pepper strands between her fingers. "To heck with him. Jerk." She set her empty glass on the floor amid the crumbled tissues and a previously emptied bottle. A whimper bubbled free from her lips.

"Are you okay?" I asked. "Maybe you shouldn't be alone."

She cuddled the new bottle on her lap and tipped herself against the chair's cushioned arm. "I've been staying here alone since the minute Wallace found out about his kidney failure. He started running off every night he could. Behaving like a fraternity boy."

"Your husband was sick? I'm so sorry. I had no idea." Kidney failure was serious and hardly motivation for finding a mistress. Didn't sick people cling to their loved ones? Get a new lease on life?

"Wallace struggled with high blood pressure for years. Diabetes came later, but we got a handle on that with diet and exercise. He did well for a while, then everything changed." She rubbed a wrist under her drippy nose.

I slid to the edge of my seat for better concentration.

"The same routines weren't working anymore. He needed a new kidney." She choked on a sob. "He told me he made a bucket list, but I never expected finding another woman was on it!"

"Do you think his diminished health contributed to his death?" Illness might explain how one night in the freezer had killed him, if the blow to the head hadn't.

Mrs. Becker swiveled upright and latched her unsteady gaze on me. "No. His friend hit him over the head. Can you imagine? He's fighting for his life with all these physical challenges, and a man he trusted knocked him dead."

I bit the insides of both cheeks. "I'm sure that's not true. What could possibly be his friend's motive?"

"Who knows why criminals do anything? Maybe the guy's a psychopath. Maybe he has rage issues." Her bloodshot eyes narrowed into slits. "You look awfully familiar. What'd you say your name was?"

"Uhm." I sprang to my feet, purse in hand. I looked just like my mother, who Mrs. Becker had thrown out yesterday. "You know what? You've clearly had a terrible day. I'm going to see myself out." Sweat beaded on my forehead. "Don't worry about me. I remember the way."

She followed me through the house, weaving and bouncing off walls and furniture. "What's your name?" she demanded in a loud, crackly voice. Boxes marked for donation scattered and slid over the polished floors as she barreled into a stack by the stairwell. "Lisa? Linda?"

I moved more quickly, checking over my shoulder as she gained on me. Her small, pleasant features had morphed into a wild and dangerous expression.

"Good-bye." I waved to Dimitri Midnight Gregori, now perched in the bay window, and barreled onto Mrs. Becker's porch, racing toward the sidewalk. "Sincerest sympathies."

"Lucy!" she screamed, barring her teeth. "It's Lucy! Lucy what?"

I ducked into my car and drove away. I could suddenly picture the whole bull-riding thing. The animals were probably terrified of her, especially if she'd had a few shots before her run. Bulls probably rolled over in submission.

I slowed at a stop sign and heaved a sigh of relief. Slowly, a smile spread over my lips. The trip had been a little scary, but well worth the trouble. One bottle of bourbon had bought me two new suspects. An angry drunk wife and a mysterious young mistress. Not bad work for a pet clothing designer.

Chapter Eight

Furry Godmother's advice on cocktails with your mother:
Make yours a double.

The alarm on my phone beeped and pulsed in my handbag. I fished it free at the next stoplight to see what I'd forgotten. A line of blue letters on the screen spelled: Operation Cheer Dad Up.

In other words, dinner with my parents.

Unlike most things in my life, this was excellent timing. I dropped the phone on my passenger seat and hooked the next right toward the Conti-Crocker abode. I couldn't wait to see how much Dad knew about his friend's poor health and sketchy extramarital behaviors. And had he ever seen Mrs. Becker liquored up on bourbon? *Yikes.*

I added some pressure to the accelerator, easing over the speed limit. No wonder Dad had looked so troubled. He was probably keeping Mr. Becker's secrets. Maybe they'd even argued about the affair. Dad had a zero-tolerance policy for infidelity.

I cruised through the district on autopilot, mentally rehashing all I'd seen and heard at the Becker house and avoiding the main streets, already teeming with evening activity. The sky had marbled into a lovely gray-and-cobalt combination. The moon peeked from behind strips of fast-moving clouds, and a colony of bats swooped majestically through the cool evening air. I cast a wayward glance at my phone, lying idle on the passenger seat. Did Jack know everything I knew now? What did he think about another dead man with a blonde mistress who was half his age? Would Mrs. Becker have been so candid with the detective on her husband's case? Should I ask him? I tapped my thumbs against the steering wheel as I pulled into my parents' driveway. If I told Jack I'd visited Mrs. Becker, he'd gripe and complain and likely accuse me of messing with his investigation. Whenever I'd gotten the scoop over him in the past, he'd thrown around his favorite word: *obstruction*.

I settled the engine and weighed my options. Jack needed the information, but wasn't he a detective? Shouldn't he know more than I did? I rolled my head against the seatback and groaned. I knew firsthand that wasn't always the case. If he knew about the mistress and I told him, he'd complain that I was digging. If he didn't know, how could he figure out who she was and look into her alibi? And if I didn't ask, how would I know if he knew? Furthermore, given the mistress's existence, Mrs. Becker's alibi could definitely use a second look as well.

I released my seat belt and brought Jack's number up on speed dial, unable to motivate my thumb to press call. Did I really want to be yelled at five minutes before listening to my mom complain through dinner?

"What are you doing?" Mom's muffled voice warbled through the glass. "Are you planning to come inside or sit out here all night?" She peered into my window with one hand at her brow, working as a makeshift visor. "Are you ill?" Her apricot blouse brought out the flush in her cheeks.

I cleared Jack's number from my screen and hiked my purse over one shoulder. If anyone was doing anything she didn't understand, she assumed they were ill, mentally or otherwise. She was obsessed with illness. Probably part of the reason she'd pushed me into premed at her alma mater.

"Hi, Mom." I climbed out and beeped my doors locked. "Sorry, I was thinking of calling Jack, but that can wait."

We ghosted into the dining room like two women with too much on their minds and sat silently at the table. The spicy scents of Cajun seasoning wafted from the kitchen and hung in the air around my head, inciting an immediate Pavlovian response. "Something smells amazing."

Mom glanced sadly at the kitchen door. "It certainly does." She poured two glasses of ice water from the pitcher on the already set table. "Why are you dressed like that?"

That was a story I'd hoped to tell her and Dad together.

Something clattered in the kitchen.

"Is Dad in there?" I stared at the door, willing him to appear. The most I'd ever seen Dad accomplish in the kitchen was tea.

Mom waved her hand dismissively. "Imogene insisted on cooking so I could spend time with my husband."

I smiled. "I love her."

"Yes, but where's my husband? I'll tell you. He's in his office tending to imaginary pets. Does he think I don't know he's alone in there?"

"Maybe he's taking time to process. It's been a rough couple of days."

"You think I don't know that?"

The back door creaked open and snapped shut, sending Mom into silence. A moment later, Voodoo jogged through the room and collapsed on my feet.

"Hello, Imogene." Dad's voice sounded in the kitchen, followed by running water.

Mom fluttered her hands in the air. "He's washing up. Act natural," she whispered.

I folded my hands on the table, suddenly unsure how to comply. "Hi, Dad," I trilled when he pushed through the swinging door from the kitchen. "Hungry?"

Mom shot me a pointed look.

I lifted my shoulders to my ears. "What?" I mouthed.

He kissed my head. Peppermint and aftershave filtered through my hazy mind. Dad smelled like home. Like joy and nostalgia. My heart clenched with reminders of the awful things people were saying about him online. He had a seat at the head of the table. "How are you two holding up?"

No one answered.

"Silly question." Sadness crept into his tone. "I'm sorry this is so hard on you both." He shook his head and muttered, "I'm sure it will get much worse before it gets better." The sincerity in his face broke my heart. "It will get better."

"Dad," I started, unsure how to ask the things I wanted to know, other than to simply come out with them, "did you know Wallace Becker was sick?"

Mom frowned. "What do you mean? How sick? How do you know?" She shifted on her seat, eyeballing Dad. "Was he contagious?"

I answered her question, but kept my eyes on Dad. "I've recently learned that Wallace Becker had ongoing health problems that led to kidney failure."

"Kidney failure!" she squeaked.

Dad nodded. "I knew. How did you?"

Heat crept over my cheeks. For the first time since I had the bright idea to visit Mrs. Becker, I felt guilty for the intrusion. "I stopped to pay my condolences."

Mom guffawed. "Well, that's ridiculous." Offense sharpened her words. "I can't believe she spoke to you." I could practically hear the subtext. *She wouldn't speak to me, and I brought her a casserole!*

"I didn't give my last name, and I brought her a bottle of Jack Daniels."

"Lacy, really." Mom scolded. "That's terribly inappropriate."

"I know." I pressed a palm to my neck, hoping to subdue the growing heat of embarrassment. "I was desperate. She also said Mr. Becker had fidelity issues."

Dad closed his eyes. "It's not what she thought."

Mom made a disgusted throaty noise. "*You* knew? This is the sort of thing that normally outrages you. What did you say to him?" She looked away before he could answer, venting to me instead. "What is wrong with people these days? Do vows mean nothing anymore?"

I made a weird sound, suddenly unable to articulate my thoughts on the matter.

"Do I know this woman?" She turned her fury back to Dad. "Did *you*?"

He scoffed. "Of course not." He covered Mom's hand with his on the table between them. "Wallace was a fool," he whispered.

She softened. Dad cradled their adjoined hands with his free one, and she stroked his fingers with her thumb. "I can't believe he'd do something like that," she said. "Secrets are no good, and that goes for you too. We've let you sulk in your office long enough. Now please let us help you. No matter what is happening, you aren't going through this alone. We're Team Crocker, and we need you."

I smiled. Team Crocker sounded like exactly the type of thing I wanted to be part of. I added my hand to the pile. "Team Crocker."

Dad smiled.

I pulled my hand back and asked the thing that was eating away at me first. "Who was Mr. Becker seeing?"

Dad didn't answer.

Mom leaned in. "Well?"

He shook his head. "That's not for me to say."

"You just said no more secrets," she balked.

He gave a sad, apologetic face.

I could appreciate Dad's loyalty, but Mr. Becker was dead, and the information was vital. "You have to tell someone. What if this woman was the one who killed him? Or what if Mrs. Becker had enough and did something about it?"

Dad look conflicted, but remained silent.

I sat straighter and pulled my shoulders back. "I'm not going to let you go to jail for this. I'll get answers one way or another. If not from you, then however else I can."

Dad unbuttoned the top buttons on his dress shirt with a long groan. "Leave it alone, pumpkin." He turned pleading eyes on Mom. "Tell her, Violet."

Mom made a droll face. "As if she'd listen. She's your daughter. Stubborn as the day is long."

And Mom was so laid back and easygoing.

"You might as well tell her what she wants to know," she said, "before she winds up in the ER again."

My tummy dropped. Images of the night I'd broken my leg while escaping a killer sent glaciers of fear through my chest. Cool beads of sweat formed on my temple. Memories of my screams rang in my ears.

"Lacy?" Dad's voice broke me from the silent nightmare. "Honey?"

"I'm okay," I lied. I refocused on the trouble at hand. "Please tell me what you know."

Dad stretched free from Mom's hands. "I don't know what I know. Maybe nothing more than you." He pinched the bridge of his nose. "Wallace was agitated, but he wasn't one to talk about personal things, so I didn't press the issue."

"He didn't give any indication about why he was upset?" I asked.

"Nothing direct, no. I mentioned his unusually dire disposition at dinner, and he said women would be the death of him. I asked if he and his wife were fighting, but he said the situation was nuanced, and he didn't want to talk about it. He was clearly in no mood for a lecture, and he knew where I stood on the topic of infidelity, so I didn't press."

"Did he say anything else?"

"Only that he nearly had everything taken care of, whatever that meant. He'd had a few drinks by that point."

"No guesses?"

Dad shook his head. "I'm afraid not, but I'm better with pets than people. You know that. I enjoy listening, but he wasn't in the mood to talk, and I'm not good at prodding people to open up. I figured he'd tell me more when he was ready, so I didn't ask. I wish more than anything that I had."

Imogene pressed the kitchen door open with one hip and delivered a steaming tray to the table. "Dinner is hot and ready." She clapped her hands and admired the feast. "There's nothing better than that to brighten a day."

The platter was lined in mounds of white rice and topped with piles of steaming shrimp and crawfish in a spicy tomato-based roux. Scents of garlic and onion set my mouth to water. I checked discreetly for drool.

"You've outdone yourself as usual, Imogene." Dad whipped a napkin in the air and settled it over his thighs. "Let's eat." He winked at me, and my heart lifted. He would beat this. And I would help.

Imogene kneaded her hands in her apron. Her attention moved to me, and the hairs at the back of my neck stood at attention. "What are you up to, Miss Lacy?"

"What do you mean?"

Her gaze traveled over my head and torso, just shy of looking directly at me. "Something's gone cockeyed with your juju." She tipped her head like a puppy trying to understand a new phrase. "You're about to get yourself in a mess of trouble."

"No, I'm not." I widened my eyes in a show of innocence and turned my palms up for proof.

She clucked her tongue and moved into my personal space, still looking over my head. "If I had to guess by whatever's going on up here"—she waved her hands over me—"I'd say you've got one foot in the thick of it already."

I didn't have to ask what she meant by "it." *It* meant trouble, and I had a lifelong pattern of finding *it*. Almost always by accident.

Mom pressed her palms to the table and wrenched upright. She marched into the kitchen and returned with a sheet of paper. "This is the meeting schedule for the NPP Welcoming Committee." She dropped the paper on the table in front of me.

Imogene frowned. "You think that was the mess I saw in her future?"

Sounded like a mess to me.

"Of course not," Mom said, "but it might keep her out of trouble. She might even meet an eligible bachelor or two."

I filled my plate with crawfish and stuffed a forkful of rice into my mouth before I said anything I'd regret about Mom's plan to marry me off at her first opportunity.

"That reminds me," she continued. "Have you found a date for your father's dinner Friday night?"

"Yes. Chase said he'd go and help out."

Imogene took the seat beside me and stole a crawfish from my plate, the way she did when she was my nanny.

"Hey!" I shoved a hand between us. "You don't have to trick me into eating anymore. I want this meal."

She grinned. "I'm just enjoying the conversation."

Mom smiled. "Thank you, Imogene."

Imogene toyed with a fat Cheshire grin. "I hear Eunice Peternick's grandson is newly single. His lazy eye is barely noticeable since he gained all that weight."

I pinched her, and she erupted in a loud hoot of hysteria. Suddenly, I could imagine her forty years younger, traveling the country with friends. She probably stole their food too.

"I swear"—Mom heaped rice onto her plate and fought a smile—"you're both impossible."

I stabbed a shrimp with my fork and savored the delectable scent. The next hour would likely amount to a rundown on the district's single men under fifty and their manageable baggage, but at least the food was excellent.

I only wished the smile on Dad's lips would reach his eyes. I couldn't help wondering, as he pushed food around his plate, pretending to eat, if the deep lines cutting through his brow were signs of grief or if there was something more that he wasn't telling me.

Chapter Nine

Furry Godmother's words of wisdom:
When running with the big dogs, wear track shoes.

Work was slower than I'd expected for a Monday morning, but at least I had time to give the place a thorough cleaning after the deluge of weekend shoppers. There were at least fifty fingerprints on my bakery display and twice as many on the turtle tank. Poor Brad and Angelina. My habit of overlooking their enchanted lagoon retreat was shameless. How could they see anything through all those smudges? "There." I cleared the last print from their glass walls with a sigh. "Now you have a lovely view of my world." I curtsied to the reptilian couple. A handful of heirloom strawberry slices from my minifridge should make up for their temporary inconvenience.

Imogene handed a logoed garment box over the counter to a customer. A wide satin ribbon hugged the shiny white center. My personalized *Thank you for choosing Furry Godmother* card was tucked lovingly beneath the bow. I smiled at the woman as she turned for the door.

"Who was that?" I asked once the shopper was on the sidewalk. "I didn't recognize her."

Imogene wiped the counter. "Pickup for Sommers. She sent her PA."

I deflated a bit. I preferred to see the customer's face when they opened the boxes, but personal assistants were taking over the day-to-day tasks of busy locals. "I'll give Mrs. Sommers a call tomorrow to follow up." I scratched a reminder onto the hot-pink notepad beside my register.

My little rolling rack of custom couture was thinning nicely again. I could barely keep it filled these days. Pet parents didn't dawdle about picking up their orders, and that seemed especially true with the National Pet Pageant on its way. Mrs. Neidermeyer was at the door when I'd arrived this morning, eager to lay eyes on the military mock-ups. She ordered seven little army costumes on the spot. The district's collective enthusiasm was hard to ignore. I'd even found myself wondering about the process the Welcoming Committee would use to choose an ambassador, and against my sensibilities, I was looking forward to the first meeting.

Imogene dusted her way through the shop, straightening shelves and doing her best not to trip over Roomba Spot and his jockey, Penelope.

I stepped out of the way. "You know what bugs me most?" I asked rhetorically as a frustrating notion did another lap through my head.

Imogene shot my legs a motherly glance. "Panty hose?"

I tugged the hem on my little red dress, which was perfect for the upcoming holiday and, as a bonus, matched the shop's current marketing theme. "No."

"I see your knees."

I pressed my arms against my sides. The dress was more than fingertip length and completely appropriate for my age and position. Mom and Imogene, however, believed no one over twenty-five had any business showing their knees in public. Short skirts were apparently a sign of immaturity and sent a childish message, if not an indecent one. I supposed that depended on the skirt, but as long as I was twenty-four-and-a-half at heart, I planned to wear whatever I wanted. The knee rule was meant more for proper society anyway, and all those people knew I was a rule breaker, Mom's personal look-alike and fixer-upper project. I met Imogene near a rack of handstitched pillows. "No one wears pantyhose anymore. I own thigh-highs and tights, but neither are appropriate for this outfit or the weather." I'd accumulated a rainbow of colored tights during my time in Arlington, but those were better suited for climates where the heat index doesn't hit "tilt" before breakfast.

Her eyebrows rose over her forehead. "Thigh-highs? Have you joined a cabaret or is this the nineteen fifties? Maybe you don't know pantyhose have been invented yet."

"I'm aware. The thing that's bugging me is Mrs. Becker, not my bare legs."

She gave my knees another look. "I'm just saying is all."

"Noted." I leaned my backside against a display table and crossed my ankles in front of me. "I don't think Mrs. Becker would kill her sick husband. What would she gain? The man was facing dialysis. Whatever he was up to was going to stop soon one way or another." I pressed my lips at the grim suggestion. "He was sick, maybe even dying. I don't think she'd murder him."

"Crimes of passion don't always make sense outside the killer's head. You of all people should know that."

I did, but the scenario didn't ring true. She followed him to the reception hall, whacked him on the head, and tossed him in the freezer? Why? To stop him from cheating? "I wonder if Mr. Becker's girlfriend knew how sick he was? Could she have a motive to kill him?" Then again, what motive did Tabitha have for slowly drugging Jack's grandpa until his heart gave out?

"Depends. Who's the girlfriend?" Imogene asked.

"I don't know. Scarlet's source said the woman was from his work." It made sense that he'd meet someone at the office. He probably spent more time at work than at home, and the bulk of Cuddle Brigade nannies were under thirty like the woman Mrs. Becker described. "Mrs. Becker said she was half his age and blonde. I need to get a look at those nannies."

"You need to let Detective Oliver handle this. Save your parents and myself a whole lot of worry."

I turned to the rolling rack, struck with inspiration. "I think Dimitri Midnight Gregori would look stunning in this. Don't you?" I plucked a velvet top hat and peacock-themed vest from the rack. "I should deliver it to Mrs. Becker at the Cuddle Brigade."

Imogene cocked a hip. "I don't know who that is, but you should stay away from angry Mrs. Becker and the Cuddle Brigade."

I slid the outfit into a garment bag. "Dimitri is the Beckers' Russian Blue. You should see him. He's beautiful."

Imogene dropped her duster on the counter and blocked my path. "What good will delivering that to the offices do? What's your plan?"

I grabbed my purse, phone, and keys from under the counter. "No plan. I'll go take a look at the nannies, and if any young blondes seem especially upset, I'll offer my condolences and a cup of coffee. Maybe the mistress needs someone to listen."

She wagged her head slowly left to right. "This is a bad idea."

"Do you mind watching the shop for an hour?"

Imogene relented her position with a sigh. "I'll burn some sage while you're out. Cast off some of that bad juju before you do something even dumber than this." She followed me to the door on squeaky orthopedic sneakers. "What about the hat and vest? Does Mrs. Becker even ever go to the Cuddle Brigade?"

I certainly hoped not.

The Cuddle Brigade offices were cheerfully decorated with photos of nannies and pets in every shape and size. A zippy jazz tune played softly through hidden speakers as I navigated the building in search of Wallace Becker's office under the ruse of kitty costume delivery.

I lingered at directional signs, eavesdropping on nanny conversations whenever possible. No one seemed especially upset, despite losing their leader over the weekend. Where were all the pitchforks and torches from those online commenters? I moved onward, slowly realizing a flaw in my plan. Clusters of empty cubicles. Some nannies were already at job sites. I wouldn't get to see them all in one trip. I'd need a reason to come back.

"Hello." A middle-aged woman with bad posture caught me staring and narrowed her eyes. She'd been whispering to a crowd of wide-eyed coworkers in matching khaki pants and logoed polo tops when I'd arrived on the floor. The group scattered when she turned her focus on me. "Can I help you?" She took a few eager steps in my direction. Curvy penciled-on eyebrows arched over each eye like fallen question marks in a startling look of surprise.

"Hello." I positioned my brightly colored kitty ensemble between us. "I'm looking for Mr. Becker's office." *Or more preferably, the young blonde with whom he was allegedly enjoying a tryst.*

Eyebrows feigned shock. "Haven't you heard? Becker's dead." She whispered the final word.

I stilled in a momentary flux, hating to lie, but also not willing to lose my advantage by saying too much.

She curved her small mouth into a little bow and proceeded to recap the weekend's horrific discovery with campfire-grade enthusiasm.

I admired the flair and practiced storytelling but didn't learn anything new. Though, for someone who wasn't present at the crime scene, she'd gathered quite an arsenal of details. I had the distinct feeling she made it her business to know what went on in her world.

"Look at that," she chuckled. "I've stunned you silent." Pleasure oozed from the words. "Becker's office is just around the corner. Would you like me to show you?"

"No, thank you." I followed the wall signs to a wide reception area with a white desk and puffy-haired woman seated behind it. Her tanned skin was heavily lined from too many years in the sun. Pinch marks along her mouth suggested she'd spent most of that time with a cigarette.

She waved me closer, gaze locked on my hands. "What a lovely costume. May I help you deliver it somewhere?"

I swallowed twice to clear the nerves from my throat. "Yes, please. A delivery for Mr. Becker." I glanced at the open set of French doors a few feet away. Photos of Mr. Becker lined the walls inside the room. Grand built-in shelves and a large mahogany desk made the perfect centerpiece. "May I?"

The woman's smile fell. "Who did you say you were?"

"I'm from Furry Godmother." I wiggled the bag. "This is for the Beckers' Russian Blue, Dimitri Midnight Gregori."

She tapped a pen to the desk and scrutinized me from head to toe, fixating, it seemed, on my long blonde hair.

No points for knowing the name and breed of their cat then. She was on to me as a fraud, but what could I do? Turn on my heels and say, "Never mind?" I brightened my smile. "Mrs. Becker said I could leave the outfit here when she placed the order last month."

"Why don't you leave it with me, and I'll see that she gets it?"

I waffled, not ready to part with a perfectly good costume unless I gained something substantial in return. Even then, it would take hours to re-create the ornate piece meant to anchor my new Mardi Gras line.

She tapped the empty spot on her desk beside a cluster of small framed photos.

The largest of the photos was taken with Mrs. Becker. The two women were on a boat holding cocktails. *Uh-oh.* They were friends, and I was busted once they'd had a chance to compare notes about intrusive blondes bearing gifts. "You know what? Why don't I deliver it to her home instead? I can see now that that would be best."

I hustled back in the direction from which I'd come and nearly toppled over Eyebrows.

"That didn't go well," she whispered. Her dimpled fingers curved around the side of a Cuddle Brigade mug. Steam rose between us.

"You were listening?" I gasped.

She paddled a tea packet through the hot water, unaffected by my accusation. "Are you a reporter? Are you here undercover to investigate the murder?"

I weighed my options. Logic dictated I flee the scene. Curiosity begged me to stay and glean new intel before the woman I'd just spoken to realized I hadn't left. I moved against the wall and Eyebrows followed.

She pressed the mug to her lips in hungry anticipation.

"My name is Lacy Crocker," I confessed. "My father was with Mr. Becker the night he died. People are saying he had something to do with what happened, but that's nonsense. I'm trying to clear his name before he's arrested for spending time with a friend on the wrong night."

Her eyes twinkled. "Oh, I love a good intrigue."

"Is there anything you can tell me that might save my father? Anything at all. Even if you think it's insignificant, I'd love to hear it. I'm desperate."

She smiled behind the rim of her mug. "Have you checked with his girlfriend?"

My heart leapt. "Do you know who that is?"

"I have my suspicions." She shot a pointed look at an empty cubicle several yards away. "Kinley's out sick today. Curious, no?"

"I don't know. Is Kinley young and blonde?"

"Yep." She winked.

"Do you know where Kinley lives?"

"You!" A vaguely familiar voice boomed nearby. Mrs. Becker charged in my direction like a tiny rhino in a fitted black dress, giant black glasses, and four-inch designer heels.

Eyebrows scurried away.

"This is her," Mrs. Becker growled.

I followed her gaze over my shoulder.

The woman who guarded Mr. Becker's office stood behind me. "I thought so. Security's on the way."

Mrs. Becker marched closer, until the adorable top hat and vest were all that could fit between us. "Let me tell you a story. A young blonde pays a grieving widow a visit and liquors her up. Sound familiar?"

"Nope." I baby-stepped backward. "But I'm sure it's a lovely story with a huge misunderstanding."

Mrs. Becker moved with me in a threatening waltz. "How about a question instead? The homewrecker I'm looking for is young and blonde. Know anyone who fits that description?"

Kinley the Absent came to mind, but that was my clue, and Mrs. Becker couldn't have it. "No."

She pointed a finger to the tip of my nose. "It's you!" Her sunglasses hid the effects of last night's bender, but the tremor in her frame couldn't be masked. She should be somewhere dark, sleeping it off, not out hunting blondes. She might do something she'd regret. "That's why you wouldn't give your last name. You're the homewrecker!"

"No. I swear." I shook my head too fast, dashing my cheeks with pale ringlet curls. "I've never even met your husband."

Eyebrows inched out of her hiding place around the corner. "Mrs. Becker?"

Mrs. Becker whipped her head around in search of the voice.

Eyebrows moved toward me. "This is Lacy Crocker."

Mrs. Becker went slack-jawed as my name registered through layers of grief and an alcohol haze. "Crocker!"

I spotted a glowing exit sign above a gathering crowd of pet nannies. "I'm just trying to find out what happened to your husband."

"You mean you're trying to save your father's hide." The elevator was behind Mrs. Becker, and there was no getting past her without a tussle.

I never tussled, and she'd kick my butt if I tried, so I'd have to take the stairs. "Saving my father and finding justice for your husband are the same things."

She scoffed. "You're as bad as your mother and her guilt casserole." She stuck her nose in the air. "Oh, dear." Her voice climbed two octaves into a childish mocking tone. "My husband killed your husband. Have some chicken. Call it even, shall we?"

Indignation burned in my pores. "That's not what she was doing, and you know it."

"And what exactly were *you* doing? Coming over after I'd already told her to kick stones? Pretending to be someone you weren't."

I ground my teeth and forced civility into my voice. "I never lied about who I was, and I've already told you. I'm trying to help."

The elevator dinged and the shiny metal doors swept open. A pair of men in black slacks and jackets stepped out. Their grave dispositions and earpieces gave them away as security.

I squeaked and ran for the stairway, bumping through the thick of gawking nannies and professing my regrets as I crunched over multiple toes. I clutched the little garment bag to my chest as I burst from the building into blinding sunlight.

I jogged across the lot and toppled into my driver's seat. Mr. Becker's mistress's name was Kinley.

Chapter Ten

Furry Godmother's tip for avoiding a catfight:
Divide the kibble.

I arrived on time to my first National Pet Pageant Welcoming Committee meeting. Mom had reserved the private upstairs room at Coquette, a restaurant on Magazine Street with gorgeous floor-to-ceiling windows, exposed brick walls, and miles of polished wood floors.

She was busy directing ladies to their seats and distributing three-ring binders in pastel colors when I sneaked in a few minutes early. Each unit was polka-dotted with tiny paw prints and personalized with the committee member's name.

I lowered myself onto an empty chair and admired the scene around me. A series of small round tables were organized in a seemingly random pattern. Though I imagined her having the pieces moved inch by inch to the perfect locations. Coordinating pastel linens and wild flower bouquets gave each table a unique personality while maintaining the uniform look. She'd outdone herself.

A waitress arrived with my place setting. "Today's personalized cocktail is the Lady's Petunia." She set a curved glass before me, filled to the sugarcoated rim with a blended sherbet-colored drink. A tiny edible flower clung to the edge. "We've also prepared chicken skewers with peanut sauce, sticky rice, and peppers." She set a tray on the table with piles of tantalizing meat and a trio of small bowls. "I'll be back to check on you in a few minutes."

She vanished in a delicious plume of sugar and spice.

I savored the medley of delectable scents and sipped the Lady's Petunia, trying not to laugh at its name.

At the front of the room, Mom clanked a spoon against her glass and the space fell silent. "Thank you for coming, ladies. I trust you've all been working hard on the assignments we spoke about at the last meeting, I certainly have been. As you can see by the folders in front of you, I've taken every suggestion to heart and broken the larger tasks into little steps. I've also divided us into two-woman teams to make things more manageable. I know how busy you all are. So"—she set her drink aside and clapped her palms together—"find the lady whose binder matches yours. She is your teammate."

The room burst into a flurry of activity and excitement as women in fancy floral dresses and light, muted colors chatted their ways through the little banquet room, seeking their new teammate.

I didn't have to look for mine. Mom had a pair of lavender binders in her arms and a coy smile on her lips. Not coincidentally, her vintage Chanel wrap dress was almost an exact match for the folders. "Why aren't you looking for your partner?" she asked.

I pointed to the folders. "I think I found her."

She set the binders on our table. "Isn't this grand?"

She returned to her podium before I could answer. I helped myself to a forkful of sticky rice.

"Take your seats," Mom instructed from her position near the fireplace. "Now that you've found your new teammate, let's discuss the points from last meeting."

The room calmed in a flash. One hand rose. The woman stood a moment later. "Before we begin, should we address the elephant in the room?" I recognized the woman as Roberta Wells, a local snob. She'd made her fortune in real estate and, according to Mom, didn't understand the workings of the district, but that didn't stop her from trying to put her mark on anything and everything she could.

The room froze. Every woman seemed to hold her breath. Roberta Wells hadn't, apparently, gotten the memo that Violet Conti-Crocker was the queen of all things and not to be trifled with.

Mom cast her gaze on me.

I gave an encouraging smile.

Roberta continued, "Dr. Crocker is rumored to have had a part in the death of Wallace Becker. What do you have to say about that?"

And there it was. I braced myself, unsure if I should hurry Mom away from the room before she did or said something she'd regret later or dial Jack and wait for police assistance.

A dozen curious faces fixed on my mother, wife of the man who gossips said murdered his friend.

Mom's jaw set. She raised her chin and turned her face away from Roberta. "The first order of business is to vote to confirm the pageant date." She fanned through a stack of loose papers in her hand before settling on one. "The Welcoming Committee will hold an event, meant for the purpose of crowning a local pet ambassador to the National Pet Pageant, on Easter weekend. All those in favor?"

Confusion wrinkled Roberta's brow.

The women murmured for several seconds before tapping their glasses in acceptance, the way guests encouraged newlyweds to kiss at a reception.

Mom's smile returned. "All opposed?"

Silence.

Roberta sat down. No one made eye contact. Except me. I raised my Lady's Petunia. *Welcome to my world, lady.*

"Very well." Mom rearranged her papers. "The date is set. Last order of business."

That was it? Two topics? I could get used to ten-minute meetings with an open bar and finger foods. Why hadn't I signed up for this job sooner? I sipped my fruity drink and emptied a skewer of its savory glazed chicken.

"Color scheme," Mom said in a dramatic singsong. "I believe we've chosen pastels in homage to traditional Easter flair. I love that you've all dressed accordingly." She made a point of not looking my way.

In keeping with my life, the little red dress I'd chosen to coordinate with my shop's valentine theme was both too little and too red for the committee's dress code. Worse, I'd get a big *I thought I told you to wear something pink* from my mother as soon as the meeting ended.

"From now through Easter, all members of this committee shall pledge to dress in accordance to the pastel code, whenever possible, for ease of identification as a committee member and in support of our purposes. All those in favor?"

More tapping of glasses.

I raised my hand, unsure of how to vote against.

Mom sent me a look that could've stopped a weaker woman's heart. I lowered my hand.

"We'll use the palette to coordinate flyers, banners, and flags with the venue decor," Mom explained.

I deflated against my seat. I had to wear pastels for weeks? I looked longingly at the nearest exit. I could take my Lady's Petunia and leave, but Mom would hunt me down and kill me.

"Don't even think about it." Mom took the seat beside mine.

"Hello." I shoved another bite of chicken between my lips.

"Thank you for coming. I hope you don't mind being my partner." She scanned the room as she spoke, carefully averting her gaze from mine. "That's why you were thinking of running, right?"

"What? No." I wiped my mouth and set the napkin beside my plate. "Of course not. Why do you always assume the worst of me?" Probably because I'd been the worst for years growing up and then I'd left. "I thought we were getting past all that these last few months."

She heaved a sigh. "You weren't thinking of leaving?"

"I was admiring the architecture," I fibbed.

She cast a regretful glance my way. "I can reassign you to another team if you'd like. Maybe one of the younger members would be better suited as your partner." A fresh flush darkened her cheeks.

"Hey." I grabbed her hand. "Mom." I stared at the side of her face until she gave up and made eye contact. "I'm glad to be your partner, and I'm in love with this committee. The food's great, the drinks are free, and the meetings are insanely short. What's not to love?"

She hitched one perfectly sculpted brow. "You're having fun?"

"Yes, but please don't make me wear a month of pastels."

Her lips twitched. "Soft colors are lovely on you."

I released her hand. "I guess I can't look any worse than I do now, showing up in scarlet while everyone else is dressed like a basket of Easter eggs."

"I told you to wear pink."

I bit my tongue as a foursome of smiling women formed a crescent around the face of our table.

Mom introduced them with great poise.

I shook their hands and tried to remember their names. "Nice to meet you."

The tallest of the group focused her attention on me. "We were thinking. Wouldn't it be great if the ambassador's court dressed as local flowers?"

I looked to Mom for details. "There's going to be a court? Like the prom queen's court?"

"Yes!" the woman and her little group enthused. "We think flower costumes will be perfect for the court. Maybe we can even have an ensemble fit for Mardi Gras royalty as the official ambassador's attire. Something to represent the city."

Mom nodded. "That's a delightful idea. What do you think, Lacy?"

"I think it sounds fantastic."

"Then it's settled," Mom said. "Lacy makes lovely costumes. I'm sure she can create whatever we'd like."

I wanted to protest on principle. It would have been nice to have been asked instead of simply assigned the job, but a parade of pets dressed as flowers danced through my mind. "I'd love to." A bubble of excitement filled my chest. The court would be darling. My fingers itched for a charcoal pencil and sketch pad. I would get to design a Mardi Gras–grade royalty costume. My heart hammered with possibilities.

"Really?" The women clapped silently and looked to my mom for confirmation.

"Really," I answered, already imagining six ways to make a proper pet bouquet.

"Wonderful!" Mom stood with a flourish. "I'll let everyone know." She headed back to the podium.

Three of the four women returned to their seats.

The speaker of the group took Mom's newly vacated chair on my right. "Thank you so much." She dipped her head close as Mom delivered the news to the group. "I practice dermatology at the clinic on Fourth," she whispered, angling her body toward mine. "I'm sorry your dad's being given such a hard time. He's a kind and honorable man. I'm sure this will all be cleared up soon."

"I hope so, thank you."

"Roberta was out of line. She's always sticking her foot in it. No one really thinks your dad hurt Mr. Becker."

Her words were an unexpected balm to my nerves. Heat rushed over my cheeks. "Thank you for saying that."

She frowned. "I hope the police find out what really happened to Mr. Becker. I didn't know him personally, but he seemed like a nice man. He always had a smile when I saw him at the clinic."

"What do you mean?" Did Mr. Becker also have a skin problem? He didn't seem the sort to visit a dermatologist for a face peel or Botox. How sick was this man?

"He had my respect. Most men his age won't see a therapist. They think men are supposed to be superhuman or emotionally stunted or something in between. And heaven forbid they need to talk to anyone about it. But Mr. Becker never missed a week."

"Mr. Becker was seeing a therapist? Why? Did he go alone?" He'd definitely needed marriage counseling.

"I'm not sure. He seemed to be alone."

Maybe his decaying health had taken a mental toll? Job stress? Keeping a woman on the side became an unmanageable emotional burden?

"Whatever the reason," she said, "he came into the clinic every Tuesday, and he always had a smile."

A glorious thought occurred, clogging my mouth with two dozen words, all fighting to get out at once. "Did you say the clinic on Fourth? Beside the chocolatier?" Karen's practice was at that clinic. I knew the place inside and out. Had Wallace Becker and I shared a therapist?

"That's the one."

Surely his therapist knew who might want to kill him. I steepled my fingers. Karen wouldn't willingly tell me anything that Mr. Becker had said in confidence, but I had a new lead!

I excused myself to take a pretend phone call, and the moment I was out of earshot, I made an appointment for some therapy.

* * *

I shouldn't have been surprised to see Jack's truck outside Furry Godmother the next morning. I parked behind him and approached with caution. He was dressed in his urban cowboy gear. I especially enjoyed the black boots. They reminded me of the time he'd driven me home on his motorcycle. He gripped a drink carrier with two cups from Café Du Monde in one hand.

"Are those apology coffees?" I asked.

"No."

Good. He wasn't here to deliver bad news. "Come on in." I unlocked the shop and disarmed my alarm, then flipped the "Open" sign around and hit the light switch. Not that I needed extra light with the fierce Southern sun beating through my big shop windows. The row of little white chandeliers flickered to life overhead, purely aesthetic but lovely nonetheless.

Jack set the cups on the counter, then released Penelope from her carrier for me.

I took my time getting over to the counter where he stood.

He trailed me with his gaze.

My hands dampened with nerves upon approach. I was clearly in trouble. The question was, why?

I cracked the top off my travel cup and tendrils of sweet steam rose into the air. "To what do I owe the pleasure?" I attempted to look more inviting and less sleep deprived than I felt. A busy mind was hard to quiet, especially at bedtime. On the upside, I was ahead on my baking and flower costume mock-ups.

Jack stared, blank faced. "You seriously don't know?"

I pursed my lips and concentrated on the heavenly scent of café au lait.

"Let me jog your memory," he offered. "Did you happen to do anything interesting yesterday?"

"I attended a committee meeting with my mom."

"Anything else?"

"I made an appointment with Karen."

He cocked his head. "Your therapist?"

"Yep."

He pressed the tip of one finger to the corner of his twitching eye. "That's good. I'm glad you did that. Anything else? For example, did you happen to run into Mrs. Becker anywhere? Perhaps at the Cuddle Brigade?"

I made a duck face. "Actually . . ." My harried mind scrambled to create a twist on the events that might make me look less like a pest, but I had nothing. "Yes."

He rubbed his face roughly with one palm. "And did you show up on her doorstep the night before? Invite yourself inside and ask personal questions about her late husband?"

The little bell over my door jingled with enthusiasm for my first round of morning shoppers.

"No." I gathered sticky curls off my shoulders and fanned my face with my free hand. "She invited me inside. Is it hot in here?" I went to check the thermostat.

Jack stalked along beside me. "Do you have any idea why I'm here yet?"

"To yell at me for bugging Mrs. Becker?" I tossed him a sweet smile and tapped on the digital temperature display. According to the device, I was having a hot flash.

"Mrs. Becker applied for a restraining order last night."

I spun on him. That was the kind of clue that could change everything. "From who?"

He mashed his handsome face into a knot. "From you," he seethed. "The judge didn't grant it. Thanks to a heavy push from me. He'd respected my grandpa, and he gave me the benefit of the doubt with you. *This time.*" Heavy emphasis on the final two words. "Moving forward, I promised to personally keep you away from Mrs. Becker."

I pressed shaky hands against my hips and huffed. An irrational pang of rejection stung my chest. No one had ever disliked me so much that they'd sought police assistance to keep me away. I was a nice lady. A proper piece of society. My chin inched upward in defiance and my shoulders rolled back. "Why on earth would she need a restraining order? There's been no threat on my part. I literally ran from her the last time I saw her."

"Your uninvited presence at her home followed by a trip to her husband's office justifies her alarm. Not to mention the man was recently murdered. She doesn't know who killed him or if someone might be coming for her. The bogus story you fed a Cuddle Brigade secretary about Mrs. Becker made everything worse. Together, the incidents can be construed as obsession, and a warrant could have been issued to you, her stalker. She could still get legal counsel involved."

"Jeez," I grumbled, hands falling from my waist. "I wasn't trying to upset her. Mom's mad enough already. I can't get in trouble with the police too."

Jack followed my lead, relenting his bossy stance. He leaned closer and locked his weary gaze on mine. "Your mother promised to whoop my behind if you got into any more trouble. I've been warned, and I don't take her threats lightly."

"You were warned," I echoed. "When?"

"When you were in the hospital after the last murder investigation you helped with." He made dramatic air quotes around the word *helped*.

A sharp realization nearly knocked me over. "Is that why you've been pushing me away?" I closed the short distance between us, containing the conversation from potentially big-eared shoppers. "My mom made you my keeper? That's not fair." And there was absolutely nothing less attractive than that. Not that I cared if he thought I was attractive. But I did.

I tilted my head back for a better view of his face from my new proximity. "Please, tell Mrs. Becker I'm emotionally distraught and seeking help. It won't happen again. I promise." I'd take care of my mother.

"Insanity? Really?" He mumbled something about the truth.

I chose to ignore it. "Stress makes people behave irrationally. My dad's been wrongfully accused of murder. The worry is taking a toll on me."

Jack made a grim face. "Is that why you're seeing Karen again?"

I didn't know where to start with all the reasons I needed to see Karen again, but this appointment was all business. "I think she was Mr. Becker's therapist too, so I made an appointment for Wednesday."

Jack pressed a hand to his chest. "*I'll* get in touch with Karen about Becker. *You* should keep the appointment for personal reasons."

"Rude."

"I'm not joking. You've been through a lot in the past year, even before you came home, and at the moment, you're clearly agitated."

"There's another killer in the district," I hissed. "Of course I'm agitated. This makes three in ten months, and my dad could wind up in jail for nothing. When is this going to stop?" I sucked air, shocked by my sudden outburst. I cupped a hand over my mouth. "I'm so sorry," I whispered. "I didn't mean to . . ." My eyes stung with embarrassment.

Jack's features softened. He ran a gentle palm from my shoulder to my elbow, leaving a trail of goose bumps on my skin. "There's always been crime in the district. You've only recently become aware of it, but it's not new." His voice was deep and strong. He gripped my elbow in his palm and dipped his face close to mine. "I know it's hard for you to believe, but NOPD does a mighty fine job without your assistance." His lips curved into a warm smile.

I chuckled. "I know. I didn't mean to freak out."

"It's okay. Understandable, like I said. You're carrying a lot of anxiety, and it would help to talk to someone who's impartial. So see Karen for you. You told me before that she helped."

"She's pretty terrific."

"Good. Try to relax. Whatever comes, take it with a grain of salt and know that I'm on your side."

I didn't like his word choice, specifically the *whatever comes* portion. Was something bad coming? Did he know what that was?

Jack released me and moved away. "Do you still have my whistle?"

The one that he'd given me at Thanksgiving? The one that had once saved my life? "Yeah." I never left home without it. "Any specific reason you're asking?"

Jack pressed his back to the wall and crossed his arms. "I just want you to stay safe." There was a fresh tone of exhaustion in his voice. Deep purple crescents underlined his eyes, and it suddenly seemed as if the wall was the only thing holding him upright.

"Have you slept?"

"Not much." He scrubbed heavy palms over his eyes. "I was up late going through Tabitha's former place and everything she left behind."

"Gain any new insight?"

Jack gave my store a long look, searching each customer slowly before turning back to me. "Maybe."

I froze. "Maybe? What?"

"It could be nothing."

Was he kidding? "You can't say something like that and then brush it off. What did you find?"

He dug long fingers into his pant pocket and liberated a square of green paper.

I took the folded cardstock in my fingertips and turned it around. Small purple silhouettes of wine bottles peppered the stiff material. A thin loop of twine ran through a little hole in the corner. "It's a gift tag." I unfolded it carefully and read the inscription. "Tabitha, keep up the good work. Sage." I returned the note to him. "Who's Sage?"

"I don't know. I found this wedged behind the baseboard in her former closet. The design makes me think the gift could've been a bottle of wine."

"That's reasonable." My eyes widened. "You think this is from one of *the* bottles. One that had drugs mixed in."

"Maybe." He exhaled long and slow. "It could also be nothing, but it's definitely interesting, all things considered."

"Agreed." I raised my eyes to his. "For a moment, when Mrs. Becker confided that her husband was seeing a blonde woman half his age, I thought it might've been Tabitha."

"She's too smart to come back here. She knows I'm looking for her."

I nodded. Jack was right. There was no way Tabitha could've been in the district enough to forge a relationship with Mr. Becker without Jack knowing about it. "We need to find out who Sage is so we can ask him about this tag."

Jack frowned. "You think Sage is a man's name?"

"I don't know. I think it's a weird one. It might be a code. What if there's a deeper meaning behind—"

"Lacy." Jack interrupted. "Stay out of this." His smile was kind, but his eyes were serious. "I mean it."

I extended a hand in his direction. "Hi, I'm Lacy Crocker. It's nice to meet you."

He pinned me with his blank cop expression.

"You know I'm going to worry about it. If you didn't want me to worry about it, why would you have shown it to me?"

He looked like I'd slapped him. "You're always saying I don't tell you things. So"—he paused—"now I'm telling you things."

"Aw." I wrapped my arms around his middle. "Thank you."

He reluctantly rested his hands on my back.

"You're finally opening up to me, and I'm definitely going to help you find Sage."

Chapter Eleven

Furry Godmother's protip:
Second banana trumps first monkey every time.

Jack held the door for Mrs. Hams on his way out.

Her bushy salt-and-pepper hair was wild with humidity as she hustled inside, keeping one eye on Jack as she passed.

He nodded at her before casting a worrisome look in my direction. "Meant what I said," he promised.

"Me too." I beamed.

I waved and pulled myself into proper shopkeeper mode. "Hi, Mrs. Hams." Mrs. Hams was Mom's nemesis and the leader of the Llama Mamas, a group of llama owners living on plantations outside the city. The Llama Mamas also raised money for charity, so when Mrs. Hams had accused Mom of being a city dweller a few years back, Mom had taken offense. How could she be faulted for the fact that her great-grandfather had sold the family plantation a century ago to build our home in the city? Mom struck at Mrs. Hams where it hurt most—her pride. She started her own group of fundraising farm animals called the Jazzy Chicks, and the war was on. Now the Llama Mamas and Jazzy Chicks battled constantly over which group has done the most good or made the biggest difference. It was silly and exhausting, but it diverted Mom's attention from me, and I called that a win. On the flip side, I worked for both groups, and that could get sticky.

I brightened my smile. "How can I help you?" Hopefully, whatever she needed wouldn't affect my mother. Mom's buttons couldn't take much more pushing this week, and I didn't want to be the one to send her over the edge.

She watched Jack pull away from the curb before bellying up to my counter. "Handsome."

"Yep."

She dug one arm into her giant quilted bag and fished around. "How's your schedule this week?"

"There's always time for you, Mrs. Hams. What do you need?"

"I'd like to do something nice for my llamas." She pulled a notepad from her bag and swiveled it to face me. "Obviously my team can't become the face of the Garden District or be crowned ambassadors for the National Pet Pageant, but they can certainly dress their part and represent the bayou."

"Of course."

She tapped an unpainted fingernail on the paper. "Eyelet lace capes and matching bonnets for the girls. Straw hats with bandanas and fleur-de-lis pins for the boys. What do you think?" She locked her small brown eyes on me.

"They're perfect." I grabbed a pink sketchpad and writing utensil from my drawer. The pencil seemed to have a mind of its own as it re-created Mrs. Hams's pictures, skating across the paper with precision. "Something like this?" My llama drawings were coming along, but the eyes were always wrong. I rubbed a gum eraser over the face, leaving its features unfinished.

Mrs. Hams watched intently as I fussed over the curve in the bonnet string. "Those are lovely. You always do such a good job of interpreting my scribbles, and you never complain. I honestly don't know how you do most of the things you do."

Pride puffed me up like a balloon. "You're very kind."

"And you're quite talented. How soon can you finish them? I can't wait to see the Mamas' faces when I present them with the finished products."

I tapped my eraser against the counter's edge. The pieces wouldn't take long once I got started, but I'd committed to the NPP court costumes yesterday. I wanted to give the committee's orders my attention first, but Mrs. Hams kept me on retainer, so I couldn't put her off. Time would be tight. I rubbed a little pile of eraser dust from the page with my thumb. "If you don't need to see mock-ups, I can probably finish them this week. I have the llamas' measurements and most of the materials to make these look fantastic."

She checked her watch. "I'll be back in town Saturday. Have them ready then." She patted the counter and left.

I hustled to the back room, hoping I had at least two bolts of white eyelet in need of a purpose.

The doorbell jingled out front. "Lacy?" Imogene's voice carried over the soft murmur of chatting customers.

"In the back," I called. I gathered the things I needed for Mrs. Hams's order and stacked them near my desk.

When she didn't come to see me, I dusted my palms and headed to the storefront.

Imogene paced behind the bakery counter, a look of exasperation on her face.

"What's wrong?"

"I can't find my apron."

I unhooked the personalized apron from a crystal knob behind her and put it in her hands. "What else is wrong?"

She slid the soft material over her head and twisted the ties into a bow at her back. "Veda's not well, and we can't reach her next of kin."

I scrutinized her disheveled appearance and the deep lines running over her forehead. There was nothing more important to Imogene than people. Her friends and family, neighbors and strangers. She wanted the best for everyone. Always. When someone in her world was hurting, her heart weathered the storm with theirs. "Have you left a message?"

She furrowed her thick brows. "We can't find her. There's no one to leave a message with."

I worked the conversation through my cluttered mind. "So the next of kin's missing?"

"Well"—she wrinkled her nose—"not necessarily."

"I'm going to need more information." And possibly a Lady's Petunia to deal with the convoluted problems of Imogene and Veda. They were, in essence, to the French Quarter what Scarlet and I were to the Garden District. Trouble.

"Veda's never met her. It doesn't work that way in her family. In fact, I'm not even sure her great-granddaughter knows she exists."

"Ah." Veda was looking for a family member who didn't know she existed. That seemed about right. I knew better than to get pulled into Imogene's whackadoodle world, but I couldn't help myself. Why didn't the great-granddaughter know about Veda? And how did Veda know about her? "If Veda's never met the woman, then what does she need her for now? Veda's one hundred, right? Is this an inheritance thing?"

"It's complicated."

My shoulders drooped. Complicated was where I jumped ship. I was swimming in complicated already. I slid one arm around Imogene's middle and tugged her against my side. "You'll figure it out. You always do."

"I hope you're right. If we don't get another Lockwood woman down here soon, all hell's going to break lose."

I'd heard her say that before, and I worried every time that she might mean it literally. "Gotcha." I stepped away and adjusted my dress. "Is there anything I can do to help?"

"No. You've got your own troubles." She nodded to window.

Across the street, Mrs. Becker came into view. She exited a restaurant holding hands with a dashing older man. "Hey." I nudged Imogene. "Who is that?"

Imogene squinted. "Looks like Mrs. Becker."

"Not her. Him."

Mrs. Becker leaned against the man's side, releasing their entwined fingers so she could wrap an arm around his back. He tipped his head against the top of hers.

"Awful handsy to be any relation."

I agreed. No wonder she was so quick to pin her husband's murder on the easiest target. She also had something to hide. A boyfriend, AKA *motive*. "Can you keep an eye on things for a minute?" I asked Imogene. "I want to say hello."

"I don't think that is a good—"

I zipped outside before she could finish her suggestion and crouched behind a delivery truck on the corner.

The happy couple kissed before climbing into an expensive-looking black car at the curb.

I patted my pockets. "Dang it." I'd left the shop too quickly. My phone was on the counter, and I didn't even have a pencil to jot down the car's license plate number.

Imogene waved from the window. I mimed taking a picture, hoping she'd get the message and snap a shot of the car and its license plate before they spotted me or drove away.

She beamed back, open mouthed, and made jazz fingers.

"Blah." I turned my attention to the happy couple. Their car pulled into traffic, leaving me hunched behind a box truck with no way to follow. "Dang it!" I creaked upright and dashed my toe in disappointment. Mrs. Becker and her dirty little secret were getting away.

I slunk back into Furry Godmother for my purse and went out again. My tummy churned. Humidity clung to my brow. I needed a cold, fruity hug to cheer me up and clear my head. The line at Frozen Banana, the smoothie shop on the corner, curled through the doors and along the sidewalk to meet me. I went to the end and leaned against the brick building for emotional support. I dialed Jack while I waited.

"Oliver," he answered.

"Hey."

"What's wrong?" he asked.

"Why assume something's wrong?"

"Have you ever called for another reason?"

"I think all information is a matter of perception," I countered. Maybe it was good news that we had a new lead and not bad news that I'd forgotten to bring my phone to capture the details. "I followed Mrs. Becker and a man from their romantic lunch date"—I paused for dramatic effect—"to his car, where they *kissed* before driving away. I didn't get the license plate number, but I can describe the car to you."

"You did what?" he asked. The eerie calm in his voice sent chills down my arms. Jack wasn't a yeller, but this wasn't my first experience with his warning voice. He didn't have to yell to make a point. He scared the bejesus out of everyone without it. "Were you even listening to me earlier?"

"Yes. I didn't go looking for the information, it fell into my line of sight. What would you have had me do? Close my eyes?"

"Yes."

"Well, it's too late for that now, and this is good news. A new lead, right? Imagine it. Two men. One woman. Fisticuffs ensued. Perhaps leading to a head injury and deadly night in the freezer. You see what I'm saying?" I crept forward with the slow-moving line.

"I'm sending you an e-mail on stalker behavior. I think you're having a tough time with the concept," he grumped.

My jaw dropped. "I followed a lead. You do it all the time."

"I'm a detective."

A young couple lined up behind me, sandwiching me in and reminding me to keep it together. I lowered my voice. "They were right outside my window. It's not as if I was waiting in her bushes with binoculars." Hurt rolled through my stomach. What did a woman have to do for an accolade these days?

"Lacy."

I waited for the apology.

"Following a woman who has tried to get a restraining order against you *supports* her argument, and it ticks me off." His voice boomed on the final three words.

"Don't use that tone. It makes me nervous."

"Oh, sure. *That* makes you nervous." He grumbled a few creative swears before settling down. "You might as well tell me about the car."

"I think it was a Cadillac. One of those decked out numbers with big shiny hubcaps and dark windows. Black. Probably new. I should also tell you I have a line on Mr. Becker's mistress." I cupped a hand around my phone and mouth, attempting to muffle my words from prying ears.

"Why didn't you tell me about the mistress when I was with you an hour ago?"

"How? You were busy scolding me about something else and then the subject changed entirely." I imagined him grinding his teeth in the silence. "While I was at Cuddle Brigade yesterday, one of the nannies suggested that Mr. Becker was seeing a worker named Kinley."

"Kinley what?"

"I don't know. Mrs. Becker came and chased me away."

Jack snorted. "None of my murder cases were this animated before you."

"Thanks." I made it through the Frozen Banana doors and sighed in contentment. Scents of spun sugar and warm vanilla encased my head, lulling me into tranquility.

"Did you just 'mmm'?"

I nodded, despite the fact he couldn't see me. "Why does it always smell like heaven and warm pound cake at Frozen Banana?"

"They make their own sugar cones."

My mouth watered. "I have to go."

"I'll run the name Kinley against the employee roster at Cuddle Brigade, and I'll see if anyone in Mrs. Becker's social circle has a new Cadillac registered to him. Meanwhile, drink your smoothie and stay out of this. At the very least, don't get caught following a woman who's accused you of stalking her."

"Fine. I won't get caught."

"Fine." Jack disconnected.

My phone buzzed immediately, and Scarlet's face appeared on the screen.

"Hello?"

"Hey, I got a new scoop on the Beckers."

Excellent. "Spill."

"A woman in my mommy and baby exercise class lives on the Beckers' block. She jogs past their house twice a day with the stroller, and she said there's always a ton of arguing going on in there. Once, the commotion was so loud, it made her daughter cry. She stopped to comfort the baby, and a minute later, the Beckers stormed into the side lawn yelling about infidelity."

"I just saw Mrs. Becker kiss a man on the street outside Furry Godmother."

Scarlet clucked her tongue. "So the new question is whether they were arguing about his infidelity or hers."

Personally, I had a whole buffet of questions on my Becker menu.

I ordered my smoothie and collected it with enthusiasm while I contemplated the most pressing theories first. "She could've wanted to get rid of Mr. Becker, but needed a way to ensure she'd get all the money. Why split the assets in a divorce when you can kill your cheating husband instead? Or maybe Mrs. Becker had had enough of his cheating and wanted to teach him a lesson. When having her own affair didn't work, she got violent."

"I should come over soon," Scarlet said. "We can make a list."

I pumped my straw in and out of the lid a few times, then sucked it flat. "Yes, please."

"Ugh." Scarlet scolded someone for eating rocks and disconnected.

By dinnertime, I'd polished everything inside Furry Godmother to a high shine and performed a handful of fruitless Internet searches on Kinley, the Cuddle Brigade nanny and potential mistress of Wallace Becker. Hopefully Jack had more luck.

A black Cadillac inched through traffic outside my window. It wasn't Mrs. Becker and her date this time, but the sight of it sent my wheels turning in a new direction. "Imogene?"

"Go on," she said from behind the counter.

I grabbed my bag and jogged across the street to the restaurant where Mrs. Becker and the man had emerged after lunch. Salu was a bistro I frequented regularly for lunch and had visited with Chase for happy hour once or twice. The food was mind-bogglingly good, and who doesn't love a two-dollar margarita?

"Hi." I bounced onto a stool at the wide mahogany bar and smiled at the bartender. Spicy scents of Cajun shrimp tickled my nose and enticed my tummy. Puffs of butter-drenched steam burst through the flapping kitchen door as servers zoomed in and out, trays of piping-hot entrées overhead. "Is the manager here?"

"Sure thing. Can I get you something while you wait?"

"No, thanks. Just the manager."

He winked one big brown eye and headed for the back room.

I tapped anxious fingers against the high-polished wood and wiggled on my seat. With any luck, the manager remembered seeing Mrs. Becker today.

A broad man with a crooked nose and round belly emerged with the barkeep and smiled when he saw me. "Lacy, how are you?"

"Hi, Stan. I'm good. Sorry to bother you."

He whipped a white towel over his shoulder. "Nonsense. What can we do for you today?" He scanned the empty space in front of me. "Where's your drink? Your appetizer? We're not making you wait, are we?"

"Oh, no. Not at all. I just came by to pick your brain. Do you know Mrs. Becker? Her husband, Wallace, owned Cuddle Brigade."

"No." He wrinkled his brow. "Why? Is everything okay?"

"Yes." I struggled for a less stalker-like reason to continue asking about her. "I saw her leaving here earlier, but I was too slow to say hello. She was gone in a flash. I hate that I missed her." My cheeks heated with the lie.

He shrugged. "I'm sorry. I wish I could help. Have I ever thanked you for sending those pupcakes to my Dalmatian, Hugo? He loved them. Couldn't get enough."

I smiled broadly. Delivering samples to every business owner on the street at Christmas had been a fantastic decision. "Hey, listen, this is going to sound strange, but did you happen to see a tall, thin, fifty-something man in here not too long ago? He was with Mrs. Becker." I chewed my lip, struggling to recall anything else about the man's appearance. "He wore a black dress coat and bright-yellow tie. Mrs. Becker is a small woman. Same age. She has short, dark hair."

Stan straightened. "The man had glasses? Round frames?" He circled a finger in front of one eye.

"Yes!"

"I think you're talking about my guy Stewart. He's a regular."

"Stewart?"

"Sure. Dr. Stewart Hawkins. Nicest guy you'll ever meet."

I shook Stan's hand and smiled.

Nice guy? Murderer? I'd be the judge of that.

Chapter Twelve

Furry Godmother's words of wisdom:
If you're feeling under the weather, check for a storm cloud.

I had to show a photo ID to visit my parents. A security guard shined his flashlight on my license and examined my face for a match. "Thank you, Ms. Crocker." He radioed someone via walkie-talkie and motioned me ahead.

I opted to park on the street for a clean getaway. There was an unidentified car in the drive, and I didn't want to get boxed in if Mom had invited a bunch of ladies over and more cars were on the way.

I hopped out with Penelope in her travel pack. The fine hairs along the back of my neck stood at attention. The sensation of being watched sifted into my bones. I checked over both shoulders, but only the guard seemed to notice me. He tipped his hat as I scuttled passed, giving him a wide berth. Not long ago, a less than stable man had posed as Mom's hired help and tried to kill me.

Mom beetled down the driveway and met me at the gate. "Come on. Hurry up."

I tiptoe-jogged to her side, trying not to shake Penelope half to death. "What's with all the double-oh-seven? Did something happen? Were you threatened?"

"Heavens no." She hustled me to the house and shoved me inside. "I told you about the added security. It's better to make a spectacle of our overdone protection than to let anyone think we can be breached."

"Ah." I freed Penelope. "In other words, you were feeling helpless and wanted to do something about it."

She frowned. "Maybe."

"Well, now you're speaking my language. The guard is probably a smart move." Assuming he wasn't a killer undercover. "If I was up to no good, I definitely would have kept driving." I turned for an inspection of the silent home around us. "Whose car is in the drive?"

"Herbert's. He's the man at the gate." She folded her hands in front of her. "Can I get you a cup of tea?"

I set Penelope's carrier on a pile of boxes near the back door. "Make mine coffee. I have an order for the Llama Mamas to take care of tonight."

"Caffeinated tea, then." She flipped her new haircut and bustled toward the kitchen. "Feel free to spill it on whatever you're making that dreaded woman and her adorable livestock."

I dropped my purse onto another box, impressed by the apparent headway Mom was making with the purging. "How's the cleaning going?" I wedged a fingertip under one box lid and peeked inside. A row of aged book spines and puzzle boxes stared up at me. "Hey! These are my things."

I pried the lids open one by one. "You can't give away my books."

Mom appeared in the doorway. "Come away from there and sit in the parlor."

I obeyed with a scowl. "Those are my books."

"The ones in boxes were piled on your floor. I packed the copies with worn covers for donation and dusted the others for display."

"The worn covers mean those were my favorite copies. I read them until the pages were soft from love and attention." I gave her my business face. "I'm taking those home."

She rolled her eyes.

That reminded me. I was already peeved at her for another reason. "Did you tell Jack you were holding him personally responsible for my safety and well-being, lest you throttle him?"

She stared defiantly.

"Well?" I crossed my arms and waited. "Why would you do that? I'm not a child in need of a sitter, and Jack has enough to do without feeling unduly burdened with your nutty requests."

Dad arrived with a tray and place settings for three. "Lacy." He set the tray on a small table before me and kissed my cheek. "I'm so glad to see you. How was your day?"

I smiled. "Good. Mom threatened Jack if he didn't keep me safe."

Dad gave her a cautious look. "She should've also told him not to mention it."

My brows rose in slow unison. "Et tu, Brute?"

His expression fell. "I'm not happy about what's happened to Wallace, or what's happening to me, but I'm thankful for all that I have in this room, and I'm not opposed to setting measures in motion to protect it."

Mom gave him a suspicious look. "I'm surprised to see you. I thought you had to work late again."

He lowered himself onto the antique Queen Anne chair beside mine. "I did, until my last two appointments cancelled. I hate to say it, but you might consider calling off the recognition dinner on Friday night."

Mom scooted to the edge of her seat, a rare look of tenderness in her normally authoritative eyes. "This will pass. I promise you. We've been through much worse, and we've survived."

Dad nodded. "I'm sure you're right."

I crossed my ankles beneath me and stretched to pour a cuppa. "What have you been through that's worse than a pending murder charge?"

"We raised you," Mom said, her troubled expression lifting. "Zing!"

Dad laughed.

I'd walked right into that, plus it was true, so I let it go. "I saw something interesting this afternoon."

"Oh, yeah?" Dad asked. "What was that?"

"Mrs. Becker kissed Dr. Stewart Hawkins outside a restaurant on Magazine Street."

He and Mom exchanged a look.

"Who?" Mom asked. "What sort of kiss?"

"Dr. Hawkins." I sipped my silky tea with delight. "A romantic one." My recently interrupted kiss with Chase crossed my mind. That moment needed to be addressed soon, but I hadn't had the spare brainpower to decide how I felt about it.

"Oh, dear." Mom lifted a cup and saucer from the tray. "Surely, she wasn't seeing Wallace's doctor on the side. How uncouth."

I gave Dad a careful look. "You don't know him?"

"No," he answered. "This is news to us." He checked with Mom for confirmation. She lifted her shoulders.

I settled my cup against my thigh. "I spent the last hour reading all about him online. He probably wasn't Mr. Becker's doctor. He's a local plastic surgeon and philanthropist who looks good on paper, but I'm wondering if he could have killed Wallace to get unlimited access to Mrs. Becker."

Mom returned her tea to the tray and rested her hands against her stomach. "You think horrible things."

"Yes, and I made an appointment to see him in the morning."

"Absolutely not," Dad said.

Mom lifted her brows in interest. "You're pretending to be a potential client? Is that safe?"

Dad shot her a look of disbelief. "Of course it's not safe. She just told us she thinks the man's a killer."

Mom steadied her gaze on me. "He can't kill her during a consultation. That would ruin his practice. Still, what do you hope to accomplish? It's not as if you can walk in and ask him about Wallace's death directly. He'd send you out on your backside." She dragged discerning eyes over me from top to bottom. "What can you get fixed?"

Dad kicked back in his chair, frustrated, disgusted, outnumbered.

I peered down at the slightly bulging button holes on my blouse. Everything was in order there. A little exercise would do wonders for anything in need of a trim or tightening. "I don't know." Aside from my height, trapped somewhere between a true petite and regular women's, I had very few complaints. "Maybe I can get that laser hair removal surgery on my legs." Never shaving again seemed like a solid time saver.

"You can always ask him about your nose," Mom suggested.

My hand flew to my face. "Hey!"

She smiled sweetly and fixed her attention on her watch.

"Got somewhere to be?" I asked.

"Imogene's picking me up for book club."

A tinge of jealousy pinched my chest. I would've loved book club. She knew that and didn't invite me. "Oh."

Someone pounded on the back door.

"Heavens!" Mom jumped.

A man's voice piped through a speaker in her kitchen. "Miss Imogene to see you, Mrs. Crocker."

She murmured about the late warning and went to open the door.

Dad turned to face me. "First of all, I don't condone you seeing this Dr. Hawkins. Second, you should know I spoke with Jack today, and he advised me to be ready for an arrest. My prints were found on the reception hall door and one of my hairs was on Wallace's shirt. It probably transferred when I hugged him in greeting."

A rock of dread formed in my gut, threatening to expel the tea. "Jack told you he might arrest you? He said that today?" I'd spoken with him twice, and he hadn't said a word. His peculiar statement flitted into mind. *Whatever comes . . . know that I'm on your side.* I gripped the teacup tighter. He'd known he might arrest my father, and he'd said nothing to me. I was running out of time, and it had only been three days since Mr. Becker's death.

"Lacy?" Imogene rumbled into the room. "I pulled this off your car window. I thought it was a parking ticket, but it looks more like a love note."

"A love note?" I highly doubted anyone would send me a love note in a nine-by-twelve manila envelope, but I took it anyway. More likely Chase had crept over from his house next door to tease me. I slid my finger under the flap and pulled the contents free. "Oh." My face and neck burned with shock and embarrassment. I flipped through the thin pile of photographs from a weekend I'd spent in New York during graduate school. Heat pooled in my gut as I raised them for closer inspection. Each picture had been sliced through at my throat, not enough to make two pieces of one page, but enough to temporarily sever my head when I lifted the photo into my hands.

Dad was on his feet with a sharp intake of breath. He marched from the room. The kitchen door snapped shut a moment later.

I stared at the baffling photos. "These were taken almost five years ago."

Mom and Imogene closed in on me, hands extended.

I passed the pictures out. "I visited New York during Fashion Week."

Imogene pinched a photo between two fingers and stretched it away from her for a better look. "What are you wearing? Are those your underpants?"

Mom gasped. "Oh, dear."

"It's a bikini."

"Who would do this?" Mom examined the careful cut across my image's throat. "It's sick."

My head swam as I sifted through the final three photos. "That swimsuit won a national competition and was featured in an article about American design schools. I wore it on a catwalk and stood for photos. These were taken at the after party." I scrambled mentally to recall details about the other guests that night. Who was there and also here? *No one.* "The event was invitation-only, but the photos were published online later. Anyone could've found and printed them if they dug long and deep enough."

I traced a fingertip over my slightly younger figure, covered in silver glitter and the perfect vintage-inspired white bikini. The tips of two shimmery angel wings framed my bottom. *Why choose these photos?*

Mom groaned at each new photo. Me on Pete's lap. The two of us canoodling in a corner.

"Pete had just proposed," I said by way of explanation. "I won the competition. I was on top of the world. It was a huge deal. I wasn't doing anything wrong. I swear."

Her face turned scarlet and then eggplant.

I turned the envelope over and shook it. A scrap of paper fell onto my lap. The top was torn away, probably to remove a telltale logo or insignia. A curlicue border in hot pink lined the sides. It was probably nothing, but the sticker on the freezer floor came to mind.

Imogene crept closer. "What does it say?"

"Stop looking into Wallace Becker's death, or your past won't be the only thing that catches up with you."

Mom pressed a hand to her chest. Imogene hugged her. Every muscle in my body tightened to the point of pain.

The back door banged open, and we all screamed.

Dad blew into the parlor with a murderous expression. "That rent-a-guard didn't see anything, and there's no one on the street to ask." He scanned our stricken expressions. "Now what?"

I passed him the note. His lips moved silently as he read. "Call Jack."

"Dad." Emotion weighted my chest. I'd wanted to help him. And I'd made it worse. The bewildered look on his face was enough to shatter my aching heart. "I'm so sorry."

He set the note on the tea tray and pulled a phone from his pocket.

Jack would be here soon.

Imogene replaced the tea with hot toddies. I helped myself to a refill or two.

Mom blew gently over the steaming amber liquid in her cup. "You never told me," she said.

"What?" I looked to Dad for translation. He stared at his shoes, utterly lost in his thoughts.

Imogene shook her head.

Mom pointed to the stack of discarded photos. "That was a huge victory for you. And you kept me out of it."

I'd carved myself out of her life the day I left for college, and I'd continued to add bricks to the wall between us for a decade, determined to find my own way, without her money, without her rules. All I'd managed to do was break her heart and make a fool of myself. Of course everyone was too polite to say the latter to my face, but it was still true. I'd gone off on an adolescent mission to find myself, and it had taken me years longer than it should have. I was a Crocker. I was part of this district. A product of my city.

I was New Orleans, and this was where I'd belonged all along. "I'm sorry."

"I wanted to know these things," she said. The words broke on her tongue. She jerked onto her feet. "I'm going to call my book club and cancel." She turned on her heels and left.

Imogene waved. "She'll be okay. I'll keep her company." She furrowed her brow. "Can I get you anything before I go?"

"No. It's okay." I closed my eyes against the urge to cry. Where would that get anyone?

Warm arms encircled me. Imogene pulled me to her chest and kissed my head. "It's not okay," she whispered, "but it will be." She gave me one more squeeze before going after Mom.

An upstairs door thumped shut as I wiped a stubborn tear from my cheek. My mother had gone to her room.

Dad paced in front of the windows, watching the street. "She'll be all right. We've just gotten you back, and you keep getting death threats. Not exactly the homecoming she'd dreamed of."

I walked to his side and leaned my head on his arm.

He wound his hand behind my back and tugged me closer. "We worry."

Jack's truck swung into view at the stop sign.

"I won't let him arrest you," I promised.

Dad kissed my head. "Whatever happens, everything will be fine in the end."

I wasn't so sure about that anymore.

Jack and Dad spoke privately in the dining room while I stewed in the parlor, fixing a mental list of anyone who knew I was looking into Mr. Becker's death. Outside of my immediate circle, there was only Mrs. Becker and Robbie, the Cuddle Brigade worker and volunteer firefighter from the crime scene. Of course, a myriad of bystanders had borne witness to Mrs. Becker confronting me at the Cuddle Brigade, and she'd probably told all her friends what a pest I was.

Eventually Jack shook Dad's hand. "I'll be in touch when I know more. Lacy"—he refocused on me—"can I walk you to your car? Maybe see you home and give the house a quick check?"

"Um . . ." I looked to Dad, not quite ready to leave him.

"Go on," he encouraged. "I'm safe here. I have an excellent home security system and a useless rent-a-guard to keep watch over me."

I kissed his cheek, longing to stay, but eager to hear what Jack thought of the strange new twist in his case. Who knew I was investigating *and* where to find me? "I'll call you before bed."

I loaded Penelope into her carrier, and Dad walked us to the door.

He wrapped a protective arm around my shoulders. "I want you to know I'm not worried about being arrested, and I don't want you to worry about it either. I want you to stay safe. Jack will figure this out."

I leaned against him. "You don't have to try to make me feel better. I can see you're hurting."

"Sweetie," he patted my shoulder. "The pain you see is for Wallace, for his family, and for mine. I hate that I wasn't there to stop this. I hate that I left when I knew something was wrong. If I'd stayed . . ." Dad's voice cracked.

He cleared his throat. "If I'd stayed and forced the entire story out of him, I might've been there when his killer came by, and my friend might not be dead. Moreover, my dear wife and precious little girl wouldn't be worried sick, receiving threats or being subjected to the gossips' spotlight, and all because I walked out on my friend when he needed one most."

I threw my arms around him and squeezed. Of course he was only worried about everyone else when he was the one in trouble. "I love you."

"I love you too." He carried Penelope to her side of the car and belted her in. "Take care of my baby," he told Jack.

"Always," Jack answered.

Chapter Thirteen

Furry Godmother's words of wisdom:
Don't like sleeping alone? Get a cat.

Jack made a thorough sweep of my home before collapsing onto my couch. He threw one arm across his eyes and leaned his head over the backrest. "You're killing me, Crocker."

I climbed onto the cushion beside him and pulled a pillow into my lap, tucking both feet beneath me. "What do you think the photos mean?"

He rolled his head to glare at me. "Really?"

"Besides 'butt out.'" I leaned toward him, eager to work through the strange situation. "What was the purpose of choosing *those* photos? A note attached to a photo from one of the best nights of my life is not very scary."

He gave me a droll look. "I wouldn't care if the note came on a candy bar. This is a problem. And how was that the best night of your life? Weren't you with your ex-fiancé in those pictures?"

"Hey, I didn't know he was a scheming, two-timing jerk at the time. I'd just won a national design competition and

been proposed to. I was high on endorphins and victory. To my younger mind, life had reached the pinnacle of perfection. Why choose a moment like that to slice up?"

"I don't know." He rubbed his eyes with one big hand. "I'm tempted to ask about the proposal and how a guy like that convinced you to accept, but I'm going to let it go."

Good thing, because Pete hadn't done anything special. I was so glad to be wanted as I was, for eternity, that I agreed to a spontaneous ask. No grand gestures. Just the party around us. I twisted on the cushion to face him. "What do you think of the pictures?"

"I liked the outfit."

"Ha ha," I deadpanned. "It was a swimsuit design competition. All the participants looked just like me."

"No." His eyes darkened. "They didn't."

A different sort of energy pulsed between us and breath caught in my throat.

"I kissed Chase." The words were no sooner present in my mind than swan diving from my lips. "I traded him a kiss for Penelope's freedom last summer."

Jack eased back a fraction of an inch. "You kissed Chase last summer?"

I bit my lip. "No. This week. I was slow on payment."

He tented his brow. A disarming look of frustration marred his handsome face. "And?"

"I don't know. We kissed and that was that. I have no idea why I'm telling you this." I decided against adding the fact Chase had requested a do-over.

Jack seemed to roll the information around. "Is this your way of letting me know you're seeing Chase?"

"No."

He narrowed his gaze, watching me so intently I temporarily forgot to breathe. "Why did you tell me you kissed Chase?"

"I don't know. Chase thinks I'm an oversharer. Plus, I don't want to lie to you," I said.

"You lie to me all the time about staying out of my investigation."

A smile tugged my lips. "Fine. I don't want to lie about the important stuff."

"You believe kissing Chase qualifies as important stuff?"

I cringed and tipped over, landing face down away from him, on the sofa.

Jack's wide palm wrapped over my shoulder and hoisted me upright. He turned my back to him and lowered my head against his legs for a pillow. He stared down at me with an unusual level of intensity. "I looked into Pete last summer."

"You did?" I gripped the pillow more tightly to my chest.

"He's not terrible on paper, but his social media accounts portray him as a playboy. He's got a ton of debt. College loans. Credit cards. A mortgage and car he can't afford, but a good education and no criminal record."

A bubble of hurt rose in my throat, and my gaze drifted away from his, studying my fidgeting hands instead as they coiled and uncoiled a loose thread from my pillow around one finger. "When we broke up, he told me he'd only asked me out because he knew about my family's money. He said he hadn't expected to fall in love with me." The burn of humiliation and betrayal was dulled but present, even all these months later.

Jack stroked a strand of hair away from my cheek. "I think love's like that. It sneaks up on us."

I smiled despite myself. "You think I'm lovable."

Jack's frown returned. He lifted me off him, setting me upright at his side once more. The look in his eyes sent shivers through my limbs. "You might as well get comfortable. I'm staying until I'm sure whoever wrote that note isn't planning on paying you a visit tonight." He pulled the throw off the couch behind him and fanned it over our legs.

Jack thought I was lovable. The truth of it was in his eyes and undeniably igniting the air around us. I set my hand in his, suddenly, overwhelmingly, thankful for him in my life.

* * *

Jack slipped out at dawn. I'd fallen asleep in front of the television watching *The Princess Bride* on DVD and slept like the dead until he wiggled me awake so he could leave. It was hard to say if he'd slept too, but part of me doubted Jack ever truly slept. He struck me as more of a persistently one-eye-open kind of guy.

I padded into the kitchen for coffee. Buttercup raced out of her tiny princess castle and swam back and forth along the glass between us. I dropped a few freeze-dried shrimp bits onto the water and blew her a kiss. Buttercup had the life. A doting friend. Fresh food from the sky. Private roomy castle. No stalkers or handsome men to confuse her life.

I headed for the shower, certain I'd never fall back asleep. I had a big day ahead, starting with an appointment to see a plastic surgeon.

I showered and shampooed while mentally inventory-ing my closet. I wanted to wear a white pencil skirt and red blouse with matching heels to keep with my valentine theme at Furry Godmother, but I was bound to pastels and florals by the NPP Welcoming Committee ladies.

An hour later, I'd paired my sleeveless daffodil-colored blouse with a pencil skirt and polka-dotted pumps. My knees were in full view, and the keyhole neckline on my blouse was just short of scandalous by Imogene's stan-dards. I'd buckled a skinny black belt around my middle and dumped the contents of yesterday's purse into a black patent-leather handbag. The outfit wasn't bad, but pas-tels were slim pickings in my closet, and florals were non-existent. I'd need to shop if I was going to keep Mom happy past tomorrow.

I checked my watch, then smoothed my skirt. Hope-fully the trip to Dr. Hawkins's office wouldn't be a total bust. I hated to lie about who I was and why I'd made the appointment, but these were desperate times, and any fresh insight into Wallace Becker's final days would be worth the deceit. Though, I was still uncertain how to get the infor-mation without being tossed onto the sidewalk. "You can do this," I told my reflection. "You're running out of leads, so make this work."

I turned for the bedroom door and caught my toe on a box of old things. "Good grief!" I planted my shoulder against the nearest wall with a thud.

Penelope came to see what the fuss was about. She leapt gracefully onto my dresser and meowed.

"Penny, you're a genius." *Dr. Hawkins wasn't the only person who might have some information on Mr. Becker. I* searched my dresser for the little business card I'd tossed aside several days before. "Found it." I waved the card at Penelope. "Resplendent, New Orleans's Premiere Thrift Shop." I dialed Claudia Post's number.

"This is Claudia," a cheerful voice answered.

"Hello, Ms. Post. This is Lacy Crocker. You probably don't remember me. We met at my mother's house."

"I remember you," she said flatly.

"Well," I stuttered, taken aback by the sudden change in her tone. "I know it's early, but I have a box of vintage casual wear that you might be interested in." I made a face at myself in the mirror. I had no such thing, unless she counted torn jeans and old band T-shirts.

"That's fine," she said. "I'm at another pickup now, but I can be there in a few minutes."

"Thank you."

We disconnected, and I set my phone aside. The boxes of old clothes I'd taken from Mom's house would have to be donated after all. A small sacrifice if our chat panned out.

I flipped through the boxes for things I couldn't live without. Not because I was a packrat, like my mom and grandmother before her, but because I was sentimental and responsible. It would be reckless to give away something I'd need later. I pulled my Louisiana State University homecoming shirt from the pile and tossed it on my bed. Halter tops were bound to make a comeback. I saved three of those, along with some plaid track shoes and a purse made from the cover of a Harry Potter novel. It had taken me forever to finish that.

Penelope climbed into a half-empty box and rolled on the significantly smaller offering.

"You're right," I said. "That's not enough to justify her trip." I grabbed my car keys and went to the driveway. I checked under the car and looked up and down the block for stalkers with camera gear before popping the trunk. I hoisted out another load of my old things and zipped back to the house. Boot-cut jeans and peasant tops. Ice skates. Pint-sized golf clubs and youth golf team apparel. No wonder the district was obsessed with anonymous donations. I arranged the boxes by my front door, fluffing and repositioning them until they looked like more.

A car door slammed outside.

I salvaged my old riding crop and helmet from the pile then ran them to my bedroom. I returned to the living room a little out of breath. Penelope had curled into an overturned trucker hat full of plastic Live Strong bracelets. I scooped her out and shut the box to hide the fact that my stuff wasn't as much "vintage" as "college-kid poor."

I counted to ten after the doorbell rang. "Hello, Ms. Post. Come inside, won't you?"

She tripped over the threshold and grabbed the wall for balance. Her pink, elastic-waist pants were capri length and in direct conflict with her structured short-sleeved blouse. The same curtain of rose hips and lavender strained the air around her. "You have a very nice home."

"Thank you. Can I get you something to drink?"

"That's not necessary," she said, dragging herself completely upright on brown Birkenstock sandals. "Are these the boxes you want to donate?"

"Yes, ma'am."

"It's very generous." Her chest rose and fell too quickly for a trip up my sidewalk. "I'm hoping to make all my last-minute pickups before lunch. There's a Valentine's Day party tomorrow night, and I want to take the most festive-looking dresses to the women's shelter before the office closes." She cast a hopeful glance at my boxes.

I jumped in front of them. "You certainly stay busy," I mused. "How long have you been doing this?"

"About six years." She sidestepped me, angling for a box.

I leaned into her path. "You probably know the locals pretty well."

She pulled back with a strange look. "Not personally, but I know some of their names. Especially the ones who have regular pickups."

I beamed. "That's wonderful." Claudia Post was an even better resource than the local beauty parlor. She probably had the inside scoop on everyone in town and didn't even realize it. "Have you noticed a big yellow Tonka truck around the district lately? Maybe know who it belongs to?"

She frowned. "Tonka? Like the toy?"

"This one is life-sized. It's an actual truck with the word *Tonka* painted over the back wheel well and dark tinting on all the windows."

She shook her head, jostling frizzy hair and looking disappointed. "No. I don't think so."

"It's fine. You drive through the district a lot. I thought you might have seen it during your pickups."

"No," she repeated.

I deflated.

Claudia gave me an apologetic smile. "Do you still want to donate those boxes?"

"Yeah." I hoisted a box onto one hip. "You've probably heard about Wallace Becker's death," I said as casually as possible. "It was awful."

Her mouth opened and closed. "Yes. It was."

"I'll bet you've heard all sorts of gossip about what happened. Everyone on your pickup route probably has an opinion." *Perhaps something useful I could use to clear my dad.*

"No." She made a stunned face. "I don't listen in on private conversations at my donors' homes."

"Of course not," I apologized. "I'm sorry. I didn't mean to insinuate that you did." The boxes I'd tripped over at the Beckers' home flashed back into mind. "You made a recent pickup from the Beckers' home though. Right?"

"I also don't discuss my clients," she whispered, checking the front door, probably for an escape.

"Right." Another dead end. Discretion was my mother's favorite thing about Claudia. I moved out of her way.

She grabbed a box and headed for the door.

I followed her down the drive.

Claudia popped the hatch on her old SUV and slid the box inside. "What's the story behind the truck?"

"I don't know," I admitted.

She frowned.

A new idea crossed my mind. I liberated my cell phone and flipped to a picture I'd snapped of Tabitha last fall. "Do you recognize her?"

Claudia made a face. "I don't know." She passed me on a return trip to the house, gaze glued to the ground. Feet moving double time.

I'd officially scared her off. What did I expect? Inviting her over, questioning her about Wallace's death, accusing her of eavesdropping on local families, then showing her amateur surveillance photos of a woman. She probably thought I was insane.

When we made it back to the house, I shut us in.

"Glory!" she squeaked, gripping the last box to her chest and peering over the top at me.

I leaned against the door and did my best to not look like a maniac. "The picture I showed you is of a woman I think might be causing a lot of trouble around here. I think the truck might belong to her, but I'm not sure. You talk to everyone, so I thought you might have some insight. I didn't mean to sound so crazy."

Claudia loosened her grip on the box. Color returned to her fingertips. "I probably overreacted," she said. "Sometimes I get carried away. Active imagination. Strong desire to live."

I smiled back. "At the risk of taking this one step too far, I have to ask. Do you know anyone who goes by the name Sage?"

Her expression slowly relaxed. "No, but can I see that picture once more?"

"Sure." I turned the photo of Tabitha to face her. "Anything you can tell me about her would be a huge help. Anything at all."

"Well," she began reluctantly, "it's possible that I've seen this woman at the coffee shop on Prytania where I like to have lunch. I can't say for sure."

"When was the last time you saw her?"

"If it's the woman I'm thinking of, then yesterday."

I sucked air. If Claudia was right, Jack had a chance of finding Tabitha there too. "You're sure you've never heard the name Sage?"

"I don't think so. Who is that?"

"I don't know." That was the problem.

My chest ached as she drove away with my things. My memories. Pieces of my life.

On the upside, I'd received a huge lead. Tabitha frequented a local coffee shop. I needed to call Jack.

My phone vibrated with a text from Chase:

> Worked late. Drove by to see if you were up. Saw Jack's truck. Hope all is well. Call me if you want to talk.

I replied quickly to assure him all was well, then stepped into the day hoping I looked more confident than I felt and that I wouldn't be late for my appointment with Dr. Hawkins.

Jack climbed my porch steps in a perfectly tailored black suit. "Morning, Miss Crocker." He smiled.

I performed a long wolf whistle. "Where are you going looking so snazzy?"

"I had an eight AM board meeting at Grandpa Smacker. I was headed home to change and thought I'd stop to see if I could catch you."

"Yeah?" In the last ten months, I'd seen Jack in everything from swim trunks to undercover goth garb, but the rich-guy look always threw me the most. Probably because it was the side of him that he was least comfortable with, and I could relate. "How did it go at the office?"

"Good. Everyone's impressed with the early response from consumers on your new line." He gave me a thorough once-over. "How's your dad holding up?"

"Good, I think. I haven't heard from him since we left my parents' house last night." I dug into my bag for car keys. "He said you might arrest him." I'd forgotten to complain about that after Imogene delivered my threat photos.

He heaved a sigh. "I'm doing everything I can not to."

"That's smart, because he's innocent." I made a show of palming my keys and tucking my bag under one arm.

Jack's expression grew dark and slightly anguished. He'd told me once that this was his thinking face, but it looked grouchy to me.

"What's wrong?"

"Your mother said you need a date for your dad's dinner Friday."

I gave him a quizzical look. "Chase agreed to take me. I thought I'd told her that."

He shook his head. "She must've forgotten." The muscle in his jaw popped and clenched.

"Hey." I moved down the steps and leaned against my car. "There's something bothering you. You can talk to me."

"Where are you going?" His voice was deeper and gravellier than normal. A tight smile formed on his otherwise stricken face.

"I have a doctor's appointment, but nothing after that. Why?"

"I thought we could have coffee before we go to our real jobs."

My tummy did cartwheels. "I can meet you somewhere in an hour if you'd like."

His trademark cop stare slid back into place. "A doctor's appointment? Are you feeling okay?"

"I'm fine."

"Are you seeing Karen?"

"No. Dr. Hawkins. I won't be long." I opened my car door and tossed my bag inside. "Can I call you when I'm done?"

He narrowed his eyes. "Dr. Hawkins?"

"Yep." I dropped behind the wheel and powered my window down. "I definitely want that coffee. I'll call as soon as I'm finished." Hopefully with a juicy detail or two, like what the good doctor was doing with Mrs. Becker.

I reversed out of the driveway, keeping an eye on him in my rearview mirror. I hated to leave, but staying meant being stopped the second Jack realized the reason for my appointment.

He pulled his phone from one pocket as I motored away.

Now I just needed a plausible cover story that would convince Dr. Hawkins to give up the information on his relationship with Mrs. Becker.

Chapter Fourteen

Furry Godmother's warning for closet cleaners:
Beware of skeletons.

Dr. Hawkins's waiting room was huge, sterile, and lined with patients trying not to look directly at one another. Half the people had visible bandages, and the rest had nervous ticks, bobbing knees, and well-chewed nails. I'd chew my nails too if I was contemplating a nose job in that room. There were at least three women still slightly black and blue from their procedures, presumably awaiting a progress check. The flipping of magazine pages mixed crudely with ultrasoft jazz.

"Ms. Doe?" An elderly nurse with flawless skin and milky eyes appeared in the doorway. Her throwback Nightingale uniform and sharply angled hat matched the doctor's white-on-white decor seamlessly.

I gathered my things and marched to her side, tingling with undue anxiety. It wasn't as if I truly planned to have any work done. But what if I was voluntarily putting myself in the same room with a killer? I hugged my purse tighter.

Mom was right. He couldn't do anything horrible to me in his office, but I was revealing my hand. If he was the one who'd sent the threat, then he'd know I was still looking into Wallace Becker's death, unfazed by the warning.

I followed his nurse to a small exam room with a sink and mirror on one wall. A complicated exam chair and little rolling stool protruded from the room's center. Two plastic seats stood beside the door. Before and after photos of successful surgeries covered the rest of the room, inter-mixed on occasion with a collage of medical school posters explaining the processes.

The nurse handed me a clipboard and gown. "Fill out the papers, both sides, and be honest. The consultation is free, but if you elect to schedule a procedure, payment is due up front."

The door swung open and Jack barged inside. His face was red and his eyes were narrowed to slits.

"Hey!" I exclaimed, jumping away from the door on instinct. I held the clipboard between us for several long beats, until my rattled brain identified him as the cavalry and not a killer. "What are you doing here?"

The nurse watched me closely before turning back to him.

Jack put on a genteel smile, rearranging his features into something less troubled and more apologetic. He extended his hand to her. "Begging your pardon, but traffic was awful," he drawled, sweet and slow. "I'm Lacy's husband."

I worked my mouth shut. Married to Jack? What on earth would that be like?

The nurse's cheeks flushed. "Nice to meet you, Mr. Doe."

She patted his hand. "Have a seat. I was just finishing your wife's instructions."

She smiled at me once more. "Remove your blouse and brassiere. Put the paper vest on. Opening in the front." She dipped her head and closed the door behind her.

Jack stared at the folded gown, stupefied. "Hawkins drives a black Cadillac."

"I know. Why do you think I'm here?" I set my pile of things on the exam table.

"With you, it's hard to say."

"How do you know about his car?" I asked, irrationally embarrassed that the nurse had asked me to undress in front of him.

"I searched his name online when you left. When I saw he was a plastic surgeon, I headed over here to stop you from doing anything stupid. Then I gave my buddy at the station a call on a hunch and asked what kind of car was registered to Dr. Hawkins. When it fit the description of the car you saw Mrs. Becker and her date getting into, I figured I'd better use my lights and siren."

"So what now?" I asked.

"I'd planned to stop you from getting yourself any deeper in this, but"—he waved to the gown—"now I'm confused."

I took the seat beside him. "Do you need a minute?"

He frowned. "You're here because you believe he was the man you saw with Mrs. Becker."

"Yes."

"How'd you figure that out? I couldn't get anywhere with the information you gave me. Do you know how many black Cadillacs are registered to men in this city?"

"Grapevine."

He made a disgusted sound. "I'm going to have to have a talk with your friend, Scarlet."

"You should. She's an excellent resource."

"Not what I meant."

A slight rap on the door halted the discussion. The door cracked open, and the man I'd seen with Mrs. Becker hastened inside. "Miss Doe? Hello, I'm Dr. Hawkins," he rattled, attention fixed to his clipboard. "I'm so sorry, but I don't have any of your information on file." He raised his eyes and started at the sight of Jack. "Oh, pardon me. I'm Dr. Hawkins."

Jack cast me a wayward look. "This the guy?"

"Yes."

Jack stood and presented his shield to Dr. Hawkins. "I'm Detective Jack Oliver, New Orleans homicide. I'm here to ask you about Wallace and Mrs. Becker."

The doctor looked to me, eyes wide. "Miss Doe?"

I shrugged. I wasn't going to give my real name. Mrs. Becker would've tried to get me on stalking again, and Jack would've complained. "I'm with him."

He blundered backward into the rolling physician's stool. "Oh, dear."

Whoever this guy was, he didn't seem like a killer, and frankly, I wasn't sure his twitchy hands belonged on a scalpel.

Jack retook his seat. "I'm sorry to spring this on you. Take your time."

"You could've set an appointment," Dr. Hawkins whispered. "You didn't need to use subterfuge." His gaze darted to me.

I pressed my lips together.

Jack crossed his legs, hooking one big foot on the opposite knee. "The new patient guise is meant to avoid drawing undue attention."

I nodded. *Quick thinking.*

The doctor's Adam's apple bobbed long and slow. "Do you mean I'm next?"

"Next?" I asked.

"Am I in danger?" His anxious gaze darted from me to Jack. "Are you here to take me into protective custody?"

Jack leaned forward, planting elbows onto knees. "Dr. Hawkins. We're here because you were seen with Mrs. Becker recently, and we're investigating the death of her husband."

My chest expanded with a quick punch of pride. *We* were investigating. *Together.*

"Wallace was my very best friend since college," Dr. Hawkins began, loosening his death grip on the clipboard. He ran the sleeve of his lab coat over his forehead. "I'm not involved with his wife romantically. I was comforting her."

"You kissed her," I said.

His cheeks turned crimson. "I repented immediately. It may have been too soon to make those sorts of advances."

"Do you think?" His best friend had been dead five minutes, and he was trying to date the widow.

"Wallace was a fool to ignore her the way he had."

Jack moved to the edge of his seat. "Why did you ask if we were here to take you into protective custody?"

The doctor's mouth opened and shut. "I assumed you knew. Wallace was being blackmailed."

"Blackmailed?" I parroted.

"Yes. I am too," he whispered, "but Wallace got sick and figured he had nothing to lose, so he stopped paying and went after the guy hard. Even hired a private investigator. I was on board with bringing this guy down"—his voice cracked—"until . . ."

"Until Mr. Becker turned up dead," I said. "Who's the blackmailer?"

"Sage." The word came so quietly off his tongue, I nearly missed it.

"Who is Sage?" Jack demanded. His gaze jumped briefly to me.

I nodded infinitesimally. Sage was also the name on the gift tag Jack had found stuck behind a baseboard in Tabitha's old closet.

Dr. Hawkins rode the stool in our direction, using his feet as pedals. "That's what Wallace and I were trying to find out."

Jack narrowed his eyes. "How does the blackmail occur?"

"We get phone calls. Letters. Sometimes packaged threats appear. Other times, a pretty lady makes the delivery."

"Describe the lady," Jack demanded.

"I don't know if I can," Dr. Hawkins said. "She wears big hats and glasses, dressed to the nines, like she's off to the Kentucky Derby or a Royal Tea."

Jack flipped through screens on his phone before stopping on a picture of Tabitha. "Is this the lady?" He turned the photo toward Dr. Hawkins.

"Maybe." He scrutinized the picture. "I haven't seen her recently, but that could be her." He lifted his pained expression to Jack. "I try not to make a lot of direct eye contact.

In the movies, these kinds of people will kill you if you can identify them."

I swept a pile of hair off my shoulders and considered the best way to approach my next question. "I've heard that Mr. Becker was seeing someone named Kinley. Do you have any idea who that is? We think she's in her twenties and blonde. I believe she works at his company."

A look of devastation flashed in his eyes. "Kinley's not a mistress. She's Wallace's daughter."

I sat back in stunned silence.

Jack tapped something onto his phone screen. "Go on."

The doctor pulled wire-rimmed glasses off his long nose and rubbed his eyes. "Wallace had a tryst early in his marriage. He was young and willful. He'd fought with his wife and left on a long weekend, hoping to make her miserable in his absence. He met Kinley's mother while he was away. He regretted his actions immediately, of course, and came right home, but he never confessed to the indiscretion because their prenuptial agreement was airtight."

"And he wasn't going to let a former rodeo star take possession of his fortune," I said.

Dr. Hawkins replaced his glasses. "They made up and went on happily for years before the woman appeared at his office with a little girl and requested proof of paternity. Wallace agreed, and he and Kinley have maintained a relationship since that day. When she finished college and moved to the city, he offered her a position where they'd have reason to spend more time together. She's not always been easy, but Wallace blamed himself when she was disagreeable."

He'd treated her like a dirty secret all her life. That sounded like motive to me. "Can you elaborate on 'disagreeable'?"

A slight knock on the door set Dr. Hawkins on his feet. "Come in."

The matronly little nurse poked her head inside. "Your next appointment is getting antsy."

He forced a smile. "I'll be right there. Thank you."

When the door closed, Jack handed the doctor his card. "If you think of anything else, give me a call. Meanwhile, do yourself a favor and don't mention our visit to anyone until we figure out who Sage is and how he's keeping tabs on you."

Dr. Hawkins tucked the card into the pocket of his white lab coat.

"One more thing." I lifted my pointer finger. "What were you being blackmailed for?"

He looked nervously at Jack.

"It's okay," I said. "I don't care about the reason. But if there's a pattern to the sorts of things Sage looks for in a money pot, we need to know. It could help us figure out who he is."

The doctor let his eyes fall shut briefly. "I enjoy the local burlesque culture and have on occasion spent private time with a particular dancer. I'm accused of paying for her companionship, which is a crime, and this is not an admission of guilt." He reopened his eyes and excused himself before Jack could respond.

I followed Jack out of the office and into the elevator.

The minute the shiny metal doors closed, I turned to face him. "So even though Mr. Becker wasn't cheating with Kinley, as his wife suspected, she was still evidence of a twenty-six-year-old infidelity. Do you think Kinley got tired of being kept separate from Mr. Becker's public life and lashed out? What about her mom? Surely she has motive to blackmail him or want him dead. Whatever stipend he gave her to raise Kinley is probably gone now that she's a grown woman."

Jack stared silently at our reflections in the doors. "I don't like the idea of the killer being a blackmailer. You asked why the photographs of you weren't taken in the present. It's because blackmailers dig things up that we don't want others to know."

My mouth dried. Jack thought the same person blackmailing old men in the district had sent me those photos and killed Mr. Becker?

The doors slid open and I stumbled out.

Jack walked me to my car with a broad grin. "I'm going home to go back through everything I have on Tabitha and give Grandpa's things another look. I need a clue to her whereabouts. Hawkins recognized her. If she's a part of this, she could be the key to finding Sage."

"Why do you look so happy?"

He tossed his keys into the air and caught them in an open palm. "My personal case has crossed paths with a work case, so I can finally take my time digging through what I know about Grandpa's death and the woman I blame."

I opened my car door to let out the heat. I didn't like the idea that another killer was sending me messages. This sort of thing never ended well for me. But there was one silver lining. "Is this enough to take my dad off your suspect list?"

"As soon as I'm sure he isn't a blackmail ringleader masquerading as the local vet."

I dropped my arms lifelessly at my sides. "You're joking."

Jack broke into a true smile. "Yeah, I'm joking." He beeped his truck doors unlocked and headed in that direction.

"Hey," I called. "What about our coffee?"

He waved and winked. "Rain check?"

"Fine." I couldn't hide the disappointment in my voice. "You owe me a coffee."

His smile widened. "Noted."

Chapter Fifteen

Furry Godmother's protip:
Everyone deserves the royal treatment, even the jesters.

I met Chase at the door that evening in yoga pants and an oversized Louisiana State T-shirt. My mind was overflowing, and my hair was wound into a knot. Messy tendrils had drifted over my ears and neck as I'd baked and sewn, sorting through the details I'd received that morning.

He looked me over with a quizzical smile. "You look a little frazzled."

"I am."

A hopeful expression lifted his brow. "Why?"

"I need to brainstorm. I have new information on Wallace Becker, and I need to know what I should do next."

He slid his jacket off and folded it over the back of my chair. "Okay. What do you have?"

"I went to see his friend Dr. Hawkins today, and I learned that he and Wallace Becker were being blackmailed." I grabbed a stack of photos off my end table and flipped them into his lap. "Someone left these on my car when I visited my folks' house last night. These are the copies I made before Jack took the originals. The ones from my car were sliced across my throat."

Chase turned them over, one by one. He swore quietly. "What are you wearing?"

"Concentrate."

"I am." He raised playful green eyes to mine. "Please tell me you still have it somewhere."

I leveled him with my most serious face.

Chase stopped on the photo of the message. "'Stop looking into Wallace Becker's death, or your past won't be the only thing that catches up with you.'" His expression fell flat.

"Yeah."

"This is why Jack was here last night?"

"Dad called him when we saw the note."

He drifted his gaze over me. "Another lunatic is after you. Is that what you were so excited to tell me?"

"No. I mean, that's only possibly true, but I wanted to tell you about the blackmail."

"How can you say it's only possibly true?" He handed me the photo of the threat and grimaced. "It's blatantly true. Where is your sense of self-preservation?"

"You're testy."

"I'm worried." He dragged the word out for several syllables. "How can you look so happy about something so awful?"

"For starters, this means my dad didn't have anything to do with Mr. Becker's death. Dr. Hawkins said Mr. Becker was being blackmailed, and when he learned he was dying, he decided to track down the blackmailer instead of spending the rest of his days worried about him."

Chase didn't look impressed. "That doesn't mean your dad didn't kill him. This is circumstantial at best." He shifted in his seat. "Look. I can accept your statement about the blackmailer as fact, but it doesn't mean your dad isn't the murderer, or that no one else wanted Becker dead, or that he didn't succumb to an accidental death as a result of an argument with someone completely unrelated to the blackmail."

I glared. "My dad did not kill Mr. Becker."

"I know. I'm just saying."

I crossed my arms and sat in my comfy chair with both feet tucked under me. "I also learned that Mr. Becker wasn't having an affair. Kinley is Becker's daughter. He was hiding the existence of a love child."

"Are you moving?" Chase moseyed to the stack of boxes against my living room wall.

I wanted to complain about the abrupt change of subject, but he'd reminded me of my latest argument with my mother. "That's round three of items expelled from my old room. Mom's found a discreet way to donate, so she's purging the house, and apparently I had too many books and puzzles. I've asked her not to give them away, so she dropped them off here."

He rifled through the boxes, reading titles from the aged spines and smiling at old board games. "I can't believe how many of these we had at our house too. Carter and I loved strategy games. He was older and wiser, but I wasn't afraid to bend the rules, so it was fun." He opened a massive tote filled with puzzles. "Holy."

"I've never met a puzzle I couldn't solve."

He shut the lid and carried a tattered paperback to the couch. "Is this where it all began? One too many Sherlock Holmes novels and family fun nights? Now you're obsessed with finding answers."

"Maybe." I took the book from him and ran my fingers over the curled edges, enjoying the feel of it in my hands. "I like knowing there are answers to be found. We only have to look."

"What's in the box with boy band posters taped to the sides?"

I smiled. "Clothes and CDs from high school."

He scoffed, a look of disbelief in his eyes. "What's a CD, Grandma? Is that like a VHS movie?"

"Kind of." I giggled. "Do you know they play those songs on the oldies station now? When did we grow up? How are we thirty?"

His smile brightened. "I'm not. I'm twenty-eight."

I hit him with a little pillow.

My doorbell rang.

Chase was on his feet in an instant. He checked the window, then disarmed my alarm and pulled Scarlet inside with a hearty hug.

A young woman in jeans and white wool pea coat stepped inside behind her. A cascade of blonde curls flowed over her back. "Hi, Chase."

Scarlet motioned to me. "Kinley, this is Lacy Crocker, the woman I've been telling you about."

"Kinley?" Kinley, Becker's daughter? Scarlet knew her? Chase knew her? "Welcome. Can I get you something?"

The stranger helped herself to the nearest chair. "Coffee."

Chase spun on his heels and vanished into the kitchen.

She watched him leave. A little smile played on her lips. "I met Chase at his family's law firm this afternoon. They're helping me legally change my name to Becker."

I looked to Scarlet. If this woman was who she said she was, why wasn't she more upset about her father's sudden death? How had she strolled into my home and presented herself like a new neighbor instead of a grieving daughter?

Scarlet sat in Chase's empty spot on the couch. "I followed the gossip until I found someone who knew where the alleged mistress lived. When I told Kinley who I was and what you and I were up to, she volunteered to help clear the air."

And announce herself publicly as a potential heir to the Becker empire.

Kinley crossed her legs and fiddled with the cuffs of her coat, apparently bored, or perhaps hoping to look bored. "Daddy hired the Hawthorne law firm to find a loophole in his prenup. He wanted an angle that would provide for me in the event of his death."

"And he was dying," I said, snapping the puzzle pieces together as they landed at my feet. He'd gone to the Hawthornes to make provisions, not to handle his business affairs as Chase had told me.

"I wasn't a match for his kidney," Kinley said. "Neither was his wife or son. The transplant wait list is long and slow. Daddy was getting his estate in order."

I wasn't sure which part of the surreal encounter was stranger. The fact that the exiled offspring of a man my dad had recently been accused of murdering was sitting in my living room or the fact that she continued to speak about her father so flatly, as if he were no more important to her than the mailman. Granted, my experience having a father was very different from Kinley's, but I doubted I'd ever be able to talk about his death so easily, even if he'd been gone many years. Kinley's father had only been gone a few days. "I'm very sorry for your loss."

She averted her gaze. "Right."

Chase retuned with a carafe of coffee and a stack of mugs. "One minute." He disappeared again, only to return with a tray. "I've got two kinds of creamer and sugar cookies."

"Are you two a thing?" Kinley asked, a glint of disappointment in her eye.

Chase broke a cookie in half and smiled. "She's way out of my league."

Kinley gave me a disbelieving look. Whether she was unsure if he was lying or how I could be out of Chase's league was uncertain. I didn't ask.

Scarlet poured a cup of coffee and held it under her nose. "I miss coffee." She inhaled deeply and sighed before setting the cup down and picking up a cookie.

"Poppet still not sleeping at night?" I asked.

"Nope."

I rubbed her back. "Why don't I hang out with the kids soon, so you can take a nap? A long one."

She tipped her head onto my shoulder and nodded it in agreement. "I love you."

"Back at ya."

Kinley poured a cup of coffee using large, deliberate gestures that drove the room's attention back to her. "Daddy sent Mom money every month until I turned eighteen, then he stopped sending the checks to her and started paying for college instead. I figured that's the same thing. I majored in business."

I bit into a cookie, trying to figure her out. We were polar opposites as far as I could tell. I'd worked diligently to cut ties with my family's money, and she'd welcomed her father's cash with open arms. Was I wrong for my response? Was she wrong for hers? "Mr. Becker offered you a job after graduation?"

She dragged a fingertip around the top of her mug. "I hated it at first. When he'd made the offer, I'd assumed I'd have a corner office with a window and everyone would finally know who I was. Instead I was treated like the other hourly workers and told to pretend I wasn't his child. He said it would prevent jealousy and that the truth would come out in time."

"Ouch." I pushed the rest of my cookie onto my tongue before I interrupted her again.

"I wasn't exactly a model employee in the early weeks, but I warmed up, especially when I learned about his health. I'd only recently become part of his everyday life and suddenly I was losing him. His sickness changed things. I hugged him on the night he told me about his kidney failure. The blackmailer must've taken the photos then. It was the first time I'd really let down my guard."

"You knew about the blackmail?" I asked.

"Daddy told me everything. Sometimes we talked for hours. I did my best to accept whatever he said without an opinion. I tried to fit into his life however I could."

"Have you spoken to his wife?" I asked.

Kinley barked a laugh. "Do you think I'm an idiot? In what scenario would that meeting go well?"

"You have a major loss in common. Maybe knowing one another would help," I suggested. "You still have a half-brother out there somewhere."

Kinley bounded to her feet, nearly spilling her coffee. "He is not my brother. She is not my mother. I don't want to meet them any more than I wanted to meet you, but since Scarlet assured me you'd find out who did this to my dad, I came tonight."

I stood slowly.

Scarlet followed suit.

Kinley's disposition took a change for the worse. Her cocky, superficial demeanor faded into something that looked more like a deer in headlights. "If you're not a complete moron, you know it was his greedy, awful wife who killed him. She's mad because she got old and thought he had a mistress. Now she's blaming the blonde bimbo who must be sleeping with him because there's obviously no other reason any woman would want to know my dad." Her cheeks flared red and tears welled in her eyes. She shook a fistful of her hair in each hand.

Scarlet brushed cookie crumbs off her fingers. "Maybe we should go."

She didn't have to make the suggestion twice. Kinley stormed onto my porch, setting off the alarm in the process.

I pushed the code into the pad as Scarlet blew past me.

"Wait. Kinley, wait!" Scarlet chased her down the sidewalk.

I peered into the night behind them. "Should we go after them?" I asked Chase.

He already had his jacket on. "I'll be right back."

I looked to Penelope. "Can you believe this?"

She walked away.

I didn't blame her. I'd call it a night if I could, but I still needed to talk to Chase and process the fact that the elusive Kinley was just having coffee in my living room. Before she'd stormed out.

Chase returned a moment later, shaking his head. "They're fine. Kinley's high strung, but Scarlet's tough. She'll see her home safely."

"You knew Kinley," I said. "You let me think Mr. Becker was seeing someone."

"I'm sorry I couldn't tell you about her. The information was privileged."

I reset the alarm. "It's fine, but I feel a little silly." I went back for my coffee.

"For what?" He followed me to the couch. "Not knowing that a pillar of our community had a love child that people believed was his mistress?" He flopped onto the cushion beside me.

"No. For believing the gossip. I'm as bad as the people buying into the rumors about my dad."

Chase squeezed my hand. "You aren't. Those people blindly believe everything they hear. You're seeking truth, and that is noble."

"You really think Mr. Becker was a pillar of the community? I thought of him as more of a *member* of the community."

"Haven't you heard death boosts us all to sainthood?"

"No, and I'd nearly forgotten the Beckers have a grown son." I freed my hand from his. "Would the son have had

motive to kill Wallace? What's his name? Where is he anyway? He wasn't at home when I went to see Mrs. Becker. Is he in the will?"

"Wally Jr. is estranged," Chase said carefully. "That's not gossip or protected information. It's just fact."

I sipped my coffee. "Are you still up for brainstorming?"

Chase stretched his long legs out and propped his hands behind his head. "Lay it on me."

"Dr. Hawkins said the blackmailer's name is Sage. Any idea who that could be? I've plugged the word into the Internet ten different times and come back repeatedly with nothing."

"Think about it," he said. "What is a sage?"

"An herb."

"A profoundly wise person," he said.

I snapped my fingers and pulled my feet back onto the cushions. "That's good. Sage might not be a name. It might have some other meaning, like a clue to the person's true identity. A wise person, a know-it-all, he knows our secrets." I waggled my eyebrows. "Blackmail. Or maybe the name is a warning, like sage advice. Maybe the blackmailer has ordained himself to judge the guilty."

"The guilty of what?"

"I don't know. Mr. Becker was unfaithful. Dr. Hawkins was accused of paying a burlesque dancer for her companionship."

Chase laughed. "A self-appointed judge for anyone committing sins of the flesh in New Orleans? Sage will soon be a millionaire."

"If he isn't already." I scooted closer. "Think about it. Whoever is doing this isn't going after everyone. He's targeting the wealthiest district in town. Sage is no dummy."

Chase snorted.

"Can you think of any disgruntled or disillusioned rich-ies around here we should take a closer look at?"

He pointed at his forehead.

"Oh, come on. What's your offense?" I teased.

He sat up straight and unbuttoned the top button on his shirt, revealing a crisp white T-shirt beneath. "There's this girl I've been waiting for over a decade to kiss, and when I finally got the chance, it wasn't my best work."

"You know we were talking about something com-pletely different, right?"

"Don't change the subject." He shot me with his most charismatic smile. "Go with this for a minute."

"Okay, well, maybe the girl didn't even notice because the kiss was perfectly lovely."

"Maybe." He screwed his lips into a knot. "I don't know how to tell if that's true, and I'd hate to think I blew my one shot at wooing her."

I smiled. "Any girl would be nuts to not be wooed by you."

"I feel a 'but' coming on."

Chase had made himself at home while I recovered from my broken leg, and I'd appreciated him for it more than I could ever explain, but now that I was well, and after our kiss, I suspected it was time to set a few boundaries. For example, comfortable as he may be, he was still my guest. I needed to answer my own door and serve the refreshments. He and I were perfectly compatible, but I didn't want to date him. Not now. Not when my life had finally started making sense.

I leaned toward him. "Our families don't care if we date other people, but if we date each other, there's going to be a lot of pressure. I'm terrible under pressure, and I don't want any more right now."

"We could be great."

I wet my lips and forced the jagged words out. "I know. Getting together would be amazing, and we'd be very happy while it lasted, but breaking up would ruin everything, and we might never get this back again." I motioned between us. "What we have is already perfect. Why mess that up?"

He mimed a knife to his chest.

"Stop."

He straightened with a smile. "What I'm hearing is that you aren't ready to marry me."

I laughed. "That is correct."

"And you feel that we"—he motioned from his chest to mine—"need to know we're the end game before we begin dating, so our families are happy forever."

I tipped my head left and right. "Kind of."

"Well, that's ridiculous, but so is life in our shoes, so fine."

"Fine?" I squinted at him, unsure what I'd walked into.

"Yes. I'll marry you eventually, and for now, you can sew your wild oats."

"Gee, thanks." I chuckled. "And you should also."

"Great." He lifted one of my hands in his and shook it. "It's a gentleman's agreement then."

I rolled my eyes theatrically. Our lives really were ridiculous.

Chapter Sixteen

Furry Godmother protip:
Share dessert with your therapist; she has to keep your secrets.

Business was pleasingly steady at Furry Godmother the next morning. Shoppers looked especially cheerful, toting boxed chocolates and swinging bouquets of brightly colored shopping bags. No midweek slump, just lots of happy people hoping to surprise their pets on Valentine's Day.

I'd dug up the last of my pastel apparel. A pale-pink fitted dress with a cowl neckline perfect for displaying my red heart-shaped paw-print pin. I'd paired the dress with a thick black belt and ankle boots. Unfortunately, the outfit marked the end of my NPP Welcoming Committee–approved wardrobe options, and tomorrow I'd be in direct violation of Mom's nutty dress code.

I slid behind the counter and lined finished bunny costumes on tiny hangers for the Creative Cavy Rescue. I positioned the rack so that I could keep one eye on the shoppers.

Claudia appeared on the corner and headed for my door.

I stood, stunned, as she hurried to the counter and tried to catch her breath.

"Hello," I said. "Everything okay?"

She lifted wide eyes and puffed for air. "I had to park"—she waved an arm wildly in the direction of my east wall—"far."

"Welcome to Magazine Street," I joked. "Is there a reason you made the trip? Looking for a valentine gift for your fur baby?"

She began shaking her head in the negative before I'd finished my question. "I heard something." The expression on her face said it was something good.

I perked. "Yeah?"

"Yeah. I heard some shoppers saying that name you asked about."

I floundered mentally for the name she meant. Tabitha? *No.* My muscles tensed. "Sage?"

She bobbed her head and fanned the material of her shirt away from her flushed skin. "I was sorting hangers at the register."

"What did they say?"

"One woman told another woman that Sage was a modern day Robin Hood."

What the heck was that supposed to mean? Was it intended to be literal? "Thank you," I said. "Did you hear anything else?"

"Yes. The women were going to a formal dinner for Valentine's Day and loved the cast-off Christian Louboutins." She looked puzzled. "I don't suppose that was what you meant."

"Not really, no. Anything else about Sage?"

Claudia leaned across the counter, suddenly mischievous. "No, but I heard about you. People say you catch criminals."

"I'm not supposed to." A wave of residual fear washed through me. Too often, the criminals had caught me. "I try."

"Well, good luck." She patted the counter and left another business card before fleeing the scene.

Imogene sauntered in my direction, a look of motherly concern on her round face. "Are you arranging a pickup too?"

"No. I sent some things with her last night. She just dropped in to answer a question I had."

I stripped my apron away from my dress and tucked it behind the counter. I couldn't help wondering if the information Claudia gave me was any good. Last night she'd claimed to have never heard the name Sage, and today it was being used in her store? What if Claudia was just lonely and mucking up my works with her need to be seen, like Eyebrows at Cuddle Brigade?

I'd think about that when I got home. Right now, I had to go. "I have an appointment with Karen," I told Imogene. "Do you mind covering the shop while I'm gone? I won't be too long."

"No. I don't mind."

I hugged her tight and put on a cheery face. "See you soon."

I motored through the district on autopilot, enjoying the view of neighbors' homes and swarms of men and women in fanny packs trailing tour guides. The thermometer on my dash said it was seventy outside. Perfect wear-what-you-like weather. Also known as enjoy-it-while-it-lasts weather. Soon, the tropical temperatures my city was known for would come and stay for the summer, making it impossible to breathe in any outfit.

Regardless of human comfort, flowers bloomed on every corner, swinging from light posts in hanging baskets and lining walkways to homes as old as the Garden District itself. Local flora thrived in our all-out crazy weather, hearty and unshakable like the people who cared for it. An herbal shop lined in bluebells caught my eye at the next light, reminding me of the blackmailer's strange name, *Sage*. No longer an innocent and delicious seasoning, the word had become synonymous with crime, heartbreak, and murder. The more I'd considered it, the more certain I became. Sage had to be an alias, a nom de plume. The word meant something to the blackmailing ringleader, whoever he was. A chef? A naturalist? I drummed my thumbs against the steering wheel.

The rebuff of a cabbie's horn hurled me back to the moment and tossed me forward. I'd missed the changing of the light. I lifted a hand to my rearview mirror in apology. He raised a rude gesture in acknowledgement.

Block by block, I worried my bottom lip, puzzling the reason to choose such a pleasant name for one's dirty work. I deliberately ignored the possibility that the fiend was bold enough to go by his or her given name. After all, blackmail was about cloak and dagger, wasn't it? Secrets and espionage? Maybe the loon didn't even think blackmail was wrong.

I pulled into the lot outside the clinic and headed for Karen's office.

The clinic bustled with activity. Every bench along the interior corridor was packed with people, some chatting excitedly, others enjoying a hasty lunch of muffuletta wrapped in sandwich paper, open bags of chips on their laps. My tummy gurgled at the familiar scents of a local favorite. Salami, mozzarella, ham, provolone, mortadella, and marinated olive salad tucked into the perfect ten-inch-round muffuletta loaf. A signature combination created and perfected in New Orleans. I popped a piece of chewing gum between my lips to keep my mouth busy.

The door to Karen's office was marked with a free-standing wooden welcome sign. A wreath of satin ribbons hung elegantly on the door, as if patients were guests at her home rather than visitors at a busy clinic. The show continued into her waiting room, where furniture was arranged in small groups; a little gathering room for old friends. The sideboard held hot pots of water for tea and coffee with all the trimmings. A "Help Yourself" sign centered above the crystal container of iced sweet tea. I signed my name on the ledger and sank into my favorite seat by the fireplace. I gripped and released the soft buttermilk fabric of the over-stuffed armchair. Someone had left a worn copy of Walt Whitman's works, cracked open like a teepee, over one arm. A little crock filled with water, cinnamon, and orange slices simmered on the mantle beside a vanilla candle. I closed my eyes and crossed my ankles, no longer anxious or driven to do anything besides breathe. Soft jazz played in the background. A tune I'd heard all my life but couldn't name. My shoulders began to sag, and my fingers uncurled on my lap.

"Lacy?" A soft voice called.

I dragged my eyelids open. Had I dozed off so quickly?

Karen stood in the archway near the reception desk. "I'm so glad you're here. Come on back."

I wrenched myself upright and willed my doubly heavy legs to carry me. The fog of sleep burdened my steps.

"You look exhausted," she said. "Are you sleeping at night?" Her brown hair was pulled back in a high bun, threaded with silver and punctured with a pencil. Rectangular-framed glasses rode high on her nose, accentuating her sharp cheekbones and close-set blue eyes.

I shuffled down the short hall to her office and slumped onto her couch with a yawn. "I'm fine."

She poured two cups of tea from a silver set on her coffee table and handed one to me. "You don't look fine."

I sat straighter. "I've been busy and trading sleep for productivity, but I'm not unwell, more like exhibiting the hallmarks of an entrepreneur."

"No more nightmares?"

I lifted the little cup to hide my face. "No."

"Good." She set her drink aside and gathered a notepad and pen. "What's new that's keeping you so busy? Business or something else?"

I considered telling her about my new position on the NPP Welcoming Committee and all the orders that had resulted from it, but Karen was sharp. She read the papers. She knew about the mess with my dad, and discussing store orders to avoid the bigger topic would only make me seem unable to cope, which would be a red flag about my emotional health. That path would also lead me away from my true reason for the appointment. I shifted forward, resting the cup on my knee. "I've actually come to talk with you about Wallace Becker. I believe you knew him."

She nodded. "Mr. Becker was a very nice fellow. His nannies watched my Schnauzers while I was in Rome."

"You've probably heard that my dad was with him the night he died."

She waited, expressionless, for me to continue.

"I'm trying to learn the truth about what happened to Mr. Becker."

"I see." She made a mark on her paper. "Do you think that's wise?"

"I think it's necessary."

"Have you considered that it was other adventures of this nature that landed you in my confidence to begin with? Not to mention in the hospital? Twice."

I slid my feet against plush gray carpeting, crossing my ankles, switching them, and then crossing them back again. "I think what matters most is that no one is left believing my father would do such a thing. It's not enough to produce evidence to clear his name because there will always be doubters and gossips. He deserves better than that and so does Mr. Becker and his family. People deserve the truth."

"And what about the other times you did something similar and it ended in danger and nightmares for you?"

"This is different."

"Is it?"

"Yes."

She smiled kindly. "How so?"

"For starters, I'm keeping my efforts under wraps. Only members of my immediate circle know what I'm up to."

Concern tugged the corners of her eyes. "Our community is a close-knit one. Think of where you're going and who you're seeing on this quest. If someone dangerous is watching one of the folks you're interviewing and you pop up, how long will it take before he or she puts together what you're up to?"

I twisted the cup on my knee. "I try not to assume the worst."

"That's a healthy way to live, normally, but under these circumstances, I wonder if positive thinking can also be interpreted as turning a blind eye." She made more notes on her paper. "Have you had any notion that you're in danger this time? Unsubstantiated fears? Direct threats?"

"What?" I stalled for time. She had me, and she knew it.

Her pen stopped midstroke. Curious blue eyes raised to meet mine. "Have there been any threats made toward you since you began your inquest?"

I exhaled audibly, unwilling to discuss the bizarre photos someone had chosen to send me. "Was Wallace Becker a client of yours?"

She stilled. "You know I can't answer that."

I set my cup aside and leaned in. "Someone saw him come here weekly."

"I can't speak to that," she said.

"If he wasn't a patient, you'd have answered no."

Karen repositioned the notebook on her lap. "I think we'd better keep this about you. How are things going with you and your friends?"

"Scarlet's good."

"I was referring to the gentlemen. Jack and Chase."

If she'd wanted to change the subject, she'd hit a grand slam. A fiery lump formed in my throat. The last time I'd seen Karen, I spent most of the hour waffling between complaints about Jack's extensive personal barriers and Chase's horrible timing.

"Has anything changed?" she pressed. "Are you dating? Putting yourself out there more?"

My spine went poker straight. Panic planted my feet firmly against the floor. Karen knew all my secrets. I'd told them to her willingly and paid her to hear. Wallace Becker probably had too, and many others with us. My mother had given me Karen's name. She assured me that Karen helped all the most discreet families in New Orleans.

"I have to go." I sprang to my feet and hiked my purse over one shoulder.

Was there any better profession for a blackmailer? A dull ache registered beneath my heart. I pressed a palm against the spot. I'd told Karen everything. Every last silly, ugly detail of my life and troubles, including the gory truth about Pete the Cheat and his completely lame proposal at that party in New York.

Karen followed me into the hallway, a note of distress in her normally placid voice. "Where are you going? What's wrong?"

"Thank you for the tea," I said, scurrying past the reception desk and through the pretend living room.

I sped back to Magazine Street and circled the block twice before claiming a freshly vacated space on the corner. I'd have to walk a bit farther than usual, but that was the price I paid for leaving and returning at lunchtime. Fortunately for me, I loved the blessed stretch of shops and would cheerfully walk it anytime for any reason. Plus my heart was racing from the possibility I'd unwittingly told all my secrets to a psychopath these last few months, and I could use a little exercise to shake off the adrenaline.

Chapter
Seventeen

Furry Godmother's advice on secret sharing:
Be careful your confidant isn't a blackmailing murderer.

A sleek-looking motorcycle cut onto the sidewalk outside my shop. The rider kicked down the stand and tugged a bulbous black helmet off his head. Jack stretched long, narrow legs onto the curb. He settled his helmet on the seat and screwed a black ball cap over unkempt hair. His fitted leather jacket and dark jeans brought a smile to my lips.

I swept the shop door open and motioned him inside.

Imogene stood behind the counter trying hats on Penelope. A small crowd had gathered to watch. "And this one," she said, "has a silver fleur-de-lis, and that makes it special." She adjusted the beret from my Vive la France! line over Penelope's left ear. "The fleur-de-lis first appeared in New Orleans on the flags of French explorers. *Three hundred years ago.*"

The crowd thickened as shoppers were drawn from racks and counters into her story.

I stooped to hide my purse behind the counter and whispered to Jack, "She was born to tell stories."

When I stood, I realized I'd been talking to myself. Jack had already been pulled into her orbit with the rest.

Penelope blinked slowly, squinting her eyes at shoppers while Imogene carried on about the silver-sequined beret and the symbol of our city. "You'll find fleur-de-lis everywhere in this city," she said. "On jewelry and souvenirs, signs and banners, helmets in the Super Dome. Even graffittied on underpasses. New Orleanians have long associated the mark with our city, but after Hurricane Katrina, the fleur-de-lis became something more."

The people drifted closer.

Imogene swept her gaze across their rapt faces, tapping a finger against the little silver embellishment. "This mark has become a beacon of hope in New Orleans. A symbol of our strength, fortitude, and perseverance. It says, 'We won't be broken. Won't be lost. We are one.'" Her voice rose slowly and steadily toward a crescendo. "We are survivors. United in hearts and minds by our love of this breathtaking city, and this symbol says, 'We are New Orleans.'"

A slow clap began. My hands joined theirs, and the sting of pride welled in my eyes. Katrina had taken so much, but the city was resilient. The people had come back stronger, like fractured bones that had fortified in the healing. We wouldn't be broken again.

Jack adjusted his ball cap, pulling it lower over his eyes. "I hope you've got plenty of those little hats," he said, finding his way back to me. "There may be a pet lovers' brawl if you run out of them after that speech."

He wasn't wrong. Imogene's audience had formed a line, money in hand.

I shifted away from the counter and met Jack on the sales floor. "I have dozens. What's with the motorcycle?"

"I'm off duty, and I can't get anywhere this time of day in my truck. The Harley's quicker."

"What happened to the other bike?" He'd driven me home on the back of a gas-blue motorcycle last summer. I thought of the experience often.

"Garage."

I wasn't sure if he meant it was being worked on or simply waiting for him at home. It didn't matter to me as long as it was still around. I liked the blue one. "So you're free today? This is a pretty serious look for a guy on a break."

"How's that?"

I gave his fantastic black motorcycle boots a pointed look. "Well, some people might say you look more like someone who belongs in the back of a squad car than behind the wheel of one."

"And you?"

"I like the look," I admitted too quickly.

His icy-blue eyes pinched at the corners. "Can I buy you that coffee?"

I sighed. "Yes, but I can't leave Imogene in a crowded store with shambled shelves. I just got back, and I should probably stay put for a while. We're swamped and everything's a mess."

Jack lifted a fallen box on the display before him and brought it to the shelf's edge. He did the same thing for the other boxes, righting toppled items and aligning them face-forward. "Was today your appointment with Karen? How'd it go?"

A cool shiver ran down my spine. "I think she's got the perfect job for a blackmailer, and she knew about that party in New York. We'd talked about that before."

He glanced up at me, long dark lashes casting shadows across his cheeks. "I'm looking into her."

"Thanks." I helped with the messy shelves. "Did you just come to ask me about coffee, or was there something else?" Our arms brushed as we worked in unison to clean the area.

"I've also come bearing good news. The coroner confirmed Mr. Becker's time of death as between midnight and two AM, which puts your dad at home with a security system that logged his arrival at ten thirty-seven."

I exhaled a week of fear. "Thank goodness. What about the cause? Cardiac arrest, right?"

He shot me a skeptical look. "Yeah. The bump on the head turned out to be superficial, the result of literally anything heavy and solid. The whack didn't kill him—hell, it might not have even knocked him out." He folded his arms. "What made you say cardiac arrest?"

Four years of premed courses and a truncated engagement to a cheating ME. "I've been reading up on Mr. Becker's health conditions. Since the lady I spoke with that morning, the one who found him, didn't mention the bump on the head, I assumed it wasn't serious enough to kill him. Then I imagined being a man his age, with his afflictions, being whacked over the head, then trapped inside a freezer. He was already under a load of stress from the blackmail and upcoming dialysis. Not to mention trying to make a place in his life for an illegitimate daughter." I snapped my fingers. I'd nearly forgotten to tell Jack about Kinley. "Who I met!"

He dropped his hands to his sides and fixed careful eyes on me. "When?"

"Scarlet brought her over last night. She seemed edgy."

"Angry," he corrected. "I spoke with her yesterday."

Dang. He'd beaten me to her. "Do you think she was mad enough to shut her dad in a freezer? Maybe she didn't expect him to die. She might've only intended to punish him."

"Or she blamed him for choosing his money and his wife over her and her mother all these years," Jack said. "Then Becker got sick and asked her for a kidney. That'd peeve me off."

"Yeah," I agreed. "Maybe."

"According to her financials, she's also broke. Probably could've used a chunk of Daddy's wealth."

I cringed. "Chase said Mr. Becker had wanted Kinley to have a proper portion of his estate, but his prenup wouldn't allow it. Would that matter if he was dead?"

"I'll find out."

I wrinkled my nose. "I'd like to know what you learn about Karen."

"I think your therapist is a long shot as a suspect. Though, I wouldn't mind a look at your file."

I pointed a finger at him in warning, and he laughed. "What about Wallace Jr.? Where's he been during all this?"

Jack turned to face me, messy shelves forgotten. "I haven't been able to reach him, but I'm sure he'll be home for the funeral, or at the very least, for the reading of the will."

"Do you think he had anything to do with his father's death?"

"I doubt it. Junior has been estranged from the family for years."

"But he's also a potential kidney donor," I said. "He wasn't a match, but he must've been mad that his dad only reached out to him to ask for something so big." A new idea sprang to mind. Hope fluttered in my chest. I smoothed my skirt, then stroked the length of my hair over one shoulder, trying not to fidget and finding the goal impossible.

"What's the matter?"

"I need a favor."

He pulled his lips to the side. "No, you can't interview Wallace Jr. or anyone else on this case. You need to take a big step back."

I shook my head. That wasn't what I wanted. "Will you make some kind of public statement to free my dad from this? Everyone's looking at him as if he's done something wrong, when in truth, he's mourning a friend and blaming himself for not staying with him longer that night."

Jack looked over his shoulder before leaning close. "I'd like to talk to your dad first."

"Why?"

"A move like that could be bad for our investigation."

I folded my hands in front of me and screwed my lips into a knot before I said something a shopper might correctly perceive as a threat to a police officer.

"Think about it," he urged. "If the killer believes he or she is in the clear, then that person might let their guard down."

"You'd let my dad be persecuted longer than absolutely necessary if it helped your case?"

He dipped his chin stiffly. "I think your dad would agree." His pleading eyes softened my frustration, as did his honesty. I didn't always like the things Jack said, but I never doubted they were true.

"Fine." I turned on my heels and headed for the stock room.

"Where are you going?" he asked.

"We're out of turtle tiaras."

Jack matched my stride easily, following me to the back room. He held the stock room door as I passed and shut it behind us.

I stacked tiny tiaras on my desk, sorting them by design to avoid doubles for the display table. "I have no doubt my dad will agree with you. He's like that. Selfless and ridiculously good. He was never worried about being arrested or what anyone thought of him." He'd trusted Jack to get the truth.

"I know you're mad," he said. "You should know we're getting close to closing this case, and I don't want to risk the setback of removing our only public suspect too soon. Your dad's out of the woods. We know he's innocent, and everyone else will see that too once the killer's arrested."

I tipped my head over one shoulder and studied him. "Who's your main suspect?"

He frowned.

"Come on. You can't ask for my blessing on leaving Dad in the trenches of public loathing, then not tell me anything about what's really going on."

Jack pressed his back to the door and kicked his feet forward several inches to support his weight. "I told you the cause and time of death."

"I guessed the cause," I said. "Besides, you only came here to get on my good side so you could leave my dad out to dry."

"Not true."

"Yeah." I nodded emphatically. "True. Is that why you asked me out for coffee?" Heat traveled up my neck and across my cheeks. I was such an idiot.

"That is not why." Jack pursed his lips. "This is a police investigation. I can't tell you the main suspect or any protected detail that hasn't been released to the media."

I leaned my backside against my desk and faced off with him from several feet away, hoping he'd mistake my humiliating embarrassment for frustration. He didn't want to see me privately over coffee for personal reasons. This was all about the case. "Fine, then tell me something else. Something you can share that I don't already know."

He drifted his expressionless gaze over me. "Mrs. Becker knew about Kinley. She found out about her years ago but never said anything."

"Whoa." I pressed upright and ghosted in Jack's direction, drawn to the turn of events like my shoppers to Imogene's practiced campfire voice. "Why wouldn't Mrs. Becker have confronted her husband over something so big?"

"She said it was his story to tell her and not the other way around."

"Will it be in tomorrow's paper?"

"No. The dirty details of his marriage aren't pertinent to the murder investigation."

I dusted tiara glitter from my palms and turned in a small circle, processing. "Who discovers their spouse has a love child but never says a word about it?"

He shrugged. "Someone who doesn't want a divorce."

Right. I kept forgetting Mrs. Becker wasn't from money. Without her husband, she was broke. "But they had a pre-nup and he cheated. Kinley is proof of that. What would Mrs. Becker lose? Even half of their money would be enough to live contentedly back home in Kentucky forever."

"Maybe she loved him," Jack said. "Maybe she didn't want to fight about the past or things that can't be changed. How would I know?" He opened the door behind him and walked slowly out, palms raised. "In case you haven't noticed, I'm not exactly an expert on women."

"What!" I feigned shock. "That is brand new information."

He cast me a furtive look. "Call me when you want coffee."

"Call me when you've publicly renounced my dad as a murder suspect."

Chapter Eighteen

Furry Godmother's secret to surviving a holiday:
Lower your expectations.

I woke with a headache Thursday morning after another fitful night's sleep. My mind had never been great at resting, and this week was no exception. My list of possible killers and blackmailers was growing instead of shrinking and slowly driving me bonkers in the process. None of my suspects had an airtight alibi that I knew of, and I couldn't mark anyone off. The wife, daughter, and son were all upset with Mr. Becker at his time of death, and my gut said whatever had been stuck to Mrs. Becker's sweater was the same thing I'd found on the freezer's floor. Though, I still had no idea what it could have been. It also occurred to me that Claudia, from the thrift shop, had access to everyone in the district. Maybe she'd been up to something when she relayed that gossip about Sage. Then there was the therapist I shared with Mr. Becker. She could've offed him if she was, as I suspected, the blackmailer, and he'd finished putting up with her. Even Dr. Hawkins, who had seemed

too nervous for any sort of confrontation, could have been the killer. People under pressure acted out of character all the time.

Suddenly everyone felt like a suspect, and what bothered me most was the very real possibility that I hadn't even thought of the true culprit yet. How did I know it wasn't Tabitha? We had evidence of her personal ties to the blackmailer, and she'd gone to ground only two months before Mr. Becker died.

I flipped the lights on in my shop and freed Penelope from her carrier. She followed Spot, the robot vacuum, lazily across the sun-splotched floorboards.

I turned the "Open" sign to face the window and dusted out my frustrations. By eleven, the shop was spotless and busting with people. Imogene and I had tag-teamed a pre-lunch rush of septuagenarians fresh off a tour bus, greeting, guiding, and ringing them up all in a matter of minutes before their guide ushered them across the street for red beans and rice. "A cultural staple," the guide proclaimed in a thick Jersey accent.

Imogene plucked the fabric away from her chest and ran a forearm over her brow. "Well, that was a whirlwind. Working here is going to keep me young." She fluffed the bottom of her puffy salt-and-pepper hair. "My grandbaby, Miss Isla, loved that red satin tunic you sent for her dog."

I smiled. "I'm glad."

"She made you a thank-you card." Imogene dug in her giant purse and unearthed a folded piece of yellow construction paper. "I almost forgot."

I accepted the paper and levered it open at the fold. "Aww." A brown circle with four stick arms and a red middle wore a smile too big to fit on its head.

"That's Beyoncé," Imogene explained. "She loved the shirt too."

I grabbed a magnet from my drawer and snapped the card to my minifridge. "Please tell Isla this is perfect. She's quite an artist."

A big yellow Tonka truck caught my eye outside the window.

I squinted through the glass in shock. A vaguely familiar tuft of blonde hair fluttered in the wind above a partially open passenger window with black tint. I hustled closer, gawking in disbelief.

Imogene craned her neck from behind the counter. "What is it?"

The fresh line of shoppers at her register turned to face me.

"Nothing." I texted the possible Tabitha sighting to Jack, then pressed my teeth into my lip until I tasted the cherry gloss. I stared at the obnoxious vehicle until it was nothing more than another set of taillights in the traffic.

Imogene crept up behind me. "Better be careful, Miss Lacy. You've got a black cloud forming over that pretty blonde head of yours, and it's got me worried."

"No." I swung my hands in the general direction of said cloud. "No cloud. See?"

She hummed a long note and went back to wiping fingerprints. "Best to shake that off before it storms."

"Nope. Everything's fine." I took a seat behind the counter, facing the window, in case the truck came back. It could've been a coincidence that a blonde, like the woman

we were looking for, drove a truck that looked like one that had harassed me, but I had a hard time believing in coincidences. I grabbed a pad of paper and a pink clicker pen. I hadn't gotten anywhere with the name Sage, but I had another idea. Maybe the blackmailer was a person the men being blackmailed had in common.

I started with a list of known victims. *Wallace Becker, Dr. Hawkins, Me.* I clicked the button on top of my pen a few times. Could the three of us have ticked off a mutual acquaintance? Who? Mrs. Becker came to mind, but she'd seemed pretty chummy with Dr. Hawkins. I selfishly hoped the blackmailer wasn't Karen, the woman who knew all my secrets.

Mom swept dramatically into my shop and looked around, unimpressed. "Slow day?" Her ivory leggings were adorable with the mint-green printed tunic and striped flats. Her new bouncy haircut was deceitful, giving her an almost playful look.

I set my notepad aside. "Actually, the crowd left right before you got here." *Coincidence?* I smiled. "What brings you by?"

She shot a pointed look in my direction. "I'd tell you I stopped by to check on you, but I don't have it in me to banter. The truth is, I'm bored. I can't take another hour trapped inside that house. The cleaning is a nightmare. My nails are atrocious. My manicure is ruined."

"Why are you trapped?" I asked. "Have you been threatened? Is someone outside that you want to avoid?"

"Don't be silly. I'm humiliated," she groaned. "I'd like to avoid the entire city. The whole district thinks I've married a killer. What does that say about my judgment?"

"Well, it is all about you," I said.

"Sarcasm is for the weak of mind," she scolded. "I raised you better. What are you wearing?"

I glanced down at my outfit. "White." The shapeless cotton dress had a braided gold belt that I'd left in the closet. I'd knotted the ends of two teal scarves together and circled them around my waist instead, hoping to imply pastel even if nothing on my body technically was.

"If you need clothes, just say so. I'll have my stylist bring you a rack."

I went back to the list. "I have lots of clothes. I just don't have a month's worth of pastels. I can't believe all those other women do either. It's crazy."

Mom pulled the paper out of my hands. "What's crazy is wearing cork wedges in February. Do you need shoes too? What's this? What are you writing?"

I longed to be with any one of the shoppers who'd escaped before Mom's arrival. "This is a list of people I know are being blackmailed. I wanted to see if they have anything in common."

"Besides the blackmail?" she deadpanned.

I bit my tongue. Apparently crabby old ladies were allowed to use sarcasm.

She returned the notepad to my hands. "How are the flower costumes coming? I'd love to see them."

I glanced at Imogene.

She looked away.

"I'm going to work on those tonight," I fibbed. I hadn't thought much about the flower costumes, or anything work related, since yesterday's meeting with Karen.

Mom's expression morphed into a gruesome hybrid of shock and repulsion. "You should have something to show the committee on Sunday. Have you even started? This is your chance to show off a little. Shine. Strut your stuff," she said. "I mean that figuratively; try not to show up in that awful bikini and wings."

"I'm sorry I never told you about that. I honestly believed you wouldn't want to know. I avoided mentioning anything that had to do with fashion design while I was away because I didn't want to argue with you."

She inhaled deeply, expanding her chest until I thought she might blow me down. "You're my only daughter."

"You wanted a doctor."

She turned her eyes to the ceiling and released the breath slowly—to a count of ten, if I wasn't mistaken. When she'd successfully deflated, she put on a civilized smile. "How was your appointment with Karen? I'm glad you made the time to see her again. She helped you so much last time."

Last time. She didn't need to elaborate. Her thoughts were written in the furrow of her brow. *The last time I got myself involved in a police investigation, stuck my nose into something that wasn't my business, got abducted.* "Fine."

She stilled. "What's that mean? Fine?" She looked to Imogene.

Imogene picked invisible fuzz off her shirt, stealthily avoiding eye contact.

"Did you at least make a follow-up appointment?" Mom asked.

"No."

"Why not? Is it the money? I've offered to pay for those sessions, and you know it."

"It's not the money. Not everything is about money."

"Then why?" she pressed. "You had the gumption to make the appointment. You knew you needed her. You went. What happened? What changed? Explain yourself. Now."

I squirmed against three decades of obedience training. Regardless of circumstance, distance, or personal choice, when Mom gave an order, I complied. Sometimes I refused temporarily, but the guilt and shame of defying her would wear on me until I caved, and we both knew it.

"You won't like it," I conceded, "but it occurred to me that she might have something to do with what's happening, and that was why I made the appointment. She had access to Mr. Becker and me. She knew about his daughter and the party in New York. She knows private things about a lot of people. Maybe even everyone on this list." I turned the page to face her.

She blanched. "Lacy." She gripped my hand. There was concern in her new, softer tone. "I know you've been through a lot, but you can't expect bad things from everyone. Why don't you leave this up to Jack and the police? Do that for me, and the most dangerous thing you'll have to worry about is an accidental stick from one of your sewing needles."

We stared into one another's matching blue eyes for several long beats. She thought I'd gone down a rabbit hole. Even after I'd helped solve two major crimes in a year, she still dismissed my efforts. She only saw the negative.

Eventually, I worked up an agreeable smile. "You're right. I'm overthinking this." And as with most things, she and I would have to agree to disagree.

"Absolutely." She released my hand when her phone rang. "Violet Conti-Crocker."

I slid my gaze to the window where locals and tourists filled the sidewalks, spilling from restaurants, happy and full, ready for another round of retail therapy, and I did my best not to wonder if any of them was a killer.

Mom waved good-bye and chatted her way out the door on her cell phone. "Tan is a neutral color, not a pastel," she instructed. "Don't you have anything floral?"

By nine o'clock, I was emotionally spent and physically exhausted. Jack hadn't responded to my text about the truck, and I hadn't seen it again either. I didn't have it in me to perform the usual cleanup routine, and Imogene had left hours earlier to meet Veda for drinks in the Quarter, so I vowed to clean in the morning. At the moment, all I wanted was a long soak in a piping-hot bath, a glass of wine, and a good night's sleep. I set the store alarm and turned the dead bolt with relief; I was sixty minutes away from my favorite comfy jammies and my blessed bed.

Penelope and I moved slowly in the direction of my car, her swinging gently in the carrier at my side, me making plans to drive home barefoot. "Another beautiful night," I told her. She meowed in agreement. The brisk, spice-scented air snapped against my skin. Sultry, ever-present jazz drifted from local cafés and a lone saxophone player on the corner.

I nearly dropped her carrier when my windshield came into view. "Oh, no." I set Penelope on the sidewalk and freed the manila envelope from beneath my wipers. I tucked the envelope under one arm while I brought Jack up on speed dial.

"Oliver."

"Hey," I swallowed hard, partially irritated that he was able to answer in one ring but couldn't bother responding to my text from hours earlier. "It's me."

"What's wrong?"

"I found another envelope on my car." I liberated the package from beneath my elbow and cracked open the top. A set of photographs lay inside. "More pictures."

"Where are you?" I heard a car door slam on his end of the line and an engine roar to life. "Are they more of the same shots or something else?"

I tapped the envelope, coaxing the photos into my waiting palm. "I don't know. I haven't looked yet." I turned the glossy black-and-white pages over with a sharp gasp. The first was a photo of Chase and me on a bench outside a bookstore. I was looking away, mouth open in laughter. He was smiling proudly at my face. I ignored my pounding heart and shifted to the next shot. Another of Chase and me. I stood on my front porch in pajama shorts and a worn-out T-shirt. He had a bottle of wine. The picture was timestamped eleven seventeen PM.

"These aren't like the last ones." I scanned the area for a big yellow truck. "These are from last week. They aren't blackmail. They're surveillance." I shifted the pages for a look at the next photo. Jack and I stood toe to toe outside the clinic. My chin was tipped upward, eyes serious and expectant. There was no doubt about my thoughts at the time, memorialized for eternity in that photo. My instinct toward embarrassment was only eclipsed by what I saw in Jack's eyes. *Desire.*

"Lacy?" Jack prompted. "Where are you?"

"I'm leaving work," I answered absently. I shoved the photos back into the envelope and pushed Penelope into the car. Dozens of worrisome thoughts scrambled together in my mind. Maybe these were blackmail after all. I definitely didn't want to show him the photos.

There was no note this time, I reasoned. Maybe they weren't evidence. Maybe Jack didn't need to see them.

"Did you get my text about Tabitha?"

"Yes. What do you think I've been doing every minute since?"

"I have no idea." *How could I?* I gunned my little engine to life, then pressed the power door locks twice. Someone had been following me. I'd been right to wonder if the ice cubes were meant as retaliation for snooping. The photos of me in New York weren't my first warning, and now the threat had been extended to my friends.

Sickness coiled in my tummy as the most paramount of thoughts pushed its way to the forefront of my breakdown. I was no longer being threatened with visual proof I was once twenty-five and victorious. *I was being followed.* And Jack and Chase were in danger now because of me.

Chapter Nineteen

Furry Godmother suggests peanut butter with
bananas and honey, but nothing pairs well with crow.

A set of blinding headlights appeared on my tail. I pressed the accelerator closer to the floorboard and gripped the steering wheel until my fingers turned white.

"Lacy!" Jack's voice boomed through the cell phone speaker on my lap. I'd forgotten to pick it up after I'd buckled in.

"Jack," I answered, unable to pull my hands from the wheel. "I'm being followed."

The headlights fell back by a car length. Custom red-and-white flashers winked at me from beneath the massive vehicle's grill. "Pull over," Jack said.

I glanced at the phone, temporarily conflicted. His house appeared up ahead, and I slid against the curb, surprised I'd wound up there.

The headlights went out behind me. "Jack?" I swiveled in my seat, releasing my belt and ramming the phone to my ear.

Someone rapped against my window.

My heart stopped, then sped forward at a runner's pace. Jack peered inside. I nearly knocked him into traffic opening my door. "I'm so sorry," I blathered, wrapping my arms around his middle and sagging against him. "I didn't realize that was you. I wasn't thinking."

He pressed warm palms against my back. "It's fine. I found you on Magazine and followed you here. You were smart to call."

I regained myself with significant effort and peeled away from him. He thought I'd done a good thing, when in fact I'd complicated his life. Knots coiled in my tummy. I didn't want Jack or Chase to see the photos, but they both deserved to know they were being surveilled. "I've upset the blackmailer, and now whoever it is has been following you and Chase too." My bottom lip quivered at the thought. A killer wouldn't hesitate to hurt them if it meant getting to me, and I couldn't allow that.

I covered my mouth, shocked by the weight of the discovery. I could be the reason they got hurt.

Jack gripped my shoulders. "Hey. Come inside."

I dipped back inside my car and fumbled to free my keys from the ignition.

Jack opened the passenger door and collected Penelope. "Bring the envelope."

I followed him up an elegant stone walkway to his home. Through the intricate wrought-iron gate and onto a breathtaking front porch, complete with regal white columns supporting flower-drenched galleries overhead. His stately mansion always caught me off guard. Outwardly, Jack seemed to be more of a cabin-in-the-woods type of guy, and maybe he was, but inheriting the Grandpa Smacker fortune had changed that. Now he was doomed to live a double life. Splitting his time equally between the endless pursuit of bad guys and protecting the financial interests of a global condiment company. Jack was the local Bruce Wayne. Reclusive. Wealthy. Determined to save his city. All he needed was a butler and a bat cave.

He unlocked the door and held it as I passed. "You're unusually quiet. What are you thinking about?"

"Batman."

"Ah." He locked up behind us and kicked his shoes onto the floor. "I often think of Batman."

I shook my head and pointed myself in the direction of his kitchen, certain I wouldn't be sleeping again tonight. "Coffee?"

He followed me until the high-polished wooden floorboards gave way to grand mosaic tiling. Jack's kitchen was nothing short of perfection. His stove cost more than my car. The endless copper backsplash of his granite countertops was embossed with the letter *S* for Smacker. "There you are," he said, lowering Penelope's carrier and swinging the door wide. "Jezebel's around here somewhere. Help yourself to food and water." Jezebel was Jack's cat. Her name said a lot about him. I just hadn't decided what that was.

He lumbered to the island where I'd climbed onto a luxurious high-backed barstool. "How about some tea? Or whiskey? Heck, maybe both. Let me see the pictures first, then I'll decide." He pressed a finger against the envelope and dragged it in his direction. "Nothing too personal in here, I hope?" he teased. "Wearing more clothes than last time?"

I was, though my goofy pajama shorts were a bit embarrassing. I squared my shoulders and lifted my chin. He may or may not be irritated by the sight of the photos, but there was nothing to be done about it now. We were all being stalked by a lunatic.

"No comment?" He blew against the paper opening and shook the photos out. "Now I'm worried." His expression turned grim at the sight of Chase and me on the bench. His eyes narrowed on the shot of us meeting on my porch.

I chewed the tender skin along my thumbnail and watched closely for his next reaction.

He tucked the pictures of Chase and me underneath, revealing the photo of me and him in what looked like the aftermath of a passionate kiss—or the moment just before one. His lips parted and his Adam's apple bobbed. He cleared his throat. "Do you want copies of these before I take them into evidence?"

I made an unintentionally strangled sound. How could I answer that without getting into trouble? Which photo would I want? And why? "I took pictures of the others with my phone. Maybe I can do that again?"

He spread the pages on the island. "There you go."

Prickles ran up and down my arms as he watched and waited. Which photo would I document first? It mattered to him. I could see it in his eyes. Feel it in the energy zipping around us. I opened the camera app on my phone and swallowed my pride. I took a picture of the one with Jack and me first.

My traitorous eyes slid in his direction, dumb and desperate to see his reaction.

His cheek twitched. "Tea and bourbon, coming right up."

Ten minutes later, Jack set a cup of hot water in front of me and a container of tea. I helped myself. While the leaves were steeping, Jack dumped in the bourbon.

"Thanks." I sipped gingerly, more interested in the liquor than the tea.

"Don't mention it." He saddled up on the stool beside mine. "What do you make of the photos?"

"We're being surveilled."

"I agree." He poured a shot into his empty mug and drank it with a heady exhale. Then he poured another. "All right. Let's go." He slid off his stool and tipped his head toward the arching hallway past the kitchen.

I gave the unlit passage a skeptical glance. "Where are we going?"

He collected his mug, bottle, and photos. "You win. I'm giving you what you want."

Oh, boy! I slid onto my feet and followed him to an elaborately decorated, but marginally disappointing, office. The overhead lights illuminated as we stepped inside. Walls were lined in floor-to-ceiling books à la *Beauty and the Beast*. I considered breaking into song, but that was probably the bourbon's doing.

He stopped at a heavy oval table near the far wall. Open file folders and loose paper covered most of its surface. He set his things on a sliver of empty space and pressed his palms to the table's edge. "This is everything I have on Wallace's death."

I rolled doe eyes in his direction. "You trust me." This was exactly what I'd wanted. "So much better than what I thought you might be up to," I mumbled.

He formed an impish grin. "What did you think I was up to?"

I took a seat at the table and pulled a file to me. "Nothing."

He sat with a snort. "You know I've got criminal informants who need less looking after than you. I'm not sure if that makes me the worst cop in town, repeatedly unable to protect one of my closest friends, or you a first-class trouble magnet."

"Neither." I straightened a pile of official-looking papers and tried to be cool, but my nerves were fully rattled despite the spiked tea. "What am I looking at, specifically?" I turned the tidy pile to face him.

"This is everything I removed from Wallace's Cuddle Brigade office. I'm trying to connect Wallace Becker to someone who'd want to hurt him. So far, I've got nothing, but I'm not finished yet." He took the papers from me and split the stack in half. "You take these." He set one portion in front of me. "Those are the notes and phone numbers I haven't had time to identify. I finished going through the things from his home office last night."

I reviewed the stack of sticky notes and scribbles, photocopies, and receipts with a bit of dismay. It could take forever to figure out why Mr. Becker had all these things and whether or not any of them had anything to do with the reason he was killed. An unpleasant thought niggled at the back of my mind. "Do you really want my help, or are you just trying to keep me here where you can watch over me?"

"Little of both." He added more bourbon to my tea. "Can you live with that?"

"I guess." I sipped the drink and traced a fingertip over a tiny mark in Mr. Becker's appointment book.

"After I got your text about the truck, I started patrolling the district in search of it. I had my guy at the station search the motor vehicle database for a truck fitting that description. He didn't find one registered to anyone in the parish, but there are half a dozen in the state. It'll take time to contact all the owners. For what it's worth, I've been busy, but I was never more than a few minutes from you after that text." The look in his eyes said something more, but my nerves were too rattled to venture a guess.

"Thank you."

"Yep." Jack's stomach growled, and he left the room. A few minutes later, he returned with a teapot and refilled my cup, then splashed another dose of bourbon in for good measure.

I set the appointment book down with a frown. "Look at this." I moved a finger over the strange little doodad Mr. Becker had scratched in several places. "What do you think this is? It's here and here." I turned the pages, pointing out a number of similar marks. "There's a little stick and a circle on top. What could it mean?"

He rested a hip on the table beside my arm and took the book from me for a closer inspection. "Are there any correlations? Do they mark a pattern of days or times?"

"Not that I can see. And it never appears with a name or number. Just this little thing." Could it be a shorthand symbol? A hieroglyphic? Something from a cipher? "Every other appointment has a note to remind him when, where, and who, but these stand alone. They must represent something important. Something impossible to forget."

Jack's stomach complained again. "Maybe it's a doodle."

"It's not a doodle. Why haven't you eaten? I thought you left to get something just now."

He patted his middle. "I'll get something later. This is important."

"So is eating. Come on." I handed him the book and collected my tea. "You have to eat. What do you have?"

He shuffled along behind me with a sigh. "Everything."

I set my tea on the kitchen island and opened his mammoth double-door fridge. "How about a grilled cheese? Those are fast and delicious." I guffawed at the fridge's contents. He wasn't kidding about having everything.

Jack appeared on my left. He bumped me with his elbow. "You sit. I'll cook. Do you like pizza?"

"What kind do you have?" I hadn't looked in the freezer, but I wasn't a big fan of a lot of the frozen brands. "I don't mind making something."

He rolled his eyes dramatically and raked a hand through his hair. "Why would you cook at my house?"

"I don't know." Why would I? Hadn't I just resolved not to let Chase serve me at my house? Here I was doing the same thing to Jack. "I'm sorry."

"For what?"

I rubbed tired eyes and suppressed a groan. "Taking over your kitchen. That was rude and presumptuous. Trust me. I know."

Jack dragged a pizza crust from the refrigerator and spread it on a baking sheet, then lined the island with veggies and cheeses. "I didn't mind."

"You didn't?"

He locked ice-blue eyes on me. "You're welcome to cook here any time, but maybe you can start on a day you haven't been threatened by a blackmailing murderer."

I rose onto my knees, balancing like a child on the big stool for a better look. "Deal."

He smiled. "For tonight, how about some spinach, tomato, basil, mozzarella . . ." He pointed to the ingredients one by one.

My stomach growled. "Yes, please."

He chuckled. "Okay. If you're still worked up after we've eaten, we can always take a swim. I do my best thinking in the water."

I'd seen that process firsthand and wouldn't mind a repeat. "I don't have a suit with me, but you can swim. I'll sit at one of the patio tables."

He lifted playful eyes from his diligent pizza making. "No suit?"

"Focus."

He brushed his hands together. "You're right. What were you saying about the little drawings?"

It took me a minute to recall. "Maybe if I find the very first symbol and follow it through, I'll get a better idea of its meaning."

He nudged my fingers away from the glass bowls of neglected toppings. "Quit stealing olives."

I stopped chewing and feigned innocence. "What do you mean?"

He laughed softly and washed his hands in the prep sink. "Did you miss dinner too?"

"No. I had fish tacos. The photos are making me hungry. I'm a nervous eater. I munch on everything when I'm in danger."

"If that's true, you ought to weigh more," he said.

"Ha ha." I sat back and turned the pages of Mr. Becker's appointment book while Jack finished the pizza. He was right. If my endless bad luck didn't change, I'd need a new dress size by breakfast.

Jack pushed dinner into the oven and set a timer.

I flipped between two pages in Mr. Becker's planner. "The meaning of these symbols is here; we just have to figure it out."

He circled the island to hover at my side. "Good luck." He fingered the line of surveillance photos again. "These are high quality. Whoever took them used a good camera and had a clear line of sight. Have you noticed anyone hanging around this week?" His kind voice and soft cologne enveloped me.

"No, but I've been distracted." Take now for example.

"Apparently," he muttered, scooting the photos of Chase and me farther away from him. "Anything new with you two?"

"No." I drew a row of the weird symbols along the edge of another paper. I drew them upside down, backward, big, and small. "Are you asking because I told you about the kiss?" I forced my gaze to remain on the paper.

"I'm just making small talk while our dinner bakes."

"No you aren't." I stopped to stare at him. "You're being nosy. Admit it." He'd told me once that nosiness was in his job description, and as far as I could tell, Jack *was* the job description.

He pulled the photo of him and me in front of him. "I'm just asking."

"I don't believe you, but for the record, there's nothing new between me and Chase. We are what we have always been. Good friends."

"Someone ought to tell him."

"I did. He said he'll wait, and we can get married later."

Jack did a monstrous eye roll.

I went back to doodling. "Does this look like a magnifying glass now that I made it bigger?"

Jack made a face. "Kind of."

I slapped the paper, overcome by an epiphany. "Dr. Hawkins said Mr. Becker hired a private investigator. I'd bet my black olives that this symbol stands for times he met with him, and the PI's number is probably one of the unidentified ones in my pile."

Jack set his cell phone on the island. "Well, what are you waiting for?"

I lined the unidentified phone numbers up and dialed them one by one. Most were businesses already closed for the night. I jotted down the company names beside their numbers. "I'm glad these aren't people's homes. It's kind of late to make calls, and I've had too much bourbon to talk to another human being."

"You sound fine to me."

"That's because you've had more than me."

He nudged the paper. "You do the dialing, and I'll decide when we've had too much bourbon."

I dialed and sniggered.

Jack made me another cup of tea.

"Hello?" A man answered the next call.

My eyes went wide. I covered the receiver and made panicked faces at Jack.

He pointed to the Cuddle Brigade letterhead and made an air circle with his finger.

"Um," I bumbled, "I'm calling from the Cuddle Brigade."

"That's my dad's company," the man said. "What do you want? Why are you calling?"

I'd called Wallace Jr.! I shrugged repeatedly at Jack, who looked thoroughly amused and not concerned at all.

"Um, I'm calling because there was a box of things in Mr. Becker's office with your name on them," I improvised. "Maybe you'd like to come and pick them up tomorrow?"

Jack gave me a thumbs-up.

"Sure," Wallace Jr. said. His voice had lost its edge. "Okay."

"Great. Ask for Jack when you get there. And Wallace? I'm very sorry about your loss." I disconnected with mixed feelings. "That was sad."

"Yes," Jack agreed, "but now I can talk to Wallace's son without his mother intervening or calling their lawyer."

The oven beeped as I dialed the next number. Jack removed the pizza and set it on the island. Tangy scents of marinara and melted cheeses buttered the air.

"Jerry Gates, PI," a voice answered.

I jumped in my seat. "Jerry Gates?" I repeated, scribbling his name onto the paper. "Private investigator?"

"Yeah. Who's this?" The sounds of live music droned in the background, making him difficult to hear.

I shot an apologetic look at Jack. This was who we needed to talk to, and I had a great idea for how to see him right away. "Someone's following me!" I burst into fake hysteria. "I need your help."

Jack crunched his face.

I huffed and puffed into the receiver. "Someone's sending me photographs of myself, and I'm frightened."

The music grew distant on his end of the line. "What's your name, Miss? Where are you? Stay calm. I can help."

"That would be wonderful. I'd really appreciate that."

Jack crept back to my side and mouthed the words, "What are you doing?"

I gripped his arm in preparation for my next bold move. "Mr. Gates, is there any way you can meet with me first thing tomorrow morning?"

"I like to sleep in," he said. "Night work is kind of my thing. Are you near the Quarter? You want to meet me at the Hotel Monteleone in an hour?"

I bounced my knees erratically, watching Jack for the blank-faced cop-nod go-ahead.

He screwed the top on the bottle of bourbon with a sigh.

I took that as a yes. "See you soon."

Chapter Twenty

Furry Godmother strongly recommends cherishing your cat.
No one knows what she's plotting.

We each had a slice of pizza and cup of coffee before Jack called a cab.

"I wish I wasn't still wearing this," I said, dotting my mouth with a napkin. "White dresses in the French Quarter aren't generally a good idea." The area was fun, but not exactly known for its cleanliness.

Jack pushed away from the island. "What size are you?"

I crossed my arms. "Yeah, right."

He disappeared down a side hall and returned with a pair of folded jeans, tags still attached. "Tabitha left boxes of brand new things in her closet when she vanished. I'd like to think she felt guilty for all the stuff Grandpa bought her while she was lying to his face and drugging him, but more likely, her getaway car was already full."

I took the pants, reluctantly. Much as I didn't want to wear a mean lady's jeans, I also didn't want to waste any more time before getting to the Quarter. "I'll put them on, but they probably won't button, and they don't exactly go with this white dress."

He produced a wad of cotton material in his other palm. "How about a rugby practice shirt?"

"Tabitha played rugby?"

He laughed. "I played when I was young."

"I can't picture it," I said, accepting the top. I shook it out and held it by the shoulders. The navy color was nice, and the material was soft. There was a big number twenty-seven on the back. The word *Oliver* stood above it. "If I wear this, will it mean we're going steady?"

"Yeah," he deadpanned. "Now put it on and let's go."

I changed in the bathroom nearest to the kitchen, surprised at how easily the pants buttoned and self-conscious about the clingy cut of the material. Rhinestones and silver thread formed elaborate crosses over each of the back pockets. I tucked the hem of Jack's shirt in and twisted for a look at myself in the mirror. Surprisingly, the top nearly fit across the shoulders. It must have been purchased before Jack's growth spurt.

He knocked on the door.

"Coming." I finger-combed my hair and checked my face for smudged eyeliner or lipstick. No problems there. Most of it had probably disappeared hours ago. I tugged the door open.

Jack leaned against the doorjamb, startling me half to death. A slow smile rose on his lips, stretching over his face until it reached his eyes.

"I think this should be your new French Quarter outfit."

"I don't think so." Though, I wouldn't have minded keeping the shirt. It was comfy, and it smelled like Jack. "I look like a little boy."

"Wrong." He turned back for the kitchen.

Lights flashed over his front windows.

"Cab's here," he said.

Twenty minutes later, thick Louisiana air raced over my skin as we strolled along crowded French Quarter streets. Sounds of laughter, live bands, and distant DJs mixed with neon lights and smiling faces from all around the world. Second-floor galleries were lined with people enjoying the same enchanted night as me. The moment was intoxicating.

Jack ran his fingers against my palm and lifted my hand into the crook of his elbow.

I lolled my head against his arm as we walked. "I love it here."

"Me too."

The Hotel Monteleone sign rose regally into the night sky up ahead, each enormous red letter supported by white scaffolding, somewhat reminiscent of California's Hollywood sign, except there were no hills here, only enough history and beauty to break my heart. "When I think of all the things these buildings have seen," I told Jack, "all the joys and tragedies that have transpired right here where we're walking . . . War. Yellow fever. Weddings. Parades. Lives. Deaths. It makes me feel like I'm being woven in the tapestry of time right beside them."

Jack pressed his free hand over mine where it rested on his arm. "I think that's exactly what happens in a city like this. We become part of it." He released me to open the grand Monteleone door. "Ladies first."

I passed beneath the majestic canopy and into the lobby. Jack entered on my heels.

Happy voices spilled from the hotel's famous Carousel Bar, where the bar not only looked like a carousel but rotated like one as well, making a complete rotation every fifteen minutes. The carousel's lights were on when we entered, and two seats opened as we approached. The couple, previously seated, had been lured away to dance. I climbed aboard an empty stool and ordered a Sazerac. Jack stuck with water, and despite our recent—albeit rushed—pizza, he requested crawfish beignets.

The bartender steadied a bottle of water in front of Jack and placed two empty glasses on the bar beside it. "A Sazerac," he explained, scooping crushed ice into each glass, "is a New Orleans tradition and one of our specialties here. It's made with Absinthe, one sugar cube, Rye whiskey or cognac. I prefer cognac." He winked. "Three dashes of Peychaud's Bitters, and voilà!" He worked methodically through the complicated process of my drink, then strained the finished product from one glass into the other. He topped it with a lemon peel. "One New Orleans work of art for another."

I blushed. "Thank you."

Jack didn't look impressed. He checked his watch. "Do you see anyone who looks like Gates?"

I swiped my cell phone to life and compared the image on my screen to the faces around us. We'd looked the PI up online during our cab ride. According to the LinkedIn profile, Jeremiah Gates was a decorated veteran with twenty years on the Baton Rouge police force and a decade working private investigations, but his picture was clearly taken in the 1990s. "What about him?" I pointed to a man sitting alone in the corner.

"No."

I squinted. "It's dark in here. I don't know." I scanned the crowded bar again. My gaze caught on a man loitering outside the window, watching a couple climb down from a horse-drawn carriage. "Him?" I pointed.

The couple moseyed into the hotel, and the man followed.

Jack lifted my phone to eye level and moved it in line with the man. "That's him."

The couple took a seat in the rear corner of the room. The man headed right for me. He was older than my dad and in worse shape. His khaki pants were belted around his navel. The cuffs didn't quite reach his black socks and white Reeboks. He'd tucked a Hawaiian button-down shirt into his khakis and topped the outfit off with a floppy brimmed hat. Next to him, I looked runway ready. "Hello, I'm Jerry Gates." He extended one dimpled hand in my direction, a business card stuck between two fingers.

"Lacy Crocker," I answered. "How'd you know it was me who called you?"

He shoved heavy glasses up the bridge of his crooked nose. "Everyone else is deep in conversation, absorbed in whatever's happening at their table. You two were obviously looking for someone. Why not me?"

"Why not?" I said. "This is Detective Jack Oliver."

Jerry looked confused. "I don't normally work with the police," he said. "I know how they can be."

"Watch it," Jack warned.

Jerry lifted his palms in peace. "I'm just saying is all."

I sipped my drink while the men sized each other up. This was my chance for a direct conversation with the man Mr. Becker had hired to search for his blackmailer. Excitement rolled over me until I couldn't wait any longer. "You knew Wallace Becker?" I asked.

Jerry swung his gaze to mine, reluctantly taking his eyes off of Jack. "Who?"

I set my drink down and leaned in the PI's direction. "We know he hired you. My dad's being investigated for his murder, and I think you can help me."

Jerry fell back, stupefied, and scrubbed beefy palms over his face, knocking his glasses around in the process. "Jeez, lady. You lied about being followed? You could've just made an appointment at my office for this."

I scoffed. "I didn't lie. I am being followed, presumably by the same crackpot who tormented Mr. Becker." I presented him with my cell phone and brought up the photos I'd taken of the ones left on my car this week. "Someone sent these to me."

He performed a low whistle at the ones of me in a bikini, then flipped slowly between pictures of me with Jack and me with Chase. "Whoa, buddy." He looked at Jack. "Tough luck, yeah? Caught cheating." He shook his head in dismay.

"I wasn't cheating." I snatched my phone back. "It's complicated. And irrelevant. The photos are misleading." I trailed off, feeling ridiculous.

Jack twisted the lid off his water. "We need to know what you know about Wallace Becker's blackmailer."

Jerry kept his attention on me. "Hey, I didn't mean to offend you. It's none of my business what you're up to. I have a bad habit of jumping to conclusions. Making inferences is part of the job. You kids these days are what the media calls progressive"—he made finger quotes around the last word—"with your relationships and things. I've seen daytime TV. I get it."

"I'm *not* progressive." My thick Southern accent soaked through each word. I barely stopped myself from declaring I was a Crocker, a proper Southern lady, or some other line my mother had spent my formative years ingraining on my psyche.

He cast Jack a funny look. "Touchy."

Jack stretched onto his feet. "Mr. Gates, this place is more public than I'd prefer for our discussion. Maybe you can accompany me to the station. It's private, and we can control the spectators."

"No." Jerry answered quickly, refocusing on the couple he'd followed into the bar. "No. This is fine." He lifted a finger at the barkeep.

The man delivered a tall glass of amber liquid to the space between Jack and me. He dropped a cherry onto the top.

"Thanks, Miles." Jerry left several folded bills on the counter in exchange for his drink. "I'm a regular at most of these places, but no one wants to give me a tab. Go figure."

I tapped my nails on the bar. "You were saying?"

He plunged a straw into the glass and paddled the cherry around. "Wallace hired me to find out who was blackmailing him."

"When was this?" Jack asked.

"A couple of weeks ago. We met a bunch of times to go over details. His suspicions, likely suspects, the usual. He never wanted to tell the whole story at once. It was easier for him in little jags, I think, so he could pretend he wasn't telling me everything. He kept saying it was important to keep the circle small. The fewer people who knew about things, the better. He led up to his big secret like he'd committed a murder or something." He winced. "Sorry. Bad choice of words. Anyway, I told him it was no big deal. Everyone's got an illegitimate child somewhere."

I made a face at Jack.

"I don't," he said.

Jerry tented his brows. "Oh, yeah? How can you be sure about that?"

Jack's frown deepened. "Back to Becker. What'd you find out during your investigation?"

He slurped his drink with a groan. "I never started. The guy kicked off before I got any further than reviewing the notes."

I curled my hands on my lap. "You didn't even start on his case?"

"Hey, I can't help it if New Orleans is a busy town for thefts and cheating. That's my bread and butter, and I've got a full plate these days. I barely squeezed in all those meetings of his."

"Did he mention a yellow Tonka truck or anyone named Sage or Tabitha?" I asked.

Jerry made a face. "You expect me to remember? That guy said a lot of stuff."

Jack dug a business card from his wallet and handed it to Jerry. "I'm going to need those notes."

"Sure thing." He backed away in a hurry. "See you later. Take care." He tipped his floppy brim in my direction and hustled through the room, regaining his tail on the couple he'd followed inside as they made their way through the lobby.

The awkward trio cut a path to the elevators. One man and woman kissing as they stumbled along in the lead, and Jerry taking pictures of them with his cell phone from ten feet behind.

I shoved his abandoned drink out of the way. "He invited us to his stakeout."

Jack's plate of crawfish beignets arrived in a puff of buttery steam. He pushed them between us. "The bread will absorb the alcohol."

I tore one in half and blew across the top. "You're the one who was plying me with spiked tea."

"That was before I knew we were going out. No one told you to order a Sazerac."

"I like watching them make it."

He laughed. For a fleeting moment, his crystal-blue eyes crinkled at the edges. Too soon, his lips fell back into their usual firm line. His eyes, now clearly troubled, focused tightly on me.

I fidgeted with my beignet, not quite sure I could eat it. The look in his eyes worried me, and I had the distinct feeling that this was where he pushed me out of his life for good. "Jack?"

The muscle along his jawline ticked. Whatever he was thinking about was big, and the longer he stared, the more anxious I became. I shoved a tuft of fluffy dough between my lips and chewed slowly, unable to look away. "Everything okay?" I mumbled.

He paid the bill and climbed down, his beignet forgotten. "Yeah. Are you ready?"

"Okay." I followed Jack onto the sidewalk. "Hey." I grabbed his hand. "I know something's wrong. What is it?"

He answered me with a regretful look, then raised his arm for a cab. "I think we need to talk."

* * *

Jack lit a fire in the fireplace and sat with me on the couch. He hadn't said much since leaving the Monteleone, and my shaken nerves had churned the pizza and tea into sickness, not to mention the beignet. What had happened? What could have driven him to leave the bar immediately and insist on this discussion?

He turned his back to the couch's arm and locked a worried gaze on me. He could have been facing a firing squad.

I held perfectly still.

Deep lines gathered over his brow, and he curved his hands together. "I'm done running from you."

I let the words settle in. "Good."

"You told Gates that the surveillance pictures were complicated. That they were misleading. I think they're pretty darn accurate."

I rubbed my palms against goose bumps rising on my arms. "Yeah?"

"I realized something during the holidays, back when everyone was still helping you get around with your cast. I didn't like it. It seems like whenever we're together, you talk and I listen."

"Sorry," I answered on instinct, suddenly guilty for filling our time together with my ramblings.

"No." He smiled. "Don't apologize. You never expect anything in return. You don't pose insensitive questions. Don't ask for more than I'm willing to give. That kind of relationship is great, and it normally works well for me"— he paused—"but it's stopped working for me with you."

"Oh." I kneaded my hands against my lap. "Is that why you quit coming around for so long?"

He bobbed his head. "I tried redirecting myself. I worked extra hours. It didn't help. You stayed on my mind. Things you'd said. Secrets you'd shared."

A strange pressure centered in my chest. What had I said? Had I offended him? I bit the insides of my cheeks to keep from asking. To give him time to say what he needed.

"I know a lot about you." He gave a small, guilty laugh. "I pulled your record last summer when you showed up at my crime scene. I asked around about you after that. Since then, you've told me more than I've ever thought to ask. I'm sure there are some things you regret telling me, and there are some I wish I didn't know."

I held my breath, uncertain and a little frightened about what those things might be. Maybe he hated that I'd been mugged at gunpoint in Arlington before we'd met. That night still haunted me, but the memory had company now. Maybe he wished I hadn't told him I'd kissed Chase or that I tried veganism once. Honestly, who knew? I couldn't possibly because he refused to open up and say what he meant. I curled my hands into fists. Whatever Jack was getting at, he'd finally started to let me in, and I wouldn't let him push me out now.

"I promised myself at Christmas that I'd stop running from you. You've never run from me. It's only fair."

I blinked, stunned. A bevy of emotions tumbled through me. Fair was of the utmost importance to Jack, and he wanted to be fair to me. "Okay."

"So ask me anything you want to know." He grimaced. "You've earned my trust over and again. It's time I said so and returned the favor."

A slow smile spread over my face. I had endless unanswered questions about Jack. Where to start? I sought the most basic ice-breaking question I had. "Why'd you come back to New Orleans?" It was the thing that puzzled me most about him. "You grew up abroad, served in the military overseas. You have enough money to start a life anywhere you want. Why'd you come here?"

Jack went pale, his face as heartbreaking as anything I'd ever seen. It was as if I'd asked the worst possible question or kicked him in the chest. He rubbed his hands on his thighs and blinked grieving eyes. "I was in a car accident in Austria. My fiancé and I."

My heart hammered. My mouth went dry. I could see the loss in his eyes, in the set of his lips. *He'd lost her.* "I'm sorry. I didn't know." I waited, hungry for more about his life before me.

"We were driving home from dinner. We'd been celebrating our engagement with friends from school. We were all so young. Fresh from college, ready to take on the world." His voice cracked, and he stopped to clear his throat. "I'd had too much to drink, so she drove. She fell asleep at the wheel." He lifted his eyes to mine. Shame creased his face. "She was tired a lot then. And she wasn't drinking."

"Oh, no." He didn't have to say it. I knew. "She was pregnant."

His eyes glossed with untold years of guilt and pain. "Not far enough along to share the news, I guess. I found the positive tests in her apartment weeks later, when I was released from the hospital. They were all wrapped like gifts. Four of them."

He hadn't even known. The knot in my chest tightened. I set my hand on his.

"I joined the army then. Spent eight years fighting my own demons along with a few tangible ones. I did three tours in the sandbox. Kuwait. Bosnia. Afghanistan. It took me that long to let her go. To accept that I couldn't go back. I couldn't save her. Them," he corrected. "When my time was up, I came home. Unsatisfied but done fighting. I took the civil service test and went to the police academy."

"Became a fierce crime-fighting detective."

He faked a laugh. "Yeah, I'm so great I can't keep one former debutante out of harm's way for more than five minutes." He turned his palm over beneath mine and entwined our fingers. "I've never told that story. The people who knew us know about it, of course, but I haven't been back to Europe, and I don't talk about it, so if there's anything else you want to know on the matter, now's the time to ask because I left that life far behind."

I squeezed his fingers. "I won't tell anyone, and I don't need to know anything else." I raised careful fingers to the pattern of tiny white dashes on his cheek. "Your scars."

He pressed rugged stubble against the tender skin of my palm. "Shards of window glass," he whispered.

I finally understood why he was so rarely clean shaven. The stubble hid those scars from nosy strangers. And himself.

He released my hand and wrapped his arms around my back instead, winding his fingers into the length of hair over my shoulder. "You shouldn't be alone tonight. Give me a chance to find out who sent those photos."

"Okay."

"Stay with me," he whispered.

"Yeah."

Chapter
Twenty-One

Furry Godmother's key to avoiding scandal:
Stop breathing.

"Nothing happened," I repeated to Scarlet. "There's nothing to tell." I'd slid out of work early to prepare for Dad's dinner and made the mistake of returning one of Scarlet's two dozen missed calls while driving. I took the next corner a little too quickly.

"Your car was outside Jack Oliver's house when I jogged past at five this morning. There's definitely something to tell."

Why was this district so small? "You should be sleeping at five AM, not out gallivanting around the neighborhood."

"Tell me that story after you have four kids," she chided.

If I had four kids, I'd be in the loony bin, but I didn't see the point of telling her. "I slept on the couch. He slept on the floor. It was all very innocent and lovely. We talked until we both fell asleep in front of the fire." The bourbon had probably helped.

"You talked." She said the words as if they were filth on her tongue.

"Yes. Grown people do that. He's stayed at my house before. You never assumed the worst then."

"Honey, I highly doubt what I'm suggesting would be the worst."

"Scarlet," I scolded. "Really."

"Yes. Really. Now if you don't start telling me what I want to know, I'm going to have to find another way to get the information. Maybe I'll call him."

"Do not."

"I can hear you smiling."

"Cannot." I pulled into my driveway with a grin. "He finally opened up to me about his life. He gave me a chance to see who he is behind the badge and all those personal barriers he insists on keeping up. He said he trusted me."

"I've got to give it to him. The guy's smooth," she said. "Every woman wants to be the one he lets in."

"It was nice. He was real, and I felt honored. When he asked me to stay, I didn't even have to think about it. I didn't want to leave. What kind of message would that have sent if I'd left after he finally opened up?" I locked my car and hustled up the drive to my house. "I almost forgot. I went over there because I got another set of photos last night. Pictures of me and Jack. Others of me and Chase."

"Yikes." Her voice jumped an octave. "Now that's blackmail."

"Yeah. No wonder he didn't want me to leave." No sooner were the words off my tongue than the weight of them had settled on my heart. "Do you think he only told me those things about himself and asked me to stay so I wouldn't insist on going home?"

"No." She was quiet for a long beat. "Hey, even if that was the reason he wanted you to stay, it's not like anything happened between you guys. *Allegedly*," she teased. "Maybe this little scare was the push he needed to finally tell you how he feels. It's good karma. You're a great person, and even the bad things turn around in your life. As they should."

I set my alarm and flopped onto my couch. "I'm not sure karma is that simple. Imogene says there's a black cloud over my head."

My phone buzzed with an incoming call from my mom. Imogene was right. "I have to go. Mom's in meltdown mode about Dad's recognition dinner tonight. I left work early to get ready."

"Oh, you don't have to tell me about your mother. Why do you think it's so quiet over here? Your mom hired a sitter to play outside with my kids so I could call everyone on her invite list, whether they'd RSVP'd or not, and thank them personally for supporting your father."

"Wow."

"Yeah. I'd answer her call if I was you, or she'll show up at your door in ten minutes."

I shot upright, adrenaline lighting fire in my bones. "I don't have anything to wear!"

Scarlet groaned. "She's calling me now. I have to take that."

"Good luck." I disconnected and set Penelope free from her carrier. "I'm in big trouble," I told her. I filled her dishes with fresh food and water, dropped a dehydrated shrimp bit into Buttercup's bowl, then dragged myself into my bedroom for a faceoff with my pastel-depleted closet.

The phone rang. Jack's face appeared on the screen.

"Hello?"

"Hey." His voice was low and careful. "How was your day?"

I twisted the hem of my skirt around my finger. "Good. Yours?"

"Okay."

I waited through an awkward pause.

"Scarlet called," he said.

I nearly dropped the phone. "What?"

"Your dad's dinner is tonight. I told her I'd be there, but the truth is that I picked up the Becker file from Jerry Gates on my way home this afternoon, and it could take a while to weed through it all."

"It's okay if you can't come." Unexpected disappointment colored my voice. "He'll understand." I deflated at the idea of not seeing Jack in a few hours.

"Will you?"

"Forgive you? Of course."

My phone buzzed again. Another call from my mother. I ignored it. "What's in the file?"

Jack heaved a sigh. "Everything. Blurry snapshots taken by Wallace. Paranoid notes from at least three months before his death. He'd documented his suspicions fairly thoroughly, but they seem a little crazed. I'm not sure what was real and what was the result of his imagination gone wild. No pictures of the truck you've been seeing."

I'd once thought I imagined a man in a giant cat head outside my window. I could relate to the effects of stress on the psyche. "I hate to do this, but I need to call my mom and get ready for Dad's dinner. Maybe I'll see you there?"

"I'll do my best."

We disconnected.

I called Mom while I flipped through a wad of dresses in dry cleaning bags inside my closet, praying something spectacular would appear.

She answered on the first ring. "Finally," she heaved. "Where are you? Are you home?"

"Yep."

"Good. Hang up."

The phone went dead. "Mom?" I shook it and stared at the blank screen. A video call rang through from Violet Conti-Crocker. I accepted.

Mom's eyes appeared. "Are you there? Can you see me?"

"Back up," I said. "I can see your pores."

A hand flew over her nose as she pulled the camera away. She set the phone on something and stepped in front of the screen wearing a lovely, tea-length Vera Wang. The floral midnight-blue-and-lavender pattern was gorgeous against her ivory skin and neutral lipstick. "What are you wearing tonight?" she asked. "My stylist brought a rack of things for you to try. Come over and bring a black clutch and heels. Those will go with anything. Hair and makeup will be here at five."

"I'm doing my own hair and makeup," I said. Though I had absolutely no idea what I would be wearing. "You look fantastic."

The lines on her forehead smoothed. "Do you really think so?" She pulled a rack of dresses into view. "I've tried them all twice. Nothing feels right. I want tonight to be perfect for your father."

"It will be."

"What if no one shows up? What if he thinks I look like a mess?"

"He thinks you're beautiful no matter what you wear," I said. "And if no one shows up, it's their loss because we're going to have an amazing time."

She spread one hand over her collarbone. "He doesn't want to go."

"He'll go."

"What if he doesn't?"

I gave her an empathetic smile. I'd felt the same way last night on Jack's couch. *What if everything falls apart and I can't stop it?* Maybe Imogene was right. Maybe Mom and I were equally dramatic. "He'll go because it will make you happy."

She ran her hands down the length of her dress. "See you at seven." She reached for the phone and blinked out of sight.

I turned back to my closet. There was nothing remotely pastel left inside. As if Mom wasn't stressed out enough, her daughter was about to show up in a vibrant, nonfloral gown or worse. Black. I pushed elbow deep into the gowns, searching for some forgotten number that had been some-how shoved from sight.

Claudia Post's business card stared up at me from the floor. A delicate green vine of sweetheart roses formed the border. My heart quickened in a moment of creative clarity. I owned a rose-colored dress and the lion's share of appliqués and accents. There was hope for this evening yet.

Chapter
Twenty-Two

Furry Godmother's words of wisdom:
Being fashionably late requires first being fashionable.

I took a cab to the Elms Mansion and arrived fashionably late. By the looks of the parking lot and line at the valet, things weren't as dire as I'd assumed. Half the district had turned up to honor Dad's contribution to the community. The cynic in me said they'd only come to stare at the murderer or see if he'd go cuckoo during his speech, but the rest of me—the parts that understood what it meant to belong here—knew that neighbors stuck together and that I'd overreacted by assuming the worst.

I nodded at the doorman and slipped into the vibrant affair. The Van Benthuysen Elms Mansion and Gardens was one of the most famous historic homes in the district. Its exquisite Italianate-style architecture made it the Mona Lisa of St. Charles Street and one of the most popular venues in the city. Knots and clusters of guests sipped champagne and wandered down hallways lined in ornamental cornices and twenty-four-carat sconces. I held my wrist at hip level, keeping the small ribbon of material looped around it at an appropriate distance from the floor. The ribbon was attached to my train. Thanks to the delicate border on Claudia Post's business card, I'd turned my fashion crisis around in under sixty minutes. The red, *Pretty Woman*–esque ball gown in my closet stopped looking so *not floral* and started looking like the start of a beautiful flower. With a few tight stitches and a line of tiny silk rosebuds down one side of the plunging neckline, I'd repurposed a piece I never thought I'd get to wear again. I smiled at a pair of whispering women as they pointed to the length of material flowing beneath my gloved arm.

"Miss Crocker," a woman in a pantsuit speed-walked in my direction. "This way. Your mother has been worried sick." Her strained face and clipboard screamed "party planner."

"I was running late," I said by way of obvious explanation.

She powered ahead, all business. "Your father's dinner is being held in the ballroom. Dessert will be served in the gardens. Get something to drink and mingle until you're called to be seated. You're sitting at the head table with your family, your date, and the men and women who nominated Dr. Crocker for the service award."

My date had called while I was sewing my dress a new look. Something had come up, and Chase needed to meet me here so as not to make me late. Given my last-minute wardrobe issues, he'd probably beaten me.

I tiptoe-ran along behind Pantsuit, unable to keep up with her long legs and ballet flats. The black-and-silver stilettos on my feet were made for show, not sport.

We passed through great arching doors at the end of the well-appointed hall. She blended instantly into the woodwork and headed away from the crowd. I slowed to admire the grand ballroom and its ornately jeweled windows. Though I'd visited the Elms many times, the view never grew less impressive.

Mom was easy to spot, shaking hands and kissing cheeks near the bar. "This home was built in 1869 for Watson Van Benthuysen II," she told an awestruck couple before her. "He was a Yankee, from New York, until he moved down here and joined the Confederate Army." She paused briefly for dramatic effect. "He died right here in this house back in 1901."

Her gaze landed on me. Her sharp blue eyes narrowed, then widened, taking me in from head to toe. She excused herself from the couple and came to my side. "You're late."

"I know. I'm sorry."

"I called. You said you were on your way." She looked me over again, more carefully this time. "This is beautiful. Where'd you get it?"

"Closet." I squirmed.

"This is one of yours?"

"I made it in design school. I'm fresh out of pastel, so I dressed it up to comply with the Welcoming Committee dress code. Now I'm a rose."

She moved around me in a tight circle, dragging gentle fingertips over the material gathered at my waist. "Could you make another in periwinkle before the National Pet Pageant?"

I forced my gaping mouth shut. "You want me to make you a dress?" Mom only wore couture. Period. If the designer wasn't a global name, she didn't have time to look at it.

"That's what I said, isn't it? If you can't, that's fine. I know you're busy with the flower costumes." She hiked a brow. "You have started the flower costumes. Right?"

"Sure." I'd start as soon as I got home.

"Is Jack coming?" she asked.

"I don't know. He said he'd try."

She made a face. "After last night, I assumed he wouldn't miss it."

The words floated loosely in my mind for several beats as I dialed. "What happened last night?"

Her expression fell. "Don't be coy. Everyone on the street saw your car at his house all night. Surely you didn't think that information would somehow elude me."

"Nothing happened." I grabbed a flute of champagne from a passing waiter. "Where's Dad?"

"In the gardens. He's telling dreadful stories about our early years—taking over his dad's once failing practice and other times of struggle."

I smiled. Dad loved telling those stories. To him, they were badges of honor, times he'd persevered and overcame the odds. To Mom, hard times were an embarrassment, representing places in her life where she'd fallen short somehow, either directly or by association with someone else who'd also struggled. Mom thought life should be easy.

Dad thought life should be a challenge. And they wondered why I was conflicted.

"Hello, gorgeous." Chase cut through the crowd to Mom's side and kissed her cheek. "You look beautiful, Mrs. C. What a lovely party you've planned."

"Hello, Chase," Mom said. "You look dashing as ever. Where's your valentine?" She shot me a pointed look. Tomorrow was Valentine's Day.

He smoldered. "I'm available if you are."

"Are you familiar with Eddie Haskell?" she asked.

"No, ma'am." He scanned the room. "Is he here tonight?"

"He was a character on *Leave it to Beaver.*"

An incorrigible one, if memory serves. I smiled at Mom. Chase made a puzzled face.

I cast him a meaningful look.

"Never mind." She waved at someone over my head. "The Cummings are here." She rolled her eyes to the ceiling in quiet exasperation. "She's obsessed with her son. It's ridiculous. You should probably go."

"Me?" I asked, confused by the sudden change of subject.

She tossed back the remainder of her drink and grabbed another. "Cora," she sang, "thank you so much for coming. This must be Max."

A woman with white beehive hair and a forty-something escort greeted Mom with air kisses. "Darling, yes. This is Maximillian."

Maximillian dragged a slow, creepy gaze over my neckline. "Nice to meet you," he told my floral accents.

I turned my train-carrying wrist discreetly in his view and pointed upward. When he found my eyes, they were slits of warning.

He coughed and looked haphazardly around.

I took a few steps in Chase's direction. The path was intersected by Kinley. She grabbed Chase's face and kissed his lips with a smack. "You were right! The band will take requests. I asked them to play 'Old Time Rock and Roll.'"

Mom closed her eyes for a long beat. I could almost hear her thoughts on the expensive string quartet she'd hired playing a Bob Seger cover. "Maybe you'd like to dance," she suggested.

I baby-stepped backward, putting more distance between myself and Maximillian.

He advanced on me, stroking his thin black mustache. "Do you like to sail?" he asked. "My yacht is participating in the Bahamas regatta next month. I keep a house on the island."

I recoiled farther, accidentally bumping into Mom.

Kinley smiled deviously. She'd twined her arm with Chase's and pressed herself against him.

"Excuse me," I said, ducking my head and making an abrupt escape I was certain to hear about later.

Chase was at my side in a minute. "I didn't mean to spring the Kinley thing on you. It happened kind of fast. Not that it's anything serious," he assured. "I meant to talk to you about it before dinner, but I was running late today, and you weren't home when I stopped by last night."

I blushed at the implication. "So tell me now."

He glanced in Kinley's direction. "I ran into her at the grocery. We talked until the store closed. I was so engrossed I forgot to buy anything. The clerks kicked us out, and I followed her home. She offered me sweet tea, and we sat on her porch until almost four this morning."

"Well, she seems nice," I fibbed. Honestly, she seemed a little hostile, and I hadn't fully released her as a suspect in Mr. Becker's murder, but I'd be angry too if I'd just lost my dad.

He pierced me with sincere green eyes. "Are you sure you don't mind? I mean, you said this wasn't the right time for us."

"I don't mind." I smiled. "I'm sure she's a great girl."

He sighed. "Probably won't last," he said. "She's not the one I've been chasing all year."

"I think when it's meant to be, you won't have to chase her."

He bent forward to kiss my temple. "Well, back at you. Be sure to pack an extra towel for the Bahamas."

"Shut up." I shoved his shoulder. "You're such a jerk."

"Definitely get the sun block that sprays on." Chase moseyed back toward his date, wiggling his fingers.

I covered my mouth and shook my head. Maximillian wasn't getting anywhere near me with sun block or otherwise.

A flash of gold swept through my periphery. I turned with a start. I'd been hyperaware of women in gold dresses since the night I'd first met Tabitha. She'd chosen a slinky gold number for a gala I'd attended. In the distance, a blonde in shimmering taffeta moved toward the kitchen and disappeared from sight. "Why not?" I asked myself.

I gave chase. If I was wrong about the woman's identity, I'd simply apologize. If I was right . . .

I rounded the corner to the kitchen, immediately assaulted by a cacophony of clanging pots and sweltering temperatures. The woman was gone. I checked under linen-covered carts and behind the counters. "Did a woman in gold just run through here?" I asked loudly.

A man in a partially flattened chef's hat pointed to the back door.

"Thank you." I hastened into the gardens via the service exit.

White bistro lights were strung through treetops, along a picket fence, and around a central gazebo. Black chairs with white-cushioned seats circled a sea of small round tables. Replica lanterns with battery-operated tea lights formed the centerpieces.

Dad stood at the garden's center with a circle of men his age, all smiling over something he was saying. He lifted a hand when he saw me and flashed the most genuine smile I'd seen on him in days. "Lacy!" He moved in my direction with open arms.

I was drawn in like a wave to the sea. "Hi, Dad." I squeezed him quickly, scanning the area for another glimpse of gold.

"Your mother throws quite a party." He chuckled.

"True, but all these people are here for you," I said proudly.

"I'm just glad you're here." He rested a palm on my shoulder. "If there was only you, your mother, and I, I'd still have the night of my life."

"Well, that's because we're awesome." I lifted onto my toes and kissed his cheek. "I'm glad everyone came. I think it helps to be reminded that we're important from time to time." I looked him square in the eyes. "You are very important."

"Pst!" The sound came from the bushes. "Pst! Pst!"

"Will you excuse me?" I asked Dad, already texting Jack.

I think Tabitha is at the Elms.

I crept in the direction of the sound, and crouched to peer through leafy green shrubs.

Tabitha came into view at the mansion's edge several yards away. Her back was pressed to the stone. "We need to talk."

I doubted this conversation would go as well as the one I'd had with Jack when he'd uttered those same words.

She motioned me to join her beside a table holding at least four hundred champagne glasses stacked into impressive but precarious pyramids. "I'm being blackmailed," she said.

"Ha." I spoke the word, unamused. "Funny."

"I'm serious." Her flushed cheeks and fidgety appearance tempted me to believe her. "My mama is in a nursing home in Bon Temps. She's got Alzheimer's. She's getting worse all the time, and she needs special care." Her face turned red. "I came down here looking for a man with money to fall in love with me and take pity on my mother. Her savings were gone. Mine were gone. I couldn't afford to keep her in a nice facility, and moving her to one of those preapproved holes on the Medicare list seemed cruel. They're understaffed. Not clean. Not homey. There are fewer full-time nurses and doctors at each location. I was desperate."

"So what?" I scoffed. "When Jack's grandpa wouldn't bend to your will, you decided to kill him?"

"Are you insane?" she seethed. "That man had a heart attack."

"He was drugged."

"Heart attack."

I hesitated, unsure if this was part of her game. Hoping if I kept her talking long enough, Jack might show up and find her. "You had spiked wine together every night."

"I don't drink." She lowered her voice. "I've been sober seventeen and a half years, and I have *never* done drugs."

I guessed it made sense that she wouldn't drink drugged wine, but he'd definitely had plenty of both. We stared at one another.

"The wine," she sobbed.

I moved closer. "Sage sent it?"

Surprise flashed in her eyes. "Yes. A delivery arrived every Sunday from his favorite vineyard. The bottles always had a note. Sometimes instructions. Pour him a glass after dinner and ask a question about someone I'd never heard of. It was simple, and he liked the wine. Who was I hurting? I'd write down the answers and leave them in the mailbox at dawn."

"Who is Sage?"

She made a desperate face. "Sage was the name on the first envelope. The one meant for me."

"Photos?" I guessed.

She wetted her lips and nodded. "Pictures of me when I was drinking. Awful ones. Those pictures would've ruined my life."

I was tempted to ask about the photos' contents, but how could I believe anything she said? "Why are you here? Why tell me this?" I watched her carefully, hoping to learn as much from her body language as her speech. She seemed genuinely shocked.

Fat tears rolled over her narrow cheekbones. "Did I really kill him? There were drugs in the wine?"

I dug a tissue from my clutch and offered it to her. "The coroner found a buildup of GHB in his system. We think the doses were masked by the wine. Eventually, it led to heart failure. I'm sure his age didn't help."

She wrapped her arms across her center and dabbed her eyes with the tissue. "I think I'm going to be sick."

"You need to talk to Jack," I said. "We already know about Sage. Jack's trying to find him and stop his reign of terror. Too many people are being hurt. At least two people are already dead. I know you want to help, or you wouldn't have come here to see me."

She sniffled. "I came to you because I knew Jack would arrest me. I can't go to jail. There's no one else to look after Mama."

I chewed my lip. "You have to tell him what you told me. Think of all the other people Sage is puppeteering. You can help them."

"She'll kill me," Tabitha said flatly.

Jack sauntered into view. He shook hands with my dad and searched the crowd. His keen eyes stopped when he found me. He started immediately in our direction, leaving Dad to look on.

"He'll understand," I said. "He needs to know."

Tabitha batted tear-filled eyes, unsure. Her body tensed when she saw Jack coming. "I wanted to tell him at Christmas, but I knew he'd never believe me. He wants revenge."

"He wants the truth."

She stuffed the tissue down the top of her dress and shook her hands out at the wrists. "Your dress is absolutely stunning. I am so sorry about this."

"Thank you." I spouted the knee-jerk response before her pained expression registered. "Wait. Sorry about what?"

She pulled both arms back, bending the elbows out to her sides, before slamming her palms against my shoulders.

I squawked. My arms circled in the air like the coyote in the old Road Runner cartoons. My stilettos had sunk into the ground at different depths, eliminating any possibility of staying upright. I hit the table of stacked glassware with a scream.

Jack skidded to a stop before me. "Lacy!"

"Go!" I pointed to Tabitha's fast-disappearing figure. "She's headed for the lot!"

He froze, unsure.

"Go," I said more calmly. "I'm not hurt. Catch her, then come back and arrest Mom for my murder."

His frown deepened before he turned for the lot and vanished in her wake.

A too-familiar groan broke through the accumulating chaos. Mom stood ten feet away, white as a ghost and quickly turning purple.

"I'm sorry," I mouthed. Piles of broken glasses twinkled at my sides. I searched for a place to plant my hands and lift myself upright without being cut.

She dropped her shoulders and let her hands fall to her sides. "For heaven's sake," she muttered. "Can we get a little help over here?" Her no-nonsense voice grew by the decibel, drawing instant silence from onlookers.

People broke into a flurry of activity. Men poured forth, eager to assist in my aid. Women in uniform swept up the glass.

Mom clapped her hands and barked orders at the band to continue playing. She sent the waitstaff into motion, filling empty hands with drinks and hors d'oeuvres.

Chase pushed a path through the crowd and hoisted me to my feet with one strong arm. He wrapped me in a warm embrace and rested his chin on top of my head. "There's never a dull moment with you, is there?"

I buried my face against his jacket. "Can I die of humiliation?"

"Not tonight." He turned me away from the gardens and walked me straight to his car.

Chapter Twenty-Three

Furry Godmother's hard truth:
Egg on a face is hard to wash off.

I woke on Saturday morning with a sleep deprivation headache. I'd insisted Chase bring me straight home after I wrecked Dad's dinner. He'd complied and left me to my humiliation. I'd changed into something with less glass and waited for Jack to call.

He didn't.

I showered, dressed, and gathered Mrs. Hams's finished products for pickup. If insomnia had an upside, it was productivity. I pulled white boxes of fresh pupcakes and tuna tarts from the fridge and stacked them on the counter.

The drive to work was quiet. Penelope lazed in her carrier on the passenger seat, enjoying the sunlight on her face. I rehashed the humility of being extracted from a collapsed table of champagne flutes while wearing a ball gown and five-inch heels, half the town looking on. The silver lining,

I supposed, was the fact that half the town had shown up to support Dad.

I angled my Volkswagen against the curb on Magazine Street. I loaded my hands with bakery boxes and a cat carrier, then hobbled to Furry Godmother's door and wedged my key into the lock. I made my way to the counter to unload. Penelope stretched slowly from her carrier. Tired. Bored. I shoved a mug under the Keurig seated on my minifridge.

The door jingled open before I'd had time to flip the sign or switch on all the lights. Jack strolled in, wearing last night's white tuxedo and looking a lot like I felt. Exhausted. "You okay?" he asked.

"Yeah." I wrapped Mrs. Hams's lace llama bonnets and eyelet capes into tissue paper and boxed them for pickup. I piled the straw hats into a logoed bag with the accompanying bandanas. "I finished a ton of projects last night while I waited to hear from you. What'd you do?"

"Chased a ghost."

I pulled the finished coffee off the Keurig and handed it to Jack. "Sorry to hear that." Tabitha certainly was a slippery one. "Did you learn anything from your talk with Wallace Jr.?"

"Yeah. He was in Vegas last Friday. He's got photos, receipts, and a call log to prove it. He couldn't have killed his father." Jack turned his phone over for a look at the screen. "Your pet line at Grandpa Smacker just got another huge preorder. If this keeps up, you can quit your day job."

"No thanks," I said.

He put the phone away and gave me an appraising look. "Sorry I didn't call. I haven't stopped moving in twelve hours. I'm glad to hear you got a lot of work done."

"Thanks. I also read everything the Internet had available on Robin Hood, so if you're ever in a pinch for extremely specific literary trivia . . ." I waved a dismissive hand.

He raised the mug to his lips, a slight tremor in his hand. "What about Robin Hood?" He rested his elbows on the counter and gulped the hot, bitter liquid.

"Something Claudia Post said. She's the woman who runs a high-end thrift shop called Resplendent," I explained. "I thought she might recognize the Tonka truck or Tabitha because she's on the road in the district a lot and visits a lot of local homes."

"You were hoping she was a gossip."

I rolled my eyes. "She was as tight-lipped as my mother promised when it came to her donators, but she recognized Tabitha from a picture I have on my phone."

Jack cocked his head. "Not bad, Crocker. What'd she say about her?"

My chest puffed with childish pride. "She thinks she's seen her at the coffee shop where she has lunch."

"Where?"

"Somewhere on Prytania."

He grinned. "I know that place. I've taken her there myself in the past. Okay, so what did she hear about Sage?"

"Someone compared him to a modern day Robin Hood."

"What's that mean?"

I smiled back. "I have no idea." I made another cup of coffee. "I have so much to tell you."

He pinched the bridge of his nose between a thumb and forefinger. "Hang on. I've got something for you, and I don't want to get called away and forget." He left his coffee and walked outside.

Imogene passed him on her way in. "Happy Valentine's Day!" Her red cardigan had pink hearts sewn on it. Her matching maxi skirt nearly hid her shoes.

I smiled at the sight of her. "Good morning. Do you want coffee?"

"No thanks." She dropped her bag behind the bakery counter and huffed. "I'm running on pure caffeine. Veda and I were up half the night, but we finally got a bead on her granddaughter."

"Oh," I sagged. "I was supposed to help. I'm sorry."

"It's no problem. She's safe and sound. Living in Ohio."

"That's fantastic. Is she coming to visit? I can show her around," I offered.

Imogene gave me a strange look. "I'm afraid Veda's family doesn't work that way. She'll reach out to her when she dies."

I twisted that sentence in my head a few ways, but it never made more sense. "Do you mean Veda? Veda will reach out to her when Veda dies?"

"That's right."

Jack returned with an accordion folder, and I cheerfully redirected my attention to him.

Imogene gave him a questioning look. "Either you're overdressed for this time of day, or those are your walk-of-shame clothes."

He snorted. "I wish. I've only been home long enough to grab this and head over here before you got busy."

Imogene tied a striped apron around her neck and grabbed a feather duster. "Won't be busy today, except for a trickle of Last-Minute Lulas pretending they didn't put off their valentine shopping until the morning of."

Jack opened the file and lifted out a flat box tied in red ribbon. "I figured I ought to bring a gift if I wanted you to work on a holiday."

I nearly spilled my coffee. "This is for me?" I lifted the box for a closer examination. "I didn't get you anything."

"You've done more than you realize," he said with a grin. "Open it."

I slid the ribbon off and loosened the tape along one end.

Imogene dusted a quick path in our direction.

Jack kept his eyes on me. "They're for your designs," he said. "For sketching."

I slid the paper away and marveled. "Colored pencils."

"The lady at the art store said these are the best. She said an artist would know."

He'd gone to a store and asked which colored pencils to buy. I pressed my lips into a smile, then stepped aside to open the drawer at my waist. I lifted out a matching, but extensively tattered, box of sharpened pencil nubs.

He smiled. "These are the same ones you use?"

Imogene ran her duster down his sleeve. "You two want to be alone with those pencils?"

He barked out a laugh and shook the rest of the contents from his file. "No, ma'am. I think Lacy was about to educate me on Robin Hood."

I hung my head. "I reread the legend, skimmed the stories, watched the movie. I searched for news articles on modern day instances like local high-end robberies and anything else I could think of in an effort to make sense of

what Claudia overheard, but nothing panned out. Everything was a dead end."

"Maybe this won't be," he said. "This is everything I've
dug up on Tabitha."

I fingered the smattering of loose papers on the counter. "She said her mom's in a facility for Alzheimer's patients
in Bon Temps. Maybe you can track her through her
mother."

Jack typed something into his phone. "That's good.
What else did she say?"

"Sage dragged her into this. She had no idea about the
GHB in your grandpa's wine. Apparently, she hasn't had a
drink in seventeen and a half years." I piled receipts into
a neat stack.

He went slack-jawed. "She thinks she's the victim?
Grandpa's dead, and she thinks she's not to blame?"

Fresh adrenaline pumped in my veins. "Yes, and guess
what else? I think Sage is a woman. When I tried to convince Tabitha to tell you everything she was telling me, she
said, '*She'll* kill me.' *She*, not he."

"More maybes." He rubbed his face. "I need to find
Tabitha. Same thing I've been trying to accomplish since
Christmas. Look where that's gotten me."

"You'd better get something to eat," I said. I gave the
street a cursory glance, knowing full well that no restaurants would open for another hour, maybe two.

"Don't worry about me. I'm headed home to shower and
change. I'll check long-term care facilities in Bon Temps for
Tabitha's mother and see if I can get a bead on Tabitha that
way. Maybe she listed herself as the emergency contact."

The bell over my door jingled. Mrs. Hams walked inside with a smile. She rubbed her palms together with vigor. "Are my babies' hats and capes ready?"

"Yes, ma'am." I smiled as she opened the box and bag, oohing and ahhing over my work, but my thoughts were elsewhere.

I checked my phone regularly for a text from Jack that never came.

The number of last-minute Valentine's Day shoppers increased by the hour, slowly clearing out my stock of Cupid costumes, heart-shaped pillows, and boxes of treats. By closing time, I was hard pressed to find anything red or pink on the sales floor.

I carried my phone all the way to bed with me at half past midnight. Jack never called, but I slept like a baby.

* * *

I picked Mom up after work on Sunday for the NPP Welcoming Committee meeting. I'd dug up pale-gray satin slacks and a white wrap blouse to pass as pastel and added a floral silk scarf to the strap of my purse for flourish. Mom met me at the door wearing Nina Ricci and a frown. "You didn't call."

"I told you I'd be here at two," I said. "I'm early." I spun my key ring on one finger, a little disappointed. I'd hoped to win her over with my impressive punctuality and a sincere apology for causing a scene at Dad's dinner.

She stuffed a stack of pastel folders into her shoulder bag, obviously avoiding eye contact. "How was I to know you'd come at all? You left the dinner party in a blaze of glory, and I haven't heard a peep from you since."

The humiliation of landing on my backside in formal wear struck anew. The memory of my gown's fabric flowing over a broken table. A halo of shattered glass circling me like a bull's-eye. The moment was hardly glorious. "I called as soon as I got home so you wouldn't worry. I left a message."

She shooed me out the door and locked up behind us. "It's fine." Her tone sharply implied that it wasn't. "Chase came back and explained everything. He said he'd been showing off for you and tripped."

"He did?"

"Indeed. I'd swear that boy made a point of apologizing to each guest individually. He seemed truly humbled by his blunder."

My heart melted. I was so lucky and undeserving of my amazing friends. "No one saw what really happened?"

"No. Chase stuck to his story with me, but I saw him arrive after you were already on your keister." She walked to my car's passenger door and looked at me over the roof. "We could've taken my car."

"I know." I loved Mom's Mercedes, but I had a stop to make, and my car was already loaded. "I shouldn't have left without saying good-bye. I should've been the one to reassure your guests that the fiasco was no fault of yours."

She buckled up, careful not to ruin the pleat of her skirt, and arranged her bag beside her feet. "Like I said. It's fine."

"It's not fine." I pulled away from her house with renewed vim. She'd claimed she wanted to know all about my life. Maybe it was time I tested the statement. I started talking at the light on her corner and didn't stop until we'd arrived at the district's end. "So that's what really happened," I concluded. "That's what I've been doing since I learned about Mr. Becker's death and Dad's threatened reputation."

She didn't speak for several blocks. Her cheeks were pink, and her lips were parted. I hoped it was a look of exhilaration and surprise, not the beginning of a lecture. "Say something."

"And you think Jack's dead grandpa's ex-girlfriend is a murderess who is blackmailing wealthy men in the district and aiding a second woman who is threatening to kill you?"

"Basically," I said, slowing for a family to cross at the intersection. "I haven't heard from Jack since he went home to track her down with the new information I gave him. He's a real pain about keeping me in the loop. It's completely willy-nilly." I stopped at a changing light and double-checked my phone for missed calls or messages.

"So you don't resent me for putting you on the NPP Welcoming Committee?" she asked, eyes trained on the windshield in front of her.

"Not at all. In fact, I kind of like it. I had fun talking about costumes with the ladies and feeling plugged into the community." Getting to know my mom as an adult was pretty great too. "It's nice being able to tell you things about my life without being sent to my room."

She looked at me from the corner of her eye. "Believe me, if I thought it'd work, I'd try. Just because I'm listening and not screaming doesn't mean I'm okay with any of this. Your curiosity has gotten you hurt more times than I can count. I lived in a constant state of panic while you were growing up. Remember when you jumped off the limbs in our oak tree with a sheet overhead? You kept climbing higher and higher. Jumping over and over."

"It was a parachute."

"It was a five-hour visit to the emergency room. I thought you were dying. A broken arm was luck. I imagined you in traction or permanently in a wheelchair, with brain damage, a lifetime of pain, and repeated surgeries."

"That's a little over the top."

"You aren't a mother."

My heart broke a little. "I didn't mean to worry you. I had a plan. I even made a pile of leaves for a landing target."

She scoffed.

"I had to know how high I needed to be before the air would catch in the sheet like a sail. *I had to know.* Once the question was in my mind, there was no other way of getting it out."

She feigned interest in passing scenery. "It's a sickness. All those reckless behaviors. All the boys," she expelled the last word on a groan. "Lord only knows what else you've gotten into since you left my care."

"Doesn't matter. I'm home now, and I'm settled, and I'm going to be fine."

She turned glossy eyes on me, giving me her full attention for the first time since I'd arrived to pick her up. "I guess I'm glad your obsession with puzzles finally paid off. You certainly spent enough time reading up on the topic."

"Then you'll be proud to know I'm not driving aimlessly away from our destination. I'm actually headed for Resplendent to drop off a trunkful of things that should've been given to folks who could use them a long time ago."

She smiled. "Good."

"Do you still want me to make you a dress like the one I wore Friday night?"

"I do, but you can't write my measurements down. You'll have to memorize them. I don't want that sort of thing documented."

I laughed.

She didn't. "What are you wearing today anyway? Do you really not own enough pastels to last until the pageant?"

I made a face. "I really don't."

"You make enough money to buy yourself some new things, don't you?"

"Yeah." For the first time in a long time, I had the money. What I didn't have was the time or desire to go somewhere with fluorescent lighting and countless strangers to try on fifty unflattering things in the hopes of finding one or two I liked enough to trade my cash for. "I'll work on it."

"You only have a few weeks before we crown our pet ambassador. If you don't have something appropriate by then, you'll have to accept a gown from my stylist."

"Yes, ma'am." I slid my car against the curb outside Resplendent. "I hope Claudia's here. I didn't think to call ahead."

"She's always here, unless she's making a pickup."

An odd thought circled into mind. "The last time I talked to her, she said something about a modern day Robin Hood. Can you think of anyone in the district like that?"

"Like Robin Hood?" Mom grimaced. "No. Thank heavens. I never liked him. Robin Hood is one of the most grossly over glorified villains in the history of literature. I'm sure there were plenty of wealthy families who'd have given to the poor if there was a proper initiative made for collection. Instead he took it upon himself to steal from those who had and distribute it to those who didn't. He was a socialist. And a brute. Yet readers sing his praise. Praise for a criminal."

"I had no idea you were so passionate about Robin Hood."

She folded her hands delicately on her lap. "How are the flower costumes coming? I hope you've brought samples or sketches or something along for the meeting."

I perked. "I have. You're going to love them. I've completed four so far and have three mock-ups ready for review, plus a pad full of sketches with the costumes drawn on varied pets. I can have whatever the committee decides upon ready in a few days."

"Good." She pulled oversized sunglasses from her bag and traded them for the smaller, less distracting ones on her face. "Tell Claudia I'll have another pickup for her next week. I'm going to wait here. If anyone sees me inside her shop, they'll speculate about which of the things were mine."

I doubted that, but there was no convincing her otherwise, and we didn't have time to fool around. We'd be late for our meeting. "I'll be right back." I left the car on with the air conditioner going and popped my trunk.

After several awkward trips, my trunk was empty and my back was kinked. Meanwhile, there were no signs of life inside the store. I dinged the silver bell near the register and had a look around.

The shop was gorgeous, decorated in antique and high-end pieces. Either district residents had donated some very costly items, or Claudia Post had more money than I'd expected. The state of her hair and clothing suggested otherwise, as did the aging SUV she drove around town.

I hit the little bell again before strolling through the racks. The thrift shop could have easily been a private boutique in Manhattan. Claudia must've had a partner or at the very least a decorator to display and disguise the hand-me-downs so handsomely. I fingered a row of last season's designer fashion and died a little inside at the amazing resale prices. Was it my imagination, or did the thrift shop have a distinct Robin Hood feel?

I pulled my cell phone from my pocket and dialed Jack.

"Sorry!" Claudia arrived in a flurry of hangers, dresses, and exasperation. "I'm so sorry. I'm here!" She attempted to unload her arms onto the counter, but my boxes were in the way. Her burden slid onto the floor. "Drat." Hangers clattered into a wide mess. "I was in the back ticketing a new round of markdowns," she sputtered. "I started up front when I heard the bell, but I dropped everything and had to start again." She gave the fallen dresses a long look and a deep sigh.

My call connected. "Oliver," Jack barked.

"Hey," I told him, unsure how to say what I'd wanted to before Claudia's bizarre entrance. "I thought of something you might find interesting." I hustled to Claudia's side and began collecting dropped hangers. "Give me a minute. The timing couldn't be worse."

She looked as if she'd seen a ghost.

I shook my head at her and pointed to the phone at my ear.

"What is it?" he asked.

"Well, now isn't a good time."

"You called me, Lacy. So what is it?"

I set my collection of hangers on her counter and raised a finger to let Claudia know I'd only be a minute. I moved casually to the far window and cupped a hand over my mouth to contain my voice. "Do thrift stores seem very Robin Hood to you?"

"It's funny you bring that up because I just had a long talk with Tabitha this morning."

"What?"

"I found her mother in Bon Temps like you said. Tabitha was telling the truth about that. I called the emergency contact number listed with the care facility, and an answering service took my information. Tabitha called back a few minutes later. She used a burner phone that I couldn't trace, but she told me everything. She wants immunity in return."

"You're kidding? That's amazing! What did she say?"

"A lot. I've been building a case and petitioning for a warrant since we hung up the phone."

"Mom and I are on our way to a committee meeting now, but are you free later? I want to know everything."

"I'd like that. You'd probably like to know that I agree with what you said before. I don't think she's a killer. Not a cold-blooded one anyway. She seemed genuinely horrified to know she'd been serving the wine that likely lead to his death. She maintains that Sage is the truly unhinged and dangerous one. I hope to have enough evidence to prove that soon."

"Who is she?" I chewed my lip and pretended to admire the shop's contents while Claudia continued dropping things behind the counter.

"You'll never believe it." He barked a hearty laugh. "It'd be comical if it wasn't so damn brilliant." The engine of his truck rumbled to life in the background. "I'm on my way to pick up the search warrant right now."

"You have to tell me," I said. "I'll implode if you don't."

The brass plate below a massive oil painting caught my eye. "Margaret Olivia Sage," I read. Tension knotted my muscles and fear twisted my gut. "Oh, no," I breathed.

"What did you say?" Jack asked, his voice suddenly tight.

My attention jumped to the quote positioned below her name: "A woman is responsible in proportion to the wealth and time at her command . . . While one woman is working for bread and butter, the other must devote her time to the amelioration of the condition of her laboring sister. This is the moral law.'" The thrift store was Sage's way of helping women. "It's Claudia Post," I whispered.

"Where are you?" Jack demanded.

"Resplendent." I spun for the door.

Something blunt pressed against my spine. Heavy scents of rose hips and lavender assaulted my senses. "Hang up." Claudia's voice was low and demanding. The bumbling worker bee was gone.

I removed the phone from my ear and dropped it into my pocket. "What's going on?" I asked, hopefully loudly enough to be heard by Jack. "Is that a gun?"

A hand appeared beside my cheek. "Hand over the phone."

"Okay." I took my time complying. "I don't know what's going on, Claudia," I said. "I came to make a donation. My things are on the counter over there."

"Give me the phone!" she ordered. "Who were you talking to?"

I hit the disconnect button as I lifted the cell phone over my shoulder to her.

She turned me by my head and shoved me forward. "March!"

"Where?" I watched in horror as she flipped the "Open" sign to "Closed" and pulled the blinds.

"To the stock room." Hot-pink price tags clung to the cuffs and elbow of her sleeves. They were the same bright color as the sticker I'd found on the floor of the freezer where Mr. Becker had died. She poked the back of my arm with her gun. "Move."

I jumped away, plastering a protective palm over the spot where the barrel had met my skin. The worst of memories bubbled to the surface of my mind, like a geyser of horror, as I marched away from my mom and civilization. Into Claudia's stock room of doom.

I crept through the doorway with trepidation, nausea, and regret. If only I'd made the Robin Hood connection sooner. If only I'd taken the call with Jack outside.

Her stock room was the size of a small warehouse. Fluorescent lights hovered overhead, suspended from high ceilings by thick chains. Rows of metal racks overflowed with things waiting to be sold. There were no windows and at least six light switches on the wall plate beside me. No one would see what she did to me here. No one would know.

My chest tightened to a painful ache. Mom would come looking for me and meet a similar fate once she tired of waiting in the car and Claudia couldn't explain where I'd gone.

Claudia caught her toe on a misplaced box and cursed. She stumbled against the now closed door behind her, flailing for balance. A powerful rush of déjà vu overtook me. Mrs. Becker had taken a similar spill while chasing me from her house. Claudia had her eyes and ears everywhere. Her hands, meanwhile, swung wide, bracing against the exposed brick walls. Her gun was no longer trained on me.

I had the space of a heartbeat to decide. Would I fight? Or would I die?

She wobbled upright, straightening with effort. "Don't get any ideas. You're finished causing me problems."

She was wrong.

I held my breath and hit the row of light switches, sending us and the room into total darkness.

Chapter
Twenty-Four

Furry Godmother's secret for avoiding tardiness:
Don't go.

I ran blindly through the dark for several seconds, cutting between overstuffed merchandise racks and smacking my knees against boxes. The storeroom was a lot like I imagined the inside of Claudia's brain to be. Jumbled. Overstocked. Dangerous. The frantic smacking and pawing noises behind me pushed my feet faster. I presumed Claudia, in all her bumbling glory, would soon find the switch plate, then shoot me.

The broad beam of a flashlight cut across the floor ten feet away. "You thought you had me," she said. "But I know this room. I've filled and emptied this room. I practically live in this room. I don't need light in here." The beam bled forward, sweeping left and right in search of its target. "But you do."

I cracked my head on a wooden shelf or coat rack and stopped short from the burst of pain. I bit my lip and grabbed the thing to steady and silence it. Definitely a shelf.

"I bought this gun for protection when I moved to New Orleans," she said. "The Big Easy. Ha!" She laughed maniacally while I patted my pockets forgetfully in search of the phone she'd taken. "There's nothing easy about making a place for yourself down here. This city's hard. Just like all the others. People only see what's on the outside, and we can't all look like you with your big Disney eyes and your long princess hair. Cute little figure. All the right clothes. Money. Money. Money. Mommy runs the town."

I shot an ugly look in the direction of her infuriating voice and considered plowing over her like a bulldozer.

"I bought this handy little silencer later."

I reconsidered the bulldozing.

"I needed to protect myself. This isn't a woman's world." Her footfalls shuffled closer. "We have to help one another." She stopped moving.

Killing me seemed the opposite of helpful, but I was admittedly biased, and she was clearly crazy.

I circled back toward the door. My only exit. My escape. The shelving contents felt different than they had on my way in. I turned in a blind circle. Had I gotten into a different aisle somehow? Did the whack from the shelf send me in another direction? A strange sense of vertigo overcame me. My eyes had nothing to focus on, and my stomach crashed and flopped like ice chunks against my spine.

"That's how I met Tabitha, you know? I helped her." Claudia's voice drew closer. "She was looking for a man and his money to save her mother, but men only want one thing, and I don't mean a relationship. She never could've made it here without me. I knew all about the locals. I knew who was single. Who was generous with their money, and who would fall to their knees over someone like Tabitha, with her big blonde hair and her narrow little backside. I had what she needed. So we made a deal. I provided her with names, and she got close to the men. Everyone has a secret they'd pay to keep hidden. She dug them up, and I collected for the both of us."

The broad cone of light moved in my direction, forcing me deeper into the darkness.

"Tabitha dated a lot of men, and we made good money until she fell in love with Old Man Smacker. They weren't even supposed to meet. He wasn't on my list, but she thought he hung the moon. She and I were friends until he ruined everything."

I felt along the shelves, moving steadily in the opposite direction of her voice. My steps were tentative and slow. Hers were heavy and quick. My breaths were too loud. My shoes were too loud. The makings of a panic attack tightened my chest and clogged my throat. I needed to get away. I needed to think. I stubbed my toe on what felt like a floor lamp. My hands wrapped around it on instinct, stopping the fall. Instead, I swung it into place behind me, right in the middle of the aisle.

"You don't know what it's like," Claudia complained. "I grew up with nothing. Not like you. My mama cleaned for people like you. I had to watch wealthy old men paw at her when they thought their wives weren't looking. It was disgusting," she said. "No woman should have to go through that."

Something toppled a few feet away, and Claudia cursed. "That lamp was antique Tiffany!"

Shoot! She was closer than I'd thought. I kicked my shoes off and pressed myself between the shelving units. I sucked in my breath and shimmied until I popped out on the opposite side.

"Marco!" she called. The flashlight's beam bobbed a zigzag across the floor. "You're supposed to say 'Polo.' Come on," she taunted, "be a good sport."

I tossed something that felt like glass as far from me as possible, and Claudia's footfalls ceased.

"Stop breaking my stuff!"

I sprinted forward, only to tangle my feet in who-knew-what and fall. My hands splayed before me, slapping the concrete loudly and starting Claudia's footfalls anew.

"Tabitha and I had an agreement," she continued, sounding sickeningly satisfied. "Once she married the old man, she'd funnel his money into my store, and I'd never let him find out who and what she really was. Then he died."

My tummy rolled and knotted with indignation and sickness. Claudia said she wanted to help women, but she'd intentionally manipulated Tabitha. "You made her a victim," I blurted. Panic shot through me like lightning. I clamped both hands over my big mouth and darted around what felt like a grandfather clock, praying fervently for an intervention or instant-onset laryngitis.

The light swept an arc in my direction. "I knew you couldn't keep your mouth closed. It's not exactly your specialty."

I slid my hands over the face of the clock, which turned out to be an armoire. I opened the door and climbed inside the makeshift refuge. I needed time to gather my wits, make a plan, find Narnia.

"Once he was dead, I told her she should do the right thing and come back to our original arrangement, but she thought she was too fancy to do that again. She didn't want to be with other men. She was grieving. She loved him." Her voice slid into a faux whine. "Nonsense. Their relationship was built on lies. I threatened to tell Smacker's grandson everything if she didn't come back to me, but she ran."

I could see why. Claudia was a lunatic.

"In hindsight, I could've handled that better, but enough chitchat. You might as well come out," she grouched. "You won't leave Wallace Becker's death alone, so I can't let you live. You must realize that."

I curled into a tight ball, praying for invisibility.

Light flashed over the cabinet, piercing the small crack between doors. "Your time on Earth is over, but I'm sure princesses like you get special treatment in heaven too."

I moved my hands in front of my face, prepared to defend myself when she opened the doors if she didn't just shoot me and go back to sorting hangers. To my great surprise, her footfalls moved away. Blood rushed in my ears. My heart pounded with relief. I swiped a renegade tear from my eye and steadied my breaths before she heard them.

"What happened to Wallace was unfortunate," she said. "I lured him into the fridge for privacy, swatted him with a frozen box of dog biscuits, and locked him inside. I'd hoped a night in the freezer would give him time to think about how badly he wanted to poke the bear. I wanted him to get some perspective and reconsider how he spent whatever

time he had left, but that didn't work out." Her voice grew muffled from the increased distance. "But he wasn't well. He was going soon anyway."

I slipped out of my hiding spot and weighed my options. Claudia was far enough from the door for me to escape, but I'd have to run right past her to get there.

"I was a mess the morning we met. Do you remember?" Her flashlight beam danced over racks and walls. "My scheduled pickup at your parents' home was horrible timing. I didn't want to see any of Wallace's friends. I didn't know who he'd told about his suspicions of me, but I had to go on as if nothing had changed. When I saw your car in the drive, I thought it was a detective come to tell Dr. Crocker the news or to arrest me when I arrived." She stopped moving. "I was having the second most horrific day of my life, and you bounced down the driveway like little bluebirds followed you through life. Not a care in the world. Baking cupcakes for animals. Making tiaras for rich little pets. Judging me."

I bit back the rebuttal on my lips.

"In the end, I think one life was worth the sacrifice. Losing Wallace Becker meant I could keep the shop going. Keep helping women afford nice things and find better places in society." The beam sliced a circle through the room. "I'm lifting up new women every day. What kind of a spoiled brat can't see that?"

I moved silently along the racks behind her, eyes trained on the line of light beneath her shop door. Prepared to reach the only visible exit by any means necessary.

"I suppose that was harsh." Her voice had turned sugary and pleasant, far too detached and carefree for the situation. "How could someone like you understand what it is to struggle?"

I balled my hands into fists. The accusation hit home in powerful, infuriating ways, cutting into every fiber of my being. I couldn't control the life I'd been born into any more than she or any of the women she used as her patsies could, but I could control what I did with it.

Despite my family's wealth, I'd never stopped trying to make my own path in this world. I'd tried fruitlessly for years to escape my heritage, my name, my money. But I couldn't because I was a Crocker. I was proud of who I was. Who my mother was. Who my grandmother was. Proud of my dad and his family. I came from a long line of people who made a difference. So what if they sometimes used their money and influence to do it? My mom also paraded chickens across the county, entertaining and educating children and retired people. She didn't need wealth to do that, only a big heart. She brought joy to strangers' faces and delivered the profits to children's hospitals. My chest swelled and my fingers curled. Who was this hateful, self-serving woman to tell me I was less than her or anyone else?

"Lacy?" Mom's voice swept through the room inside a thick swath of light from the shop outside the stock room. Her silhouette appeared in the doorway.

Pain seized my chest, deflating the pride and replacing it with fear. *Should I call out and warn her? Would Claudia leave her alone if I stayed quiet? Would Mom flip the switches and find Claudia with a gun?*

Only ten feet from the light beam now, I had no choice but to move. I locked my jaw and made a run for Claudia.

If I reached her before the flashlight turned in my direction, I could take her down.

Something pounded against my throat, and I went backward, coughing and choking. I groped a nearby shelf for leverage, but the overfilled monstrosity came tumbling onto me. The flashlight I'd been running toward rolled onto the floor beside my head. Another beam pointed at my face, and I squinted against it.

"Lacy!" Mom called again. "What was that? Are you okay? Your things are on the counter. Where are you? Why does the shop's sign say 'Closed'? Where are the blessed lights?"

"Run!" I screamed through an aching gravelly throat. "Run, Mom, run!"

Claudia clicked a flashlight on beneath her chin, illuminating her face like the ghouls in old horror flicks. "Now you've done it."

Heavy metal shelving pinned my legs to the ground. Something sharp pressed into the flesh of my side. Her fallen flashlight, the one she'd tricked me with, slowed to a stop, its beam shining against the side of my head. Board games, sports items, and random camping supplies were scattered over the floor.

Massive blinding light erupted overhead. "Finally," Mom yelled.

Claudia growled like an animal. "You ruined everything," she seethed. "Do you know how long it will take me to start over? I'll need a new name. New store. New resources. New everything!" She tore at her wild hair with one hand while training the gun on me with the other.

"Get over here, Mrs. Crocker," she called. "You're just in time to say good-bye to the princess."

"Lacy!" Mom cried. From the sounds of her voice, she could see me clearly now. I couldn't see much beyond the fallen shelves and my captor.

Claudia spun toward the door. A sinister smile spread over her crazy face. She braced both hands on the gun, taking aim in the distance.

I dragged a fallen golf club into my palm and swung it against Claudia's ankle.

The gun went off, and both women screamed.

My heart stopped beating. "Mom!"

The bark of police sirens exploded outside the building.

"Mom!" Tears flowed over my cheeks. "Answer me!"

"Here," Mom called. "Here! We're here!" Her voice was distant and getting farther away.

Claudia hobbled to her feet and made a run for a narrow hallway I hadn't noticed earlier. A deluge of marbles and board game pieces scattered over the floor like thunder as she clunked between shelves. Her gun clattered to the ground, and she followed with a shout.

"Lacy!" Jack's voice sent my heart and mind into overdrive.

"Jack!" I captured the pink handle of a ladies' golf club and swatted Claudia's gun as far from her as possible. "I am not a princess!" I yelled, turning the nine iron on her feet and legs as she rolled onto all fours and tried to crawl away. "I'm a Crocker!"

Mom blurred into view and dropped onto her knees beside my head. Tears streamed over her trembling lips.

"Yes, you are." She gripped my hot cheeks in gentle hands and sobbed.

I pulled her to my chest, fervently thankful for the fact she wasn't shot by the bumbling lunatic on the floor beside me.

A pair of uniformed officers arrived seconds later and stopped to gawk at the scene.

"Well?" Mom snapped, wiping tears and righting herself. "What are you waiting for? Get this thing off my daughter."

The men jumped into action.

"Have you called an ambulance?" she asked.

The officers looked at one another. "Yes, ma'am," they answered.

Jack laughed, and the distinct sound of locking handcuffs was followed by nine precious words. "Claudia Post, you have the right to remain silent."

Chapter
Twenty-Five

*Furry Godmother believes in fairytales, second chances,
and forgiveness, especially in New Orleans.*

A month had passed since officers pulled a rack of toppled
sports paraphernalia off my bruised body. All visible marks
from the trauma had vanished. There was no longer a place
for them on the canvas of my body. My mind was another
story. Nightmares of being somewhere endlessly dark would
likely haunt me into the future, beside other things I'd prefer to forget, but I refused to dwell on the negative. Given
a repeat of the circumstances, I'd do it all again. I liked
to believe that freeing Tabitha and the men she'd blackmailed was worth a little emotional unsettlement on my
part. Undoubtedly, Karen would get me through it with a
few short years of therapy.

I crossed my ankles beneath rose-colored linen and
absorbed the moment. Surrounded by family, neighbors,
and friends, the NPP Welcoming Committee would soon

crown the first-ever Garden District pet ambassador. Stacks of bedazzled gold crowns formed the centerpieces on a sea of pastel-draped tables. Anticipation electrified the air.

The committee had outdone themselves. While I'd recuperated from the shock of another near-death experience, the show had gone on—or at least the show preparations. The ladies were unnecessarily tight-lipped about the final details, which infuriated Mom to no end, but I assured her they were only being considerate of her recent trauma and that it was perfectly acceptable, even advisable, for her to let others carry the burden from time to time.

Dad finished his drink and dabbed a napkin to his lips. "I have a surprise for your mother. Will you be okay here for a few minutes?"

I tipped my head and rolled serious eyes up to meet his. "Dad." He'd been treating Mom and me as if we were made of glass since our run-in with Claudia. "I'm fine."

His brow puckered. "Have I told you how sorry I am?"

Sorry that a maniac he'd met once in passing had tried to kill me? "Not today."

"I'm sorry." The ache in his voice broke my heart anew.

I kissed his cheek and patted his hand. "You have nothing to be sorry for. What happened to us had nothing to do with you, no matter how you try to spin it."

"You're wrong."

Emotion plucked at my chest. Dad had to let this go in his own time, by his own will, but I'd never stop attempting to help the process along. "Mom and I are fine, and don't forget I have a whistle."

He matched my give-me-a-break expression before pushing back in his chair and standing to button his jacket. "I won't be long."

"Okay." I sipped my drink and scanned the roomful of happy faces.

As Mom had hoped, the NPP Welcoming Committee members were easy to spot in our matchy pastel ensembles. Despite the recent chaos, I'd given in and let Mom take me shopping. She insisted on buying me the most extraordinary knee-length, baby-blue gown I'd ever seen. The piece had just enough crinoline to give it zest and flounce. The wide neckline exposed my collarbone and hugged my shoulders. I was far too in love with it to reject her offer. The dress had been my gateway drug. I'd even let her hair and makeup team work me over, and I wasn't disappointed with the results. Claudia would've hated the modern Cinderella effect wearing powder blue had on my skin and hair. I could practically see the little birds following us all the way to dinner.

My favorite part of the afternoon had happened while I sat in a makeup chair beside my mother. The experience was nothing like I'd remembered. She didn't force me to repeat memorized statements that made me seem more genteel or advise me not to slouch. Today, she'd sat beside me, fussing at her stylist and asking me for advice on lipstick and jewelry.

I'd missed the exact moment it happened, but things had changed. My mom had changed. Somewhere along the line, she'd stopped being only my mother and had started also being my friend. I wondered if maybe it had happened the moment I'd finally let her in.

She returned to our table with a pasted-on smile and arranged the fabric of a soft-yellow skirt against her thighs. "Would it kill them to turn the air on in this place?" she quietly huffed. "The people are starting to smell like their animals."

I smiled. Sure, she was a bit grouchy, bossy, and occasionally judgmental, but she was my friend.

"Speaking of animals," she whispered, "here comes a fox."

A portly man in a salmon-colored jacket tested the microphone. "I suppose it's time we announce the Garden District's first ever pet ambassador."

A round of raucous applause broke out.

I gave Mom a questioning look. Maybe she'd had one too many of those pretty pink umbrella drinks. My legs had more hair than that guy.

The empty chair beside me slid away with a whisper. Telltale scents of shampoo and cologne tickled my nose and sent a wave of butterflies through my core. "Sorry I'm late." Jack's voice pulled my lips into a broad smile.

I swiveled for a look at him. His dark hair was damp from a recent shower, his cheeks ruddy from the heat. The ever-present stubble was groomed to a thin shadow. "You clean up nice," I said.

"Like a fox," Mom muttered behind me.

I smiled impossibly wider. "I didn't know you cared so much about our district's pet ambassador."

He settled the gaze of ethereal blue eyes on me. A ghost of a smile played on his lips. "That's not why I'm here."

Mom scraped her chair back and stood. "For heaven's sake."

Thunderous applause echoed through the room, drawing my unwilling attention to the stage, where Mom retook the podium with the speed of an injured sloth. Dad waited, center stage, with Voodoo in his arms. A ring of gold and white satin petals adorned her collar.

"Why's your cat dressed like a daffodil?" Jack asked.

A bubble of laughter lifted from my chest. "I think she's the new pet ambassador." I joined the room in a standing ovation as Mom tried to, politely, reject the award. Dad shook his head and lifted Voodoo overhead like the Lion King, sending the crowd into booming fits. A quick DJ played the movie's theme song.

"He seems forgiven," Jack said. "All wrongful accusation forgotten."

"Yeah." Members of the community had shown up on his doorstep with apology casseroles and humble pie every night since the NOPD televised a press conference announcing the extermination of a local blackmail ring, which had resulted in the death of Wallace Becker. Claudia's picture had made headlines for days. Dad was unequivocally off the hook.

Mom gave up her protest in an effort to quiet the crowd and graciously accepted Voodoo's appointment. Personally, I couldn't think of a more fitting cat to represent our town. No wonder the committee had kept Mom out of the last-minute details.

Jack leaned closer, clapping loudly. "Did Voodoo even compete in this competition?"

"No." I did a wolf whistle and literal catcall. "This was a total coup."

Chase slid onto Mom's empty seat and leaned across me to shake hands with Jack. "How's it going, Oliver? Congratulations, Lacy. Couldn't have happened to a better cat."

"Thanks," I laughed. "Where'd you come from?" He was wearing the kind of suit he normally wore to work. "What are you doing here?"

"Looking for you. I thought you'd want to know that we couldn't find a loophole in the Becker prenup, so Kinley isn't legally entitled to anything that was her father's."

I stilled my clapping hands and curled them on my lap. "Oh. I'm sorry."

"Me too," he said. "I was hoping to be the hero for a change." He lifted smiling eyes to Jack.

"Is she here?" I asked.

"No. Turns out she's not your biggest fan."

I laughed. "What have you been telling her?"

"All lies." He winked. "No, I'm sure she'll come around. She's a nice girl. She's having dinner with Mrs. Becker tonight."

I didn't bother hiding my surprise. "How did that happen?"

Chase's playful eyes sparkled. "They were forced to meet at the funeral, and it wasn't a disaster. I think they give one another a piece of Wallace to hold onto. They've gotten together several times now. Mrs. Becker is turning the Cuddle Brigade over to Kinley. She said the company was Wallace's baby and something he'd chosen to share with his daughter. She had no interest in overseeing it without him, so Kinley was the obvious choice for his seat on the board. She may not have gotten a check from the estate settlement, but this will change her life."

I hugged him. "That's the best story I've heard in days. People do help each other." I pressed a kiss to his cheek.

He covered it with his fingers and made a goofy face. "Careful," he stage whispered, "I think we're being watched."

"Accurate," Jack's deep voice answered behind me.

Chase lifted onto his feet and buttoned his jacket. "That's my news for today. I'm going to leave you two to it." He cast me a wink and strode away in a cloud of attitude and charisma.

I turned back to Jack's waiting face. "So Chase and Kinley. Wow."

"What do you think of it?" he asked.

"I think he hasn't dated since he got home, and it's probably killing him, so it's nice he's back out there. I think she's probably not the right girl for him, but that's up to him to figure out."

"And how do you feel about it?"

I scrunched my nose. "Conflicted. Protective."

"Jealous?"

"No." I shook my head and smiled at the peculiar expression on Jack's face. "I think Chase is trying to let go of childish things. Settle down. Be a man." I made air quotes on the last sentence. "Whatever that means to him, I want him to succeed. I worry about my friends."

Jack worked his jaw, apparently deliberating on something.

"So what brought you here tonight? You never said."

He released a long breath, as if he'd been holding one in. "I came to tell you Claudia's going away for quite a while, but she's getting court-ordered help from a counselor. Her

sanity is in question, so the jury will go easy on her, and her maximum sentence will be lower because of it."

"Good. I know she was confused. She really thought she was helping people."

"It's strange but true. She used all the money she swindled through blackmail to fund her store. Her bank accounts were thin, but her business sense was pretty good. Too bad she'd chosen racketeering as a secondary occupation."

I thought of Jack and what Claudia had taken from him. "What about you? Those women weren't only hurting the ones they preyed upon. They ruined reputations and businesses by association. Destroyed families. What will you get for your suffering?"

"Justice, I guess. At least I know it's over. No one else will be hurt by those women. And I finally have the truth, a confirmation for my suspicions and a face for the one who tore things apart."

My mouth dried. "Tabitha?"

"Yes."

"Did you arrest her?"

He tented his brows and looked away. "Her mom's in bad shape. I looked in on her."

"You gave Tabitha the immunity deal, didn't you?" I slid my palm over his hand on the table and curled my fingers beneath his palm. "Why doesn't that surprise me?"

He curved his lips into a small smile. "I didn't give her the deal, but I'm not working real hard to bring her in either."

"I can live with that," I said. "Did you ever find out who the big yellow truck belonged to?" I couldn't imagine Claudia driving it, but it didn't fit Tabitha either.

"Yeah. That belongs to Jacob Brownstein in Bon Temps. He says he and Tabitha are getting married."

"Married?" I laughed. "Does she know?"

"Yeah, but Jacob thinks her name is Hannah Goldman. He identified her from a photo for me."

My jaw dropped. "Should you warn him?"

"I'm not sure he'd care. He's about half her age and severely smitten."

"A younger man this time. Go figure."

"His dad owns a thriving chain of health care facilities across the country. I'm sure that helped the appeal."

"Jeez."

"Yep." He pinned me with a goofy grin. "Mazel tov, I guess."

A chorus of yips and click-clacking toenails flooded the room as Mrs. Neidermeyer and her troop of dancing Shih Tzus in Boogie Woogie Bugle Boy tutus took the stage. Mom pinned each of their little military jackets with a felt corsage. "May I introduce to you the ambassador's court."

A tall man blocked my view of the stage and bowed. "Miss Crocker?" His thick Russian accent and three-thousand-dollar suit reeked of power and influence. "I'm Viktor Petrov, a representative of the National Pet Pageant. Your city is hosting my event this summer."

I stretched my hand out in greeting, and he kissed it.

Jack pressed onto his feet and shook Viktor's hand. "Mr. Petrov, I'm Detective Jack Oliver. I'll be overseeing the security team for your event."

"You will?" I asked. He was a homicide detective. "How?"

He ignored the question. "What can we do for you, sir?"

Viktor gave Jack a long, careful look. "I only wanted to introduce myself to the beautiful woman in charge."

"In that case," I told him, "let me introduce you to my mother."

I caught Mom's attention as she headed for the bar. She forced herself in my direction. "Here she is," I said.

"This is your mother?" Viktor asked, obviously impressed. "Do they have a fountain of youth in your town?"

She blushed. "I'm Violet Conti-Crocker. It's very lovely to meet you . . ." she looked at me.

"Viktor Petrov," I explained. "He's from the NPP."

Mom's mouth gaped open. "Mr. Petrov, welcome!" She cast a frown at me. "I know who Viktor is." Her smile stretched into something cheerful and enthusiastic. "I've sent you how many handwritten letters?" she asked him. "Pleading for your consideration of New Orleans as the next pageant location?"

"Hundreds?"

They laughed.

"Come along," she said. "Let me introduce you to everyone and get you a drink."

He accepted Mom's arm, but turned for a last look at Jack. "I think I would also like to speak with you at your earliest convenience as well, yes?"

Jack produced a business card from his pocket and set it in Viktor's hand. "Anytime." He reclaimed his seat at my side with the quirk of a brow. "What do you think that was about? A lot of danger in pet pageantry that I should know about?"

I watched as Mom and Viktor were swallowed by the crowd. "I have no idea, but I bet I could find out."

"Do not," Jack said. "No more looking into anything. It gets you hurt and it scares the life out of me. I swear it. I'm going prematurely gray." He pointed an accusatory finger at his head.

I dragged a long blonde curl over my bare shoulder and let it fall. "I've heard spending time with a younger woman makes men feel more youthful."

He lifted his brows. "I suppose that depends on the woman."

"Or the man." I matched his poker-straight posture and tilted toward him in challenge. I refused responsibility for his gray hairs. Real or imagined. "And I assume it also depends on how they spend their time."

Jack's eyes darkened. His lips parted into a suggestive smile. "How about that coffee, Crocker?"

I grabbed my clutch and led the way.

Furry Godmother's Heart-to-Heart Smoothie Bites

Makes approximately 1 dozen smoothie bites.

Lacy wasn't always a professional treat maker. In fact, she wasn't always old enough to use the stove, but that didn't stop her from making healthy, organic treats to share with her father's furry patients on a hot Louisiana day. These bites are so irresistible, you're going to love them too!

Ingredients

6–8 sun-ripened strawberries
1 large banana

Directions

1. Peel and slice the banana.

2. Wash and hull the strawberries.

3. Drop prepared fruit into your favorite blender and blend until smooth.

4. Spoon the mixture into a heart-shaped ice cube tray and freeze for 4–6 hours or until firm.

5. Don't forget to share these delicious smoothie bites with your friends, furry and otherwise.

Furry Godmother's
Tuna Kitty Kisses

Makes approximately 2 dozen Kitty Kisses.

Why wait for Valentine's Day to show your kitty that you care? Furry Godmother's Tuna Kitty Kisses are a great way to let your feline friends know they've got their paws on your heart all year round.

Ingredients

1 can of tuna
½ cup coconut flour
½ cup rice flour
½ cup water
¼ cup coconut oil

Directions

1. Preheat oven to 350 degrees.

2. Empty drained tuna into a medium bowl.

3. Add dry ingredients and water.

4. Mix well.

5. Drizzle coconut oil over the mixture and knead until thoroughly blended.

6. Roll into ½-inch balls and press gently onto a cookie sheet.

7. Use your fingertips to dent the treats into individual heart shapes.

8. Bake for 5 minutes on each side, flipping halfway through.

Furry Godmother's Canine Cutouts

Makes approximately 3 dozen cutouts.

Everybody knows it's not a party without cutout cookies, and these all-natural, sweet-smelling treats are guaranteed to make your pet's mouth water. With ingredients like organic sweet potatoes, honey, and peanut butter, it's hard to believe they aren't meant for you!

Ingredients

3 cups brown rice flour
2 medium organic sweet potato puree
½ cup oats
2 free-range eggs
3 tbs all-natural peanut butter
1 tbs organic honey
½ tsp cinnamon

Directions

1. Preheat oven to 350 degrees.

2. Clean, peel, and cube your sweet potatoes.

3. Boil sweet potatoes in water until soft (approximately 20 minutes).

4. Remove potatoes from water and puree in a blender until smooth.

5. In a small bowl, combine flour, oats, and cinnamon.

6. In a large bowl, whisk together eggs, sweet potatoes, peanut butter, and honey.

7. Stir dry ingredients into sweet potato mixture until a soft dough forms.

8. Roll dough to ¼-inch thickness on floured surface.

9. Cut into shapes using cookie cutters. Furry Godmother recommends *X*s and *O*s for a festive valentine look.

10. Bake 30–35 minutes or until golden brown.

11. Cool on a rack.

Acknowledgments

I'd like to thank the incredible team of people who made another book about Lacy and her gang possible. My critique girls, Jennifer Anderson and Keri Ford, for reading all my words and making them better. My beloved agent and friend, Jill Marsal, for being the guide and mentor every author needs. My amazing editor, Sarah Poppe, for her incredible wit and wisdom. Thank you, friends and family who keep me going, support me, encourage me, and believe in me, especially when I find it hard to believe in myself. I wouldn't be writing this note without you.